80 003 224 484

D1434395

Copyright © 2011 George Mann

George Mann asserts the right to be identified as the author of this work.
All rights reserved

First edition

Proudly published in 2011 by
Snowbooks Ltd.
www.snowbooks.com

Paperback ISBN: 9781907777127
Hardback ISBN: 9781907777110
eBook ISBN: 9781907777509

A catalogue record for this book is available from the British Library.

GHOSTS OF

WAR

A TALE OF THE GHOST

George Mann

ABOUT THE AUTHOR

George Mann is the author of *Ghosts of Manhattan*, as well as the popular Newbury & Hobbes steampunk series, beginning with *The Affinity Bridge*. He has written fiction and audio scripts for BBC TV's *Doctor Who*, as well as numerous short stories, novellas, and audio dramas. He lives in Grantham with his wife and children.

NORTHAMPTONSHIRE LIBS & INFO SER	
80 003 224 484	
ASKEWS & HOLT	26-Sep-2011
AF SF	£7.99

DEDICATION

Once more, for Lou. Thank you for your patience.

PROLOGUE

TERROR FROM THE SKIES

As the rate of disappearances increases to epidemic proportions, New Yorkers look to the skies in fear

"Stay indoors" is the advice from the police department, as the recent spate of missing persons reaches an all-time high. There are now over fifty reported disappearances on Manhattan Island, spanning the entire festive season, and this reporter has been told that the police department is in a state of panic and has already run out of leads.

It is understood that each of the missing people disappeared in what's thought to be identical circumstances—whilst walking the streets of the city—and eyewitness accounts refer to "terrible flying creatures" that pluck their victims indiscriminately from the sidewalk, dragging them away into the sky, never to be seen or heard from again.

These creatures are said to resemble human skeletons with "batlike" wings and glowing red eyes. They swoop silently out from the shadows to abduct the good people of New York and carry them away for nefarious purposes that are not yet clear

Commissioner Montague, in his statement yesterday, assured people that the police were doing everything they could to discover who was behind the abductions and warned citizens to "stay indoors unless absolutely necessary" until the matter was resolved.

This, however, offers little comfort to the families of the fifty missing people, of whom nothing whatsoever has been heard since their abductions. There have been no ransom notes, no demands, and no bodies. Mothers, fathers, husbands and wives all over the city are holding constant vigil in the hope that news will come soon and that their loved ones will be returned to them safely.

Profilers report that there are no obvious connections between the victims—they appear to have been selected entirely at random, plucked from obscurity, representing all different walks of life. Neither is there an obvious pattern to the locations of the abductions, which have taken place at points all over the city, from Central Park to Hell's Kitchen, from the Battery to Union Square

The people of New York are therefore advised to take the commissioner's advice and remain in the safety of their homes, especially after nightfall.

It seems that in Manhattan this winter, nowhere, and nobody, is safe.

—*Manhattan Globe*, January 6, 1927

CHAPTER ONE

He was falling.

Tumbling out of the sky, his arms wheeling as the air rushed past him, his black trench coat billowing open around him like a single black wing.

He gasped for breath, but his lungs failed to respond: the blow that had sent him careening over the lip of the building had knocked the wind out of him, causing his stomach muscles to spasm and leaving him struggling to breathe. His heart was thrumming like a beating drum, pounding in his ears, drowning out the sound of everything else: the roar of the biplanes that soared through the sky on spikes of yellow flame, the coal-powered cars that hissed and sighed as they barreled down the avenues, the chattering of the bizarre mechanical things that had sent him spiraling toward his death. It was as if he had been cocooned inside a bubble, as if the rest of the world had been shut out and all that was left was him and the rush of the sidewalk that was coming up to meet him. Falling had become everything. There was nothing else.

He blinked. Raindrops sparkled in bright flashes of neon light, glimpsed in flickering snapshots as he tumbled over and over, hurtling toward the sidewalk below. He felt unconsciousness tugging at him, threatening to overwhelm him. Blackness swam at the edges of his vision. If he allowed himself to give in to it, to welcome its embrace, then everything would be over. It would only take a second.

For a moment, the Ghost thought that might not be such a bad idea. These days, he didn't have much to live for, save for the anger—that constant, burning fire in the pit of his stomach—and he wondered whether it might not be better to allow that fire to burn itself out. Better for everyone. Better for him. To surrender to it would be easy.

The Ghost felt the needles of rain lashing his face, felt it sting his eyes, wished it could somehow cleanse him of the things he had seen and done. He wanted it to be over. He wanted peace.

Then, suddenly, his lungs were working again and he was sucking at the air, dragging at it in grateful gulps. The sounds of the city permeated his bubble. He had only seconds left in which to act. He moved almost mechanically, his instincts taking over. There were people up there who needed him. He had that much to live for, at least.

The Ghost, still tumbling and spinning as he fell, reached inside the lapel of his trench coat and fought to disentangle a thin cord from among the buckles and straps of his black jacket. He yanked it hard and felt his entire body jerk as the twin canisters strapped to his calves ignited with plumes of bright orange flame and he was propelled sideways into the building.

He slammed against the wall, striking his right elbow hard while cushioning his face in the crook of his arm. He called out in pain—a short, sharp wail—and then forced himself to ignore it, to bury it until later. He rebounded, continuing his plummet toward the ground, arcing away from the building on a streak of flame as his rocket boosters propelled him through the air at a tremendous speed. He was only twenty feet from the ground. If he got the next move wrong, all he'd have succeeded in doing was hastening his own demise.

Mustering all of the strength that he had left, the Ghost angled his body, twisting in midair, forcing his legs down and around so that he was upright once again. He bucked and flailed as the upward momentum of the rocket canisters fought against the momentum of the fall. He slowed in midair, almost lost his balance, and then he was streaming upward again, riding on twin spikes of flames as he shot through the sky toward the two raptors who had forced him off the roof.

He looked up and saw nothing but scintillating raindrops and the top of the building, silhouetted against the moonlit sky. In the distance, the searchlights of numerous police dirigibles played back and forth across the rooftops, monitoring the streets, vigilant for any sign of the brass monsters. As usual, they were too slow and ponderous, and had failed to spot the twin raptors that had descended on Fifth Avenue to pluck two unwary citizens from the street.

The Ghost had been there, however, watching from his favorite vantage point atop his own apartment building, and had opened fire on the mechanical creatures as soon as he'd been able to get a clear shot— the result of which meant he had ended up being knocked over the side of the building during the ensuing tussle as the creatures descended on him, their talons bared.

He only hoped he wasn't too late. He'd been trying to follow one of the things back to its lair for weeks, but they were simply too fast, and he had yet to discern any obvious weakness. Not only that, but there were also the abductees to consider. If he could prevent the raptors from getting away with two more innocent people, he had no choice but to stand his ground.

The Ghost had lost his hat in the fall, and the rain plastered his sand-colored hair across his face. His goggles were pushed up on his forehead, and he reached up and pulled them down sharply over his eyes, welcoming the protection they offered from the rain and the definition provided by their night vision.

As he came up over the lip of the building he caught sight of one of the civilians, squirming in the grip of a raptor's talons as it lifted her off the roof once again and pitched forward into the air. The other was nowhere to be seen.

The Ghost leaned into the gusting rain and shot across the rooftop, slewing around a pyramidal skylight to careen bodily into the back of the raptor.

The mechanical creature screeched in fury as it was bowled forward, nearly dropping the woman as it freed one of its talons and twisted around, trying to rake at the Ghost furiously as he grabbed hold of two of its brass ribs and held on with all his might, trying to force the thing back down onto the rooftop. The woman screamed and held on to the raptor's other talon with both hands, dangling over a hundred-foot drop to the street below.

The raptor beat its batlike wings, trying to shake off the vigilante, who held on despite the claws that raked at his face or scrabbled at his forearms, trying desperately to pry him free.

This was the closest he had come to one of the things, and he was at once appalled and amazed by the artifice on display. It was about the size of a large man, vaguely humanoid in appearance, but with a skeleton constructed out of gleaming brass components. Two large cylinders sprouted from its shoulders, housing spinning propellers—the engines that enabled it to fly. The wings were like those of an enormous bat—taut, pink flesh stretched over elegant fingers of brass; there, he supposed, to guide its flight. Its head was a brass skull, reminiscent of that of a large cat, with long, jagged fangs and an absent lower jaw.

Somewhere in its belly the power unit hummed and crackled with a powerful electric charge.

Most disturbing of all, however, were the pentagrams and weird occult symbols daubed on its chest plate, which appeared to house a small cavity hidden behind an ornate brass door, and the fragments of what looked like human bone incorporated into its skeletal frame. Its eyes burned a demonic red, as if signifying a fierce intelligence.

The Ghost had no idea where the things had come from, but they had been terrorizing the city for weeks, if not longer. For the last two months people had been reporting dead birds found all over the city, pigeons and gulls shredded midflight, dropping to the pavement like gruesome, feathery bombs. The raptors, the Ghost had discovered, were the cause of it. The birds were being chewed up by the raptor's propellers, sucked in by the back draft and spat out again as the brass monsters soared through the sky above the city streets. As yet he had no idea of the creatures' purpose, their numbers, or their origin, nor the reasons why they continued to abduct seemingly random members of the populace, but he intended to find out.

The raptor's talon flashed as it struck out at the Ghost, catching him fully in the chest and forcing him back, straining against his hold. Grimacing as the sharp brass claws punctured the fabric of his jacket, burying themselves in his breast, the Ghost released his grasp on the ribs and clutched for the talon instead, swinging his legs up and round so that the angle of his booster jets was countering the pull of the raptor's engines.

The three figures drifted almost lazily across the rooftop, twisting and turning as the Ghost and the raptor fought for dominance. The creature emitted a chattering howl as it battered at the Ghost's head and arms, scratching and pulling, trying frantically to get away. Below, dangling from the raptor's other leg, the woman continued to scream in terror.

The Ghost knew the ammunition from his fléchette gun—the projectile weapon he had strapped beneath his right arm on a ratchet—would do nothing to harm the brass creature. Even the explosive rounds he had developed to combat the lumbering moss golems of the Roman would bounce off its metal frame, finding little or no purchase. But he needed to find a way to slow it down.

The raptor beat its wings again, the barbed metal tips and fleshy membranes striking the Ghost full in the face, disorientating him as he hung upside down clutching the raptor's clawed foot. But it gave him an idea.

Straining to twist himself around, the Ghost released his right arm and flicked his wrist sharply, causing the long steel barrel of the fléchette gun to snap up and around on its ratchet, clicking into place along the length of his forearm. The rubber bulb that served as a pneumatic trigger dropped into his palm. He paused for a moment, took aim, and fired.

A hail of tiny metal blades scattered from the end of the barrel, showering the raptor and causing it to reel suddenly, confused by the suddenness of the attack. The blades bounced harmlessly off its metal face and chest, just as the Ghost had anticipated, but where they struck the fleshy membrane of the raptor's left wing they tore through, opening large rents and causing the mechanical beast to wail in frustration.

Together, the three figures began to spin wildly out of control as the raptor's wing flapped uselessly at the air, unable to maintain the status quo any longer. It screeched and scrabbled, and then, as if realizing it needed to lose some ballast to remain airborne, casually tossed the woman away as if shedding a dead weight.

Horrified, the Ghost watched her tumble away across the rooftop like a discarded rag doll, striking the paving slabs and rolling, unable to slow herself as she bounced over the low lip of the roofline and went sliding over the edge. The Ghost heard her cry out and strained to see as the raptor spun around crazily in the air, then realized with some relief that she had managed to catch hold of a flagpole and was dangling over the side of the building. Beneath her was a hundred-foot drop, and the rain, still lashing them in a relentless torrent, made it harder to hold on. He didn't have long before she'd be dashed on the sidewalk below, but there was still time to save her.

Cursing loudly, the Ghost released his grip on the raptor's leg and peeled away from the creature, bleeding profusely from the scores of scratches that marred his face and arms. Righting himself, he pulled the cord inside his trench coat to cut the fuel line, and the flames at his ankles guttered and died. He dropped quickly to the rooftop, hitting the slabs on his side and rolling to a stop about ten feet away from the baying raptor. The creature landed softly on its clawed feet and cocked its head, regarding him as if trying to work out his next move.

The Ghost cursed again and climbed quickly to his feet. This was his best chance. The thing was damaged, its wing a mess of brass spines and ragged flesh. That would slow it down, and if he followed it now it might lead him to its lair. If he could find out where the things were nesting, who was controlling them, and why, he could save innumerable lives. Perhaps even the lives of those already taken, if they weren't already dead.

That would mean sacrificing the woman, though, and even though the odds were against her, even though it meant other people might have to die, the Ghost couldn't simply leave her to fall. He'd never be able to live with himself if he abandoned her there, dangling from the flagpole, preparing to tumble to her death.

Refusing to take his eyes off the raptor, he backed up toward the lip of the building. He saw the creature start forward, as if it were intending to follow him, and for a moment he thought his luck might be in, that it might rush him across the rooftop, leaving him enough time to haul the woman to safety before continuing the fight. But he realized with dismay that it was trying only to get enough momentum to launch itself into the air. It staggered forward, skipped lightly over the flagstones and then came down again. Then, on its second attempt, it got itself airborne once more and dropped over the side of the building, banking sharply as it soared away into the rain-soaked night.

Sighing, the Ghost turned to the woman, whose upturned face was stark and white and scared, gleaming in the silvery moonlight. She was clutching the flagpole with both hands, but he could see that her arms were already growing tired with the strain, her fingers beginning to slip on the wet metal pole.

The Ghost dropped to his knees, bowing his head against the rain so that it sprayed off his upturned collar, and reached down over the side of the building, grabbing the woman by the arms. He hauled her up, slowly and carefully, without saying a word.

She was as light as a feather—thin and pretty—and he could see how absolutely terrified she was by the ordeal. He pulled her over the lip of the building and dragged her to safety.

Then, kneeling on the rooftop in the driving rain, he allowed her to wrap her arms around him and clutch him tight, sobbing on his shoulder as she trembled with fear and relief. She felt as fragile as a bird as he wrapped his arms around her to protect her from the storm.

"Who are you?" she whispered, after a few moments. She looked up at him, studying his face for any clues. Her mascara had run in the rain, streaking her face with tributaries of black ink.

He turned his head, searching the sky for any sign of the raptor. He was too late. It was gone.

"I'm no one," he replied, his voice low. "No one but a ghost."

CHAPTER TWO

The blows were coming fast and hard.

Gabriel Cross ducked and sidestepped, blocked and returned. He caught his opponent, Jimmy Carmichael, with a swift jab to the chin; but he failed to get enough power behind it, and it glanced harmlessly off the man's iron jaw.

After his exploits on the rooftop the previous evening, Gabriel was in no fit state for a boxing match, and too many of his opponent's punches were striking home. His elbow was excruciating where he'd slammed into the side of the building, and his chest wounds kept opening every time he flexed or punched. It felt as if someone were digging hot daggers into his flesh. He'd been forced to wear a vest to hide the brace of bandages he'd had to wrap around his chest to stanch the seeping blood from the wounds.

Then, of course, there was the webwork of scratches and gouges on his face, which he'd had a harder time explaining away, to everyone from his butler Henry to Jimmy and the others at the gym. In the end, he'd fabricated a story about a mugger who'd pushed his face into a wire fence, but he could tell that none of them had bought it in the slightest.

He was beginning to get a reputation as a brawler, he knew, and he understood that many of his acquaintances thought he had developed a penchant for barroom scrapping. It could have been worse, he supposed, and at least it provided him with an explanation for his long absences. He'd heard them muttering at his parties, whispering to one another in scandalized tones that their host, a bored playboy and former soldier, had developed a taste for speakeasies, for getting roaringly drunk and starting fights. It wasn't the most salubrious of reputations, but better that than the truth.

Of course, upon hearing his story Henry had insisted he talk to the police, and so Gabriel had been forced to call his friend at the precinct, Inspector Felix Donovan, to arrange a meeting. The fact that he really did want to speak with Donovan regarding the matter was by the by—the web of lies he'd been forced to weave was as extensive as the web of scars on his unshaven face. At least Donovan knew the truth about his alter ego, and with him Gabriel would be able to speak openly and frankly.

Gabriel had decided it was time for them to compare notes. His investigations into the raptor abductions were getting him nowhere fast, and while he knew the police were even further behind, there could be something—anything—that he had missed.

Donovan, of course, was as anxious as Gabriel to bring things to a swift conclusion, and had readily agreed to meet, but had put him off until that evening, saying the commissioner was hauling him in on an urgent matter that afternoon. He hadn't alluded to the nature of the emergency, but Gabriel suspected it was also to do with the raptor abductions.

The newspapers had been going to town in recent weeks, and the commissioner had been forced to issue a statement declaring his intention to take a personal interest in the case, trying to win back public confidence in the police department. The newspapers continued to erode that confidence, however, and the numbers spoke for themselves—fifty people reported missing since the start of the festive season, and many more, Gabriel suspected, who hadn't even been noticed yet. Homeless people, waifs, strays, people who hadn't yet returned from their holidays, tourists and foreigners—just some of the people who might not have been noticed as missing. He suspected the number was at least double that being reported in the press, and he knew Donovan thought the same.

For a while the police had been able to keep a lid on the affair, playing down the near-identical circumstances in which the victims had been abducted. Soon, though, eyewitness reports began to filter out regarding the raptors, and it was clear the police and politicians were not going to be able to keep the matter buried for long. All the while they were waiting for the perpetrator to make his demands, or for one of the many pressure groups of terrorist regimes to assume responsibility for the kidnappings. No one had come forward, however, and all the attempts to talk to those who might be responsible had been met by a wall of silence. Even now, appealing to the people of the city through the media, no one had come forward, and the police were just as in the dark as Gabriel as to who—or what—was responsible.

Of course, given the current political climate, it hadn't been long before extremists were publishing pamphlets blaming the British, denouncing them as murderers who came in the night to steal away your loved ones. Gabriel knew this was only so much garbage, but was surprised by the strength of feeling and support that had swelled among the population of the city. There had been rallies calling for the president to declare war on the British Empire, with those desperate people who had lost their loved ones to the raptors held up as figureheads and martyrs for the cause. Anxious to feel like they were doing *something* to bring their missing loved ones back, many of them had been swept up in the waves of anti-British feeling, adding their names to the petitions and the calls for action.

The president, of course, was avoiding the issue, and Gabriel suspected he saw the demonstrations for what they really were—the last attempt by a scared population to rationalize what was happening to them, to find an enemy they could blame for the abduction of the people they loved.

The sooner the real power behind the threat was uncovered, the better.

Gabriel ducked left to avoid a swinging fist, but misread the feint and took a glancing blow to the face from Carmichael's other fist. He staggered back, shaking his head from side to side in an attempt to clear the dancing lights before his eyes. Carmichael wasn't waiting for him, however, and came on again, striking him twice again before Gabriel was able to get his arms up in defense and the referee stepped in to break them up.

Gabriel flexed his neck and shoulder muscles. He was desperate for a cigarette. He looked up to see Jimmy smiling at him from across the ring, leaning on the ropes, catching his breath. He was clearly enjoying himself. Rather too much, Gabriel thought, wryly.

The gym was a downtown establishment, out of the way, a place where he could escape without fear of being accosted by the press or harangued by any of his usual gang of followers. He'd been spending more and more time there of late, and he wondered for a moment if there was actually some glimmer of truth in all the rumors—if he had, indeed, developed a taste for brawling. Just not in the sense that people thought. He much preferred his brawling to be refereed, with padded gloves.

Nevertheless, he'd certainly been spending less and less time at his

Long Island mansion, where the scent of Celeste still clung resolutely to the bedclothes, and where the memories were still all too raw.

In the darkness, when he closed his eyes, unable to sleep and unwilling to drink himself into another stupor, he could still see her there at the house. He remembered the feel of her lithe, sensuous body curled around him with her feline grace; the sight of her auburn hair a bright splash on the stark white pillow; the touch of her red, full lips as she leaned in and gently kissed his neck. He was haunted by her memory, unable to shake her from his dreams.

Sometimes he sat listlessly in the drawing room and played the holograph recorder on a constant loop, watching her flickering blue image as she swayed her hips on the stage at the Sensation Club, listening as she softly sang her lament for lost love.

Gabriel didn't know what to feel anymore. He didn't feel *anything*. He was numb. The only thing that came close to sensation was the beating of another man's fists against his face, or the rending of a raptor's claws, or falling. . . .

A bell rang out, and the referee motioned them both forward.

Gabriel was feeling tired now, weary to the bones. He hadn't slept last night after he'd escorted the woman home. He'd left her with Donovan's name and told her to call the precinct in the morning. He'd check with Donovan later to make sure she'd done as he'd suggested.

Carmichael—a thin but wiry man in his mid-thirties, with dark chestnut-colored hair and a thin mustache—came at Gabriel in a frenzy. Something had stirred him—whether it was the scent of victory, or perhaps an overeagerness to impress, Gabriel couldn't be sure, but he was experienced enough and wise enough to take advantage of it.

Gabriel went on the defensive, channeling all of his energy into dodging and blocking, pushing Carmichael on to tire him out. The blows rained down and Gabriel kept it up, pacing around the ring, even allowing a few of the jabs to hit home, urging Carmichael on with little glimmers of success.

It was a well-proven strategy, and it wasn't long before Gabriel could see the other man beginning to slow. Carmichael's punches were becoming appreciably less frantic, and less powerful, too; and almost sighing with the inanity of it all, Gabriel took a step forward, feinted to the left, and finally took Carmichael down with a swift, sharp hook with his right fist.

The man, utterly dazed by the blow, spun around slowly and collapsed to the mat, semiconscious and momentarily unable to move.

The referee rang the bell and Gabriel slumped back against the ropes, still panting with the exertion. He turned when he heard the sound of someone clapping enthusiastically from behind him.

The gym was nearly empty, save for a couple of other men sparring in the far corner, but there, framed in the doorway, was a face he hadn't seen for over three years.

"Ginny?" he said, as if he didn't quite believe his own eyes. "Ginny Gray?"

The woman smiled, and her blue eyes flashed in amusement. "It's been a long time, Gabriel." Her voice was exactly how he remembered it: sugary and sweet. She was young, in her mid-twenties, with stunning blonde hair and the most perfect cheekbones he had ever seen. She was tall and slender, with shapely legs and a slim waist. Her skin was pale and unblemished, as if she'd been sculpted by a fine renaissance artist, presented in alabaster like some immaculate vision of a woman, rendered in life according to a secret blueprint of perfection. She was wearing a red felt cloche and a knee-length dress, and she looked just as stunning as she had when she'd walked out on him all those years ago.

Gabriel wiped his face in the crook of his arm. "What . . . ?" he trailed off, unable to give any shape to his thoughts. His mind was racing.

Ginny laughed. "You look terrible, Gabriel." She approached the ring, her heels clicking loudly on the tiles. She reached for a towel that was draped over the back of a ringside chair and tossed it to him. He caught it awkwardly with his gloved hands, and smiled.

"I thought about coming along to one of your parties," she said, watching him intently as he mopped his brow with the towel, "but Henry said you hadn't been home for a while. Not since Christmas, in fact. He said I might find you here."

Gabriel shuddered. Ginny was right; he hadn't thrown one of his famous parties for weeks. He'd grown tired of the interlopers, the occasional friends, the strangers who invaded his house every night searching for distraction from their own mundane existence. There was a time when he'd needed the bustle, the sense of not being alone. A time he'd thought he collected those people like others collected butterflies, or stamps, or cars. But lately he'd found their presence nothing but a drain, found the constant background noise a burden rather than a reassurance, and so he'd packed up and moved into town to get away from them all for a while.

He'd enjoyed the solitude while it lasted, enjoyed being himself, with no pretense, no need to adopt his playboy persona, to become *Gabriel Cross*. If he was truthful with himself, though, he knew it wouldn't last. Soon enough he would drift back into his old life, his old patterns, finding comfort in their familiarity, like a favorite jacket or scarf. The people would return, and they would laugh and cajole and drink and fuck and whisper and bicker and leave their tired, careworn lives behind for a short while as they threw off their shackles and revealed themselves in all of their human glory.

He'd been waiting for that. He knew it was coming. With the inevitability that he knew that someday he was going to die, Gabriel knew that something would happen to drag him back to his old life, to Long Island, to the world he'd tried so hard to forget.

And now, here was Ginny.

But Ginny was different. Ginny had broken his heart. Ginny was the girl who got away, the girl he hadn't been honest with, the girl who had known only Gabriel, and not *him*. Not really him. Ginny had been everything, and he had lost her.

The question was: what was she doing here now? Why had she walked back into his life after all these years?

Gabriel folded the towel around the back of his neck and parted the ropes, ducking his head to step through. He glanced back at Carmichael, who was slowly pulling himself up into a sitting position, still looking dazed by the blow that had felled him. He met Gabriel's gaze and grinned at him appreciatively, as if admiring Gabriel for the quality of his blow.

Gabriel nodded in acknowledgment and turned to face Ginny, who was watching him intently. "So, here I am," he said, holding out his gloved hands for her to undo the straps. She took a step closer to him and he caught her scent, drinking it in. It reminded him . . . well, it reminded him of her. Of time spent lounging in the sun by the pool, or their trip to the New Jersey shore, or holding her in a clammy embrace as they made passionate, violent love.

Ginny pulled his left glove free and set to work unlacing his right.

"What are you doing here, Ginny?" he finally said, his voice quavering slightly as he tried not to stumble over the words. It wasn't that he didn't want to see her, but more that he wasn't sure he wanted to deal with all of the emotions she was stirring inside him with her presence. It had been *three years*. A lot of water had passed under the bridge.

Ginny paused. She looked up from his gloved hand, catching his eye. He remembered gazing into those icy blue eyes. Now, they looked glassy, shining in the electric light of the gym. "Oh, Gabriel," she said dramatically. "Don't be like that. I thought you might like to go for a drink. Shall we go for a drink?" She still had her hand on his wrist. He looked down at her painted red nails, like talons.

"Now?" He glanced at the clock on the wall. "It's not even eleven o'clock."

She shrugged. "What can I say? I'm thirsty. And I'm here, and you're here, and there's a place I know just around the corner." She grabbed the remaining boxing glove and slid it carefully off his wrist, dropping it nonchalantly to the floor. She took another step closer. He could feel her breath on his cheek. "Say you will, Gabriel. Say you'll have a drink with me."

Gabriel smiled. She always had been able to wrap him around her little finger. It was one of the most infuriating things about her—and one of the things he'd loved most, too. This time, however, he didn't mind being manipulated. She had him intrigued. He wanted to know the reason for her sudden, disconcerting appearance at the gym. "Can you wait while I take a shower?"

Ginny batted her eyelids and smiled. "As long as it's quick."

Gabriel laughed like he hadn't laughed in some time. "You always were an impatient sort, Ginny."

She gave him a sly grin. "I told you, I'm thirsty!"

Gabriel pulled the towel from around his neck and dropped it over the back of the chair. "Wait here. I'll be back in ten minutes."

Ginny folded herself neatly onto the chair and produced a packet of cigarettes from her handbag. "Ten minutes?" she echoed, as, still laughing, Gabriel made his way to the locker room.

CHAPTER THREE

Felix Donovan slid a thin cigarette from the packet on his desk, placed it between his lips and pulled the ignition tab, watching the tip flare briefly before sucking appreciatively at the thick, nicotine-tainted smoke. He slumped back in his chair and glowered at the clock. It was still morning. The day was dragging, and his belly was already growling, ready for lunch. He'd been in the office since before six o'clock that morning, and the late nights and early starts were beginning to take their toll.

Donovan was dog tired. He'd barely been home these last two weeks, and although he knew Flora understood—wonderful woman that she was—he couldn't help noticing the forced smiles and sideways looks as he rolled in at some ungodly hour and climbed out of bed while it was still dark.

It was not that she suspected him of anything untoward—he'd always been faithful and wouldn't have time for dallying with other women even if he'd wanted to—but just that he could see that she was being slowly eroded by his constant absences, by his tiredness and frustration.

That was his most palpable fear, the slow rending apart of his marriage because of the job; the long periods of time spent apart, the awkwardness that prevailed whenever they did manage to spend any time together. He'd seen it happen to so many others over the years, and he had sworn to Flora that it would never happen to them.

The worst thing was that she probably didn't even see it herself. She was so ready to offer her support, so willing and understanding, that she couldn't even see what it was doing to them. If he'd been a banker, or a plumber or some other such tradesman, then perhaps things would have been different, but he was a policeman—an inspector, no less—and he had a duty to the public to keep them safe.

And now fifty people—probably more—were missing, presumed kidnapped, and it was Donovan's job to get to the bottom of what was going on and prevent any further disappearances.

Only . . . he had nothing. He knew about the brass raptors, of course—he'd even caught a glimpse of one himself—but their strikes were executed with such speed and surgical precision that even the Ghost had been unable to capture one of them, or even follow one back to its lair.

It didn't help that whoever was perpetrating the abductions was doing so for obscure reasons. Donovan could establish no motive. Typically in these cases people were motivated either by revenge or greed, and they would make their demands and have done with it. But this time, the abductions just kept coming, without warning.

He'd tried looking for a pattern in the abductions, the profiles of those taken, and could find nothing that might help him to establish a motive. He'd fingered all of the manufacturers who might have been supplying components—whether unwittingly or not—to the people responsible for the raptors, but again, he had been able to uncover nothing of use. Either the people behind the abductions were exceedingly clever, or else they had friends in high places, looking out for them from above.

Donovan feared that in this case, perhaps both were true. And now the commissioner wanted to see him. Montague had taken a personal interest in the matter, and while Donovan found it reassuring to know he wasn't working in isolation, he wasn't really sure what the commissioner could bring to the investigation, other than to bawl at him on a daily basis for the lack of progress they were making.

Donovan took another long pull on his cigarette, relishing the sound of the crackling paper as the tip glowed a bright crimson. He allowed the smoke to plume luxuriously from his nostrils, wreathing his head in rings of ethereal blue.

He turned at the sound of footsteps approaching his desk. Mullins was there, brandishing a mug of steaming coffee.

The sergeant was red faced and his small, beady eyes darted back and forth as he stood nervously looking down at the inspector. He was a large man, in his late thirties, and always looked as if he had dressed in a hurry. Today, his brown suit was crumpled and his shirt clearly hadn't been ironed. Donovan knew the man's domestic situation was unenviable—his wife had left him recently and he was sharing an apartment with one of the constables—so he'd cut him some slack. Mullins's was yet another example of a marriage pulled to pieces by the force. He was a good man, and an even better sergeant. He'd sacrificed a lot for the good of the department. More, perhaps, than any one man should be expected to.

"I brought you a coffee, sir. You looked like you needed it."

Donovan smiled and accepted the mug gratefully. "You know, Mullins, that's exactly the sort of thing that'll help you go far in this department."

Mullins frowned. "Bringing you coffee, sir?"

Donovan laughed. "Don't be ridiculous, Mullins. Reading people.

That's what I was talking about. You seem to have a remarkable knack for seeing to the heart of a matter, for understanding what a person wants. It'll stand you in good stead." Donovan took a swig of the coffee. "See? You were right. I did need that."

"Thank you, sir."

Donovan sighed heavily. "I don't suppose there have been any new developments?"

Mullins shrugged. "One of the men did take a call from a woman this morning while you were out. She asked for you by name. Said one of the brass things had tried to abduct her last night but some man in a black suit had saved her. I figured it must have been that Ghost chap again, sir."

Donovan nodded slowly. So this was what the Ghost had wanted to meet with him about. "Call her back, Mullins. Have her come to the precinct. You can take her statement while I'm in with the commissioner. She might have gotten a good look at the thing. It could be our best lead yet."

Mullins gave a curt nod. "Right away, sir." He paused for a moment, as if weighing up his next words.

"Spit it out, Mullins."

"What about the Ghost, sir? Do you think he's tied up in all this?"

The Ghost had been an ongoing cause of contention in the department during the Christmas season. The commissioner was still as keen as ever to have the vigilante caught and brought to justice, but Donovan had tried to play the matter down, ensuring as far as he could that his friend's activities were kept under the radar.

As he'd tried to point out to Montague on numerous occasions, the Ghost was a useful tool. His methods might be brutal, but they were effective, and despite what the newspapers decried at every available opportunity, the evidence only demonstrated that the Ghost had the best interests of the city at heart.

Of course, Donovan had stopped far short of revealing the true nature of his relationship with the vigilante, or the Ghost's involvement in the matter of the Roman and the affair at the museum. Nevertheless, the commissioner—and as far as Donovan could tell many others in the department—felt the Ghost was a menace who should be strung up for his crimes. Donovan suspected that, really, they were more concerned with the manner in which he showed up the police department for what they really were—a law-enforcement agency that spent more time pandering to the whims of the Senate rather than get on with their jobs.

Donovan shook his head. "You just worry about getting a statement from that girl, Mullins. Leave the Ghost to me."

"Yes, sir," said Mullins, and he clumped away to his desk on the other side of the office to make the call.

Donovan stubbed the still-smoldering end of his cigarette in the ashtray beside his notebook and grinned. Perhaps they *were* getting somewhere, after all.

—•—

Two hours later, Donovan was ushered into the commissioner's office by a desk sergeant who bore an expression of forced jollity and calm.

The commissioner's office was situated on the floor above the main precinct, and compared to the sparse, economical circumstances in which the rest of the department worked, the room was palatial. In fact,

Donovan mused as he climbed the stairs to the second floor, puffing slightly with the exertion, it would be more accurate to describe the commissioner's lair as a suite of rooms.

Decked out with furniture and fittings that Donovan always felt were more suited to a domestic dwelling—armchairs, coffee tables, portraits in gilded frames—the three connected rooms were more like those one might find in a top-end hotel like the Gramercy Park than anything one expected to find in a police station. He couldn't see how they were in any way conducive to getting any police work done—but then, that assumed the commissioner was still interested in doing any work. Realistically, Donovan knew, the commissioner was far more concerned with schmoozing politicians and showing off his pretty young wife around town.

Still, someone had to talk to the politicians, and he'd rather it was Montague than him. At least this way, Donovan could keep out of their way while he got on with the real police work.

At least, that was what Donovan had thought until he crossed the threshold into the commissioner's office and heard the desk sergeant pull the door shut behind him.

Donovan's heart sank as he saw who was sitting with the commissioner, reclining in one of the armchairs, puffing on a fat cigar. He'd never met the man, but he recognized him from the photographs he had seen in the newspapers: Senator Isambard Banks.

The man was balding, in his mid-to-late fifties, and wore a pinstriped suit and white shirt, open at the collar. He was clean shaven and full faced and his forehead was glistening with perspiration. Pungent cigar smoke hovered in the still air around him, as if concealing him behind a semitranslucent veil.

Donovan sighed. So, now the Senate was leaning on them again, no doubt instructing them to bring a swift conclusion to the matter of the abductions. Well, it wasn't as if he wasn't trying. . . .

"Ah, there you are, Felix. Come in, take a seat. Can I fix you a drink?"

Donovan gave the commissioner a sideways glance. Why the sudden geniality? It wasn't like the old fool to behave in such a fashion. Usually when Donovan was hauled into the commissioner's office it was to be faced with a series of curt commands and sage advice on how he should really be conducting his investigation. He'd never been offered a drink before. Perhaps the commissioner was showing off, attempting to impress the senator. Or perhaps Donovan was being welcomed into some sort of secret clique, and from now on he'd be expected to associate with these people and attend their drink parties and sell his soul to the devil just to keep his job. Well, he supposed he'd faced that problem before.

Donovan suppressed a laugh at his own expense. He could tell he'd just about reached his limit—he was getting cranky and paranoid and needed a good night's sleep.

Groaning inwardly, Donovan did as the commissioner instructed. "A scotch, thank you, Commissioner." Donovan nodded to the seated senator and pulled up an armchair opposite the man. He reached for his packet of cigarettes and realized, with a stifled curse, that he'd left them downstairs on his desk.

Banks, grinning wolfishly, leaned forward and pulled a large, walnut cigar case from inside the folds of his jacket. He offered it to Donovan, who thanked him and took one gratefully. He didn't much like cigars, but he supposed it was better than nothing. He pulled the ignition patch and watched it flare.

Montague talked as he set about fixing Donovan's drink, taking a decanter from a small mahogany dresser that stood against the far wall. "You don't know Senator Banks, Donovan?"

Donovan smiled at the senator. "Only by reputation, I'm afraid." He was careful to make it sound like a compliment. In reality, however, Donovan *did* only know the senator because of his reputation. His name had cropped up more than once during the investigation into the Roman's crime syndicate, connected to the cabal of corrupt individuals who had funded the crime boss's power station project down in the Battery.

There hadn't been enough evidence to haul him in on a charge, however, and unlike the other members of that small group, Banks hadn't gone and gotten himself murdered by the Roman's goons. Whether that was because he really hadn't been involved or because he'd been so significantly involved that the Roman had chosen to keep him alive, Donovan couldn't be sure.

Commissioner Montague, of course, had dismissed all notion of conspiracy, preferring to believe Banks was clean and that it was only to be expected that the condemned men would have had dealings with other, innocent members of the Senate. "Some of them had probably even met the president," he had said loftily, "and we're not about to bring him in for questioning, are we?"

Donovan had wanted to respond that, yes, if the president had been implicated in a plot to unleash a dangerous interdimensional beast on the city, he would have absolutely considered it his duty to bring the man in for questioning. Wisely, however, he had bitten his tongue.

And now Banks was here, in the commissioner's office, and Donovan had to wonder what the hell Montague was getting them involved in.

The commissioner crossed the room, handed Donovan his drink, and then took a seat in a chair beside the senator. Donovan felt like he was about to be interviewed for a job. Perhaps he was.

"Well, here's to your health, gentlemen." He saluted both men with his glass and then took a long slug, enjoying the sharp hit of alcohol, the long fingers of warmth that spread throughout his chest.

The commissioner cleared his throat. "Felix, Senator Banks is here to discuss some urgent business with us, and I hope that you will listen carefully and give him your full attention." Montague leaned forward in his chair, his gray mustache bristling. "It's a matter of national security."

Donovan blanched at the commissioner's patronizing tone but nodded heartily, sliding his drink onto the coffee table and meeting Banks's gaze. "Of course. How can I be of service, Senator?"

Here it comes, he thought. *About these abductions . . . They're making our figures look terrible. . . .*

"We have a spy in our midst, Inspector," said Banks, his tone ominous. "A British spy. We have reason to believe he is in possession of information that could threaten our national security." He leaned forward, chewing thoughtfully on the end of his cigar. "We're talking about the safety of the entire country, here, Inspector. We're talking about war with the British Empire." He sat back, allowing his words to sink in.

Donovan didn't know what to say. He took a long draw on his cigar. It tasted stale. A spy? "You mean here, in the police department?"

Banks shook his head. He glanced at Montague, who nodded, urging him on. "No, Inspector. But here in the city. He's been posing as a young philanthropist from Boston. Quite successfully, I might add. He was able to insinuate his way into various political circles here in New York, and over the course of the last year became quite influential in certain quarters." The senator pulled a handkerchief from his breast pocket and mopped his brow. "Even had him over to dinner at my own home," he said wistfully, as if embarrassed to admit he'd ever been taken in by such a dangerous scoundrel.

"So he's still at large?" Donovan asked, furrowing his brow. He wasn't quite sure where this was going.

"Quite so, Inspector. Quite so. Yesterday, it seems, he came into possession of certain . . . facts that could prove very damaging indeed if they were to fall into enemy hands. But he made a mistake, blew his cover. Now he's somewhere in the city, and I imagine by now he knows that we're on to him."

Donovan nodded. "What are these . . . facts, Senator?"

Banks frowned. "Suffice to say, Inspector, that they would leave this country very exposed if they were to come into the possession of a hostile nation."

"And you think the British mean to use them to that end?" Donovan tried to hide the incredulity in his voice. Did they really think the British were likely to invade?

Banks inclined his head, just a fraction. "I think anything that puts this nation at risk, Inspector, should be taken very seriously indeed."

"Felix, what I believe the senator is getting at is that he would like the help of this department in locating and containing the British spy." The commissioner beamed at him, as if the very thought of such patriotic work filled him with pride.

Donovan turned to face the commissioner. "But surely, sir, there's some sort of counterespionage unit who'd be much better placed to deal with something as significant as this? We're a local police force, and we have our hands full with this plague of abductions. I'm not really sure how we can help."

Montague shook his head. "Donovan, the security of the nation comes first. It must. Of course there are government men already working on the case. How else do you think we're aware of the spy in the first place? All the senator is asking for is some local assistance with containment. Our men know these streets better than anyone else in the city. We can hound this man down. We can close the borders. We can stop him getting off this island and, in doing so, prevent the outbreak of war." The commissioner took a swig of his own drink. "Once we've got him, we'll simply hand him over to the right government agency and the matter will be closed."

Donovan wanted to laugh. Montague made it sound so easy, instilled it with such romance and melodrama. Closing the borders would be nigh on impossible, and while his men did know the city like the back of their hands, they were hardly trained to be able to handle an active foreign agent. Particularly one who knew he was being hunted. The Englishman was probably armed to the teeth and would fight like a cornered animal if any of Donovan's men even got near him.

Nevertheless, he supposed he had no choice in the matter. And besides, he knew a man who might be able to help. He nodded, glancing at Banks. "What's his name?"

"Jerry Robertson. An alias, we presume. We don't know if he operates under any other names."

"A description?" Donovan prompted.

"Commissioner Montague has photographs and descriptions for you already, as well as his last known address."

"Very well." Donovan reached for his scotch and emptied the glass with another long pull. He dropped the barely smoked cigar into the ashtray, scattering dust. "I'll get my men onto it right away. Commissioner?" He glanced at the portly old man, who returned his look with a confused expression. "The photographs?"

"Ah, yes." He rose from his chair and crossed to a bureau, turning a key in the lid and folding down the writing stand. He withdrew a large, cream-colored envelope from within, holding it out for Donovan.

Donovan stood, taking it from him. It felt thick with sheaves of paper. Whoever had assembled the file had clearly been doing so for some time. But hadn't Banks said it was only yesterday that Robertson's cover had been blown? Had they been keeping a file on him for a different reason, then? Something didn't add up, but Donovan didn't have the heart, or the energy, to force the issue now.

Banks also rose from his chair, extending his hand to Donovan. "We won't forget this, Inspector."

The thought made Donovan's skin crawl. He took the senator's proffered hand. "I'll do everything in my power, Senator."

"Be sure that you do, Inspector," Banks said dryly. "Be sure that you do."

Donovan quit the commissioner's office, pulling the door shut behind him. He breathed a heavy sigh of relief. He could hear the two men still talking on the other side of the door, but didn't wait around to hear what they had to say. He'd heard enough already. The commissioner was clearly moving in more significant circles these days. It was obvious to Donovan that this was not the first time the commissioner and Banks had met. He only hoped that whatever game Montague was playing, he knew what he was getting himself into. Whatever Donovan thought of the old man, he knew he wasn't a crook.

He wasn't sure he could say the same about Isambard Banks.

CHAPTER FOUR

Peter Rutherford was feeling more than a little out of his depth.

He was alone in a hostile country, his head full of state secrets, and he knew the authorities were on to him. That much had been made clear by the reaction of the British embassy when he'd tried to report in earlier that day. They had denied all knowledge of his existence, refusing to let him in through the doors.

Just a day earlier, he'd been welcomed in with open arms and ushered to a back room where he'd been encouraged to use the holotube terminal to contact his handler back home. The staff at the embassy—people he'd been working alongside for months—had been proud to play a part in the protection of British interests, proud to welcome him into their midst, clapping him on the back and telling him what a stand-up job he was doing, how he was working on the front line for the good of the Empire.

Today, however, those very same people had refused to acknowledge him, and that, Rutherford realized, was a very bad sign indeed. That meant they'd been leant on by the US government and were now trying to protect him, to give him a signal that he needed to get out of New York as quickly as he could. If the US government knew there was an English spy in their midst, the embassy would eventually be forced into giving him up.

He was under no illusion; he would be sacrificed to prevent a diplomatic incident, and the embassy would deny all knowledge of his actions. He'd be branded a renegade and hung out to dry. They would have no other option. Otherwise, given the tensions that already existed between the two nations, there was the potential for a full-blown outbreak of war.

The irony was that war was exactly what Rutherford was attempting to prevent. If he couldn't get his warning to the people back home, everyone was in dire danger indeed.

Now, he was sitting in Central Park, wrapped against the wintry chill in a thick woolen overcoat, trying to discern his next move. He needed to find transport to England, and he needed to find a secure means of communicating with the British secret service.

Peter Rutherford had never expected to wind up working as a spy. In all his years of public school he'd trained to be a teacher, but then the war had come, and he had done what every self-respecting Englishman had done—he'd joined up.

The war had not been kind to him, and he'd seen most of his friends cut to ribbons by enemy fire, or else frozen in the trenches or blown apart by mortar fire. But, amazingly, he'd managed to make it out alive, ferried back to England by airship after the Behemoth Land Crawlers— the giant war machines unleashed by the British forces to bring an end to the conflict—had effectively rendered the Kaiser's army impotent.

Rutherford had seen one of them in action while still out on the front in France. It was like a fortified city on wheels, an enormous land tank bristling with gun turrets and machine gun emplacements. It was slow moving and ponderous, but it was utterly impregnable.

The British forces had shipped them over the channel on massive floating platforms and set them loose on the battlefields of Europe, where they had simply trundled across no-man's-land to the enemy-occupied territory. Once there, they had unleashed a storm of death, gun turrets blazing as the Behemoths had rolled over the enemy trenches, crushing those who hadn't fled or been mown down by the all-consuming gunfire. The machines had even rolled into the enemy-held cities, remorselessly leveling buildings and razing all before them to the ground.

The Behemoths were weapons on a scale never seen before—weapons of mass destruction—and while they had won the war for the Allies, they had inspired a sense of nervousness in the Americans. The British Empire was still a significant power in the world, and now, harboring such monstrous weapons and led by a monarch who was keen to reclaim the glory of her ancestors' days, many thought it was only a matter of time before they mounted an invasion of their former colony. ·

Rutherford wondered if that were really such a wild claim. Queen Alberta regularly referred to the American government as "upstart colonists," and, party as he was to many of the strategic secrets of the British government, Rutherford had himself wondered whether the reclamation of the American continent was the endgame they had in mind. Whatever the case, a cold war between the two nations had developed as they'd jostled for position in the new world order, and while things were not outwardly hostile between them, Rutherford knew the gloss of cooperation was only skin deep.

By the time he'd returned from the trenches, of course, Rutherford had given up all hope of ever settling down to become a teacher. Instead, finding himself feeling dislocated from normal life and isolated from his family and the people he had left behind, he had enlisted in the secret service. At least that way, he had felt, he could still make a difference.

As a veteran of the war he had risen quickly through the ranks, and having shown an aptitude for espionage work he was soon assigned to work in Chicago, and then Washington, and most recently New York, operating out of the embassy.

He'd been in New York for over a year now, during which time Rutherford had managed to ingratiate himself into New York politics, adopting the persona of a rich young bachelor from Boston. He'd attended parties and soirees, funded carefully selected political campaigns and written articles for the *Globe*. He'd made his presence felt, and soon enough he'd been drawn into an inner circle of senators, councilors, businessmen and statesmen. He'd played their games, taking part in their petty political squabbles, earning their confidence and trust. He'd listened to everything, recording it all in his eidetic memory, searching out each of their weaknesses and flaws in case he found need to exploit them later. They all had their secrets: booze, whores, boys, bribes. Rutherford knew them all.

For a while, little of any importance had happened: more political games, more character assassinations, more bribery and corruption. Then, when he was least expecting it, something had fallen into his lap, something so big and so startling that, at first, he hadn't known how to react.

That night—last night—he'd gone straight to the embassy to report his findings. But he hadn't been able to get through on the holotube. Transatlantic connections were notoriously temperamental, and he knew it was likely the terminal would be working again in the morning. He didn't trust anyone else with such potentially explosive information, and he knew that any calls home through an unsecure line risked being overheard. So he had returned to his apartment where he had waited, barely able to sleep, and had returned to the embassy early that morning to make the call.

But something had happened during the night. Somehow, someone had found him out. He'd been turned away at the embassy door, and the pleading look in the eye of the concierge told him everything he needed to know.

Rutherford wondered if perhaps he'd been followed to the embassy the previous day. He'd taken every precaution—heading home first, then changing and going out into town, taking in a show, visiting a speakeasy, then drifting past the embassy first before using the rear entrance when he knew the coast was clear. He wondered if perhaps he'd missed something crucial. Or perhaps someone had found his room in Greenwich Village, the little bolt-hole in a run-down apartment block where he stashed any evidence as to his real identity. That was where he kept all of his equipment, the tools of his trade.

He knew they'd searched his apartment on numerous occasions, but the place was clean—they could have found nothing incriminating there, nothing to even suggest he was an Englishman from Crawley rather than a young and wealthy Bostonian with an interest in local politics.

Regardless, it was too risky to visit either location now. So he was left wearing the clothes he stood up in, carrying only the items he had in his pockets. Luckily, experience meant he was rarely unprepared, and he had stitched a handful of useful items into the lining of his coat—a stash of dollar bills, a penknife, an American passport, a lock pick and the address of a safe house in Brooklyn.

Brooklyn was no good to him, though. Yes, he'd probably be safe there, perhaps even long enough for the whole thing to blow over and for him to make good his escape. But by then it would be too late. By then war would have been declared, and half of Great Britain would already be lost.

Air travel was the only way. A steam liner would simply take too long. He needed a berth on a transatlantic airship. And he needed to call ahead. That was his priority. Get his warning to the people who could make a difference. Get help.

If he couldn't get into the embassy—and he knew, now, that his enemies would be watching the embassy like hawks—his only other option was to head back to his room in Greenwich Village. He had a secure line there, for use in the direst emergencies. He knew it was a terrible risk and that it went against everything he'd ever been taught, all the experience he had from his years in the service. The safest thing for him to do was run.

Yet running wasn't an option. There were bigger things at stake than Rutherford's own safety. He only hoped that he was wrong, that his cover hadn't been entirely blown. All he needed was ten minutes alone in the room, and then he could focus on getting out of the country alive.

Bracing himself against the chill, Rutherford got to his feet. The walk downtown would do him good, stir some blood in his veins. He turned his collar up against the light drizzle and set off for the Village, alert for anyone who might be following behind him.

—•—

The dingy, run-down apartment block was not at all the sort of place where anyone would expect a foreign spy to set up his bolt-hole. Rutherford knew that, back home, most people's idea of the secret service was swanky dinners in posh restaurants, Monte Carlo and fast living. They thought the danger was romantic, exciting, sophisticated.

He knew better. There was nothing glamorous about poking around in other people's filth, in murdering people in alleyways and trying to scrub away the bloodstains afterwards. It was dirty work, and it left a dark impression on one's psyche.

Rutherford had lost track of the number of people he'd killed in the name of his country. There had been dozens of them during the war, scores and scores, wiped out by the rapid-fire gun emplacements he'd manned, blown apart by the mortar shells he'd fired or speared through the bellies with his rifle blade as he went over the top.

After the Behemoths had trundled over the battlefields, he'd followed in their wake, mopping up the survivors with his squad. He'd seen firsthand what their weapons had done to those young men, witnessed their eviscerated corpses, put mercy bullets through their skulls so they didn't have to suffer any longer, leaving them to bleed out in the cold, wet mud. He knew they were the enemy, but he pitied them nonetheless.

Rutherford had seen what war could do to a man, and that was why he had to do everything in his power to prevent it from happening again.

Of course, he'd killed others since the war. It was inevitable in his line of work. Whether it was self-defense or political assassination, he'd carried it out in as detached a fashion as he'd been able to muster, always doing what was necessary, always remaining calm and logical. But he knew someday it would catch up with him.

The war had changed him. The war had made him a killer, and the British government had seen that, had harnessed that. They had taught him about efficiency, about stealth. They had trained him in the art of death. They had, in short, turned him into a monster.

Rutherford knew he was damaged goods. He'd never be able to

return to a normal life. Never be able to love without always somehow compromising it, seeing the blood on his hands and knowing that he didn't deserve to be happy.

There was a dark place inside his mind, a place where he buried all of the memories, all of the sights and sounds, all of the things he wanted too much to pretend had never happened. The best thing he could do for his countrymen, he knew, was to ensure that in the future none of them had to see the things he had seen, or do the things he had done. Perhaps that, and only that, could be his benediction.

Rutherford melted into the shadows on the street corner opposite the apartment building and stood there for some time, watching, waiting. He was cold, chilled to the bone, and his breath made steaming clouds before his face.

People came and went. Cars hissed by belching trails of oily smoke. The light began to wane. Still he waited. He smoked a cigarette, and then made sure to dispose of the butt down an open drain. He didn't want to leave any evidence he had been there for even the slightest amount of time. He studied the parked cars nearby, watching for any signs that the building was being watched.

Two hours later, confident that the apartment block was clear, he stepped out from beneath the awning of a derelict store and crossed the road. He moved quickly, ducking into the shelter of the doorway and slipping the key out from a hidden compartment in the sole of his shoe.

The key grated in the lock, the door swung open and then he was inside, rushing up the stairwell toward the third floor. The stairs were covered in a thick layer of grime and the detritus of poverty. He wrinkled his nose at the smell.

Moments later he was outside the door to apartment thirty-four. A different key, this time in the sole of his other shoe. He unlocked the door and pushed his way inside the apartment.

He hadn't been here for weeks, and the place was filled with a musty scent, of dust and underuse. Everything seemed to be in order. They couldn't have discovered the place yet.

His heart was pounding in his chest. He wondered how long it would be safe to stay here. He only needed ten minutes, time enough to make the call to London and toss a few belongings in a bag. Then he'd take the train out to Brooklyn and spend the night in the safe house before trying to book a berth on one of the airships leaving for the continent in the morning. If he could make it to Paris or Berlin, he could take a train to Calais and be home in a few days.

Rutherford rushed to the small bedroom where, beside the single cot, sat the holotube transmitter he needed. He flicked the metal lever to the 'Make Call' position and sat back, waiting for the unit to warm up to capacity. The machine whirred to life, emitting a dull electrical hum. The metal box was rectangular, about two feet tall, and contained a mirrored cavity within which a holographic image of the person on the other end of the line would be relayed. It was decorated in a modern style, the side panels covered in ornate fretwork and inlaid with colored glass. Rutherford found himself wishing the manufacturers had spent more time developing a way to make it work faster and less time worrying about how the thing looked.

It would take a few moments for the transmitter to come online, and then a couple of minutes to establish a connection to London.

Rutherford slouched on the bed, willing the machine to hurry.

He cocked his head when he heard something *snick* out in the hallway. What was it? The sound of someone cocking a gun?

Cautiously, trying his best not to make a sound, Rutherford slid off the bed and reached for the penknife in his pocket. He eased the blade out of the housing and shuffled across the room to stand behind the door. The door itself had swung to on loose hinges, leaving only the slightest crack of light spilling in from the hallway. Otherwise, the bedroom was shrouded in gloom, lit only by the shimmering blue light of the holotube unit.

He glanced around the dingy room, looking for anything else he might co-opt as a weapon. It was sparsely furnished, with only the bed, the bedside table and an old wardrobe filled with different sets of clothes—everything from sharp suits to pauper's rags, depending on what he might need to help him adopt one of the many personas that his trade demanded. There were weapons—guns, knives, explosives— in the other room. He'd been intending to collect those before he left. He cursed himself for not being better prepared.

Rutherford held his breath, listening intently for any further sounds from the hallway. Yes—there—the scuff of a boot on the carpet. Someone had followed him. They must have been good; he'd been careful to take a circuitous route, and he'd been vigilant, stopping to look in store windows or to buy a coffee, using those opportunities to scan the faces of the people on the street, checking none of them were becoming familiar.

There was no doubt, however. Someone else was in the apartment.

The holotube blared suddenly, the sound ringing out like a foghorn in the otherwise silent apartment. Rutherford glanced at it. A face had resolved in the mirrored cavity. "Rutherford? Are you there, Rutherford? It's London here."

The door to the bedroom slammed open with sudden force as the intruder came running at the sound of the English voice. Rutherford fell back against the wall to avoid catching the door in the face and barely had time to catch sight of the dark-haired man framed in the opening. Rutherford dived to the floor as a gunshot rang out, the bullet splintering the plaster where he had been standing only moments before.

He rolled, doing his best to get clear in the confined space of the small room.

"Rutherford!" the man on the other end of the holotube cried as he must have heard the echo of the gunshot all the way in London. "Rutherford?"

Another two gunshots, and this time the holotube transmitter fizzed and popped, the mirrored panels shattering as the lead bullets slammed into it, sending it spinning to the floor.

Rutherford used the edge of the bed to haul himself to his feet, twisting around and leaping for the other man, his penknife clutched in his fist. He brought it down hard, catching the intruder in the top of the arm and burying the knife to the hilt.

The man screamed and struck out with the butt of his gun, clubbing Rutherford hard across the side of the head. Rutherford staggered back, dazed, refusing to let go of the penknife and ripping it out of the man's arm in the process, causing blood to fountain up out of the wound. The man let off another shot, but his aim was wide and Rutherford easily avoided it, leaping out through the open door into the hall.

He didn't have time to scramble for the weapons in the other room, however, as moments later the dark-haired man was rushing him, pistol-whipping him hard across the face with the revolver. Rutherford cried out, dropping to his knees, spitting blood. Blindly he punched up, striking the man squarely in the balls.

The man doubled over, and Rutherford, lights dancing before his eyes, repeated the motion, this time burying his fist in the man's gut, causing him to drop his weapon and stagger back a pace, gasping for breath.

Rutherford stood, his back against the wall.

Then the man was rushing him again, and it was all Rutherford could do to get his arms up in defense. He jabbed out savagely with the penknife, still clutched in his right fist, roaring in sheer, unadulterated rage. To his satisfaction he caught the man brutally in the face, burying the blade in his left eye.

The result was almost instantaneous. The man slumped, his knees giving way, and then dropped to the floor, an inanimate sack of bones. Rutherford, his back still to the wall, slid to the floor beside the body, panting for breath.

A minute passed, maybe longer. Rutherford felt numb, dazed. He was bleeding from a severe gash in his cheek where he'd been struck by the butt of the gun. His hands were trembling. In the other room, through the crack in the doorway, he could see the holotube terminal smoldering on the carpet, fizzing and popping as the electrics burnt out.

Beside him, on the floor, surrounded by a growing pool of dark, glossy blood, the corpse stared up at him accusingly. The man was— had been—in his early thirties. He was swarthy and good-looking, muscular and fit. His chin was encrusted with stubble. Blood now ran freely from his nose and his slack-jawed mouth, and the penknife still jutted rudely from his left eye. The eye itself had burst, and optic fluid trickled down his cheek.

Gingerly, Rutherford leaned forward and searched the man's pockets. The man was clearly a professional. No identification papers, no handwritten notes, no jewelry. Just a thick wad of ten-dollar bills and a packet containing a few sticks of gum. Rutherford pocketed both of these.

Then, unsure what else to do but unable to hang around in his compromised bolt-hole any longer, he gathered a change of clothes, some more cash, a gun and some ammunition, and got away from there as quickly as he could, leaving the dead man where he had fallen, bleeding out all over the carpet.

CHAPTER FIVE

The Ghost stood on the roof of the precinct building, gazing out over the thronging streets of the city.

This was *his* city. The city he had sworn to protect. The city that permeated the very fabric of his being, that coursed through his veins, an immutable part of his psyche. The Ghost was the city rendered flesh. He was its avatar, its judge, jury and executioner. It was as if the city imbued him with energy, woke him from the slumber of his daily routines, gave him purpose, meaning. Gave him a reason to exist.

In return, the Ghost watched, and waited; a silent sentinel, ready to stir into action when the city needed him.

Now, he was poised like a statue on the corner of the police building, his trench coat billowing around him in the gusting winds. A cigarette dripped from his lower lip, and his goggles glowed like red pinpricks in the darkness as he turned his head, surveying the passing cars on the street below. Searching for signs of the raptors, striking out from their nest to wreak havoc once more upon the citizens below. Searching for danger, for mobsters or burglars, muggers or rapists. Searching for valediction and redemption.

If the brass monsters showed themselves that night, he would stop them. He would down one, shredding its wings, and he would pull it apart to find out what diabolical mischief had given it life. Perhaps then he would find a clue as to their purpose, or their origin, or both.

Above, the searchlight of a dirigible shone down in a brilliant column, washing everything it touched in a brilliant white light. And farther out, all across the city, electric lights twinkled and shone in the windows of tower blocks, causing the whole island to glow, under-lighting the brooding night sky. The moon was shrouded in wispy clouds, hanging full and low in the distance.

He heard the scuff of a booted foot from somewhere behind him, and smiled.

"Get down from there, Gabriel. You're making the place look untidy."

The Ghost turned to see Donovan standing on the rooftop a few feet away, his hair whipping around his face in the cross winds, a wide grin on his face. Behind him, the door to the fire escape was wedged open, allowing yellow light to spill out across the graveled courtyard.

The Ghost dropped down from the lip of the building and walked over to greet his friend, clasping him firmly by the hand. "How are you, Felix? How's Flora?"

"Tired and overworked." Donovan said, with a shrug. "Nothing new there. I haven't seen Flora for weeks. Not properly." He ran his fingers through his hair. "But we're good. We're surviving." He flexed his shoulder. "And this is finally beginning to heal."

Donovan had taken a bullet in the shoulder back in November, during a run-in with Gideon Reece, the Roman's second in command. He'd nearly bled to death in the stairwell of his apartment building until the Ghost had come to his aid, dragging him across town to his own apartment and strapping the wound. That was how Donovan had first learned of the Ghost's alter ego, having spent the night sleeping fitfully in an armchair, waking to find the Ghost had once more become Gabriel Cross.

Since then, there had been a growing bond of trust and mutual respect between the two men, even if their methods were often diametrically opposed.

"What about you? You've been quiet." The concern was evident in Donovan's voice. He knew about the canceled parties, the fact that Gabriel had retreated from public life since the death of Celeste.

"I've been busy," the Ghost replied, attempting to draw a line under the matter.

"Haven't we all," Donovan laughed, darkly. He sounded more exasperated than amused.

"This raptor business . . . " the Ghost started.

"Ah, yes," Donovan sighed. "You look like you've been busy." He indicated his face, referencing the Ghost's scarred and scratched appearance. "A woman called Patricia Reuben called the station this morning, asking for me by name. Said she'd been abducted by one of the flying things but a man in a black suit had saved her. Know anything about that?"

The Ghost laughed. "Did she give you anything useful?"

"Not really," Donovan replied, "Nothing new. It's helpful to have a firsthand account, but she only told us what we already knew: that the things come swooping out of the sky to pluck people off the streets, seemingly at random. She was walking back from a jazz club when it happened. She was lucky you were there to help. Otherwise she'd have gone the way of all the others."

The Ghost nodded. "I only wish we knew what that was. And that I'd been quicker. There was another one, too. That one got away with a young man."

Donovan shook his head. He looked pained. "That one hasn't been reported yet." He kicked at the gravel underfoot. "I take it you've had no luck tracking the things, then?"

"No. They're too fast, even carrying a body. I damaged one of them yesterday, but I had to let it go to save the girl."

"Too bad," Donovan said morosely.

The two men lapsed into a brief, knowing silence.

The Ghost studied the policeman, who seemed distracted. He watched as Donovan glanced up at the sound of the police dirigible whirring overhead, as if worried they might find themselves caught beneath its swinging searchlight.

Then Donovan said suddenly, urgently, "Look, there's something else. Something that's come up."

"This thing with the commissioner?" the Ghost queried.

"Yeah. The thing with the commissioner." Donovan searched around in his jacket, realized he'd left his cigarettes on his desk again, and held his hand out to the Ghost, who chuckled and tossed him his own packet. Donovan slipped one of the thin white sticks out of the paper wrapper and pulled the ignition tab. He sighed gratefully as he dragged the nicotine into his lungs. "Seems there's a British spy running amok down there"—he nodded toward the bristling lights of the city below—"and the commissioner wants me to find him."

The Ghost frowned. "A *spy*? Aren't there government agencies to take care of that sort of thing? What about the raptors?"

Donovan blew smoke from his nostrils in long riffles. "That's just it. That's what's got me feeling jumpy about the whole thing. I think the commissioner's been leaned on. The whole thing seems to have been orchestrated by a senator called Isambard Banks." He paused. "Do you remember that name?"

The Ghost frowned. "Wasn't he mixed up in all that mess with the Roman?"

"That's him." Donovan nodded. "Walked away from the whole thing because we couldn't tie him back to anything specific. But his name was linked to the others, more than once. Anyway, he was there when I went to speak to the commissioner this afternoon. Pretty much gave me an order to get on with it, and the commissioner just sat by and encouraged it to happen. Thing is, I don't trust him, Gabriel."

"Who? The senator? Or the commissioner?"

Donovan shrugged. "Perhaps both . . . I don't know. There's something not right. I can't put my finger on it."

"Did he tell you what this spy was up to?"

"Counterintelligence. Apparently he knows secrets that could ignite a war with the British," Donovan replied, his voice low.

"You mean he's uncovered what Banks and the rest of those corrupt bastards are up to, and Banks is trying to stop him going public," the Ghost laughed, skeptically.

"Something like that," Donovan said, his tone serious. He reached out, catching the Ghost by the arm. "I need your help, Gabriel. If this is real, if there really is a war brewing . . . well, we have to stop it."

The Ghost nodded. He knew the horrors of war. Knew what it could do to a man. Donovan was right. If this spy really was in a position to escalate things with the British, to exploit the intelligence he'd uncovered, then he had to be stopped. "Of course," he said. "I'll start by checking out Banks, find out what he's really up to. But first I want to bring down one of those raptors."

Donovan nodded. "Thank you," he said. He flicked the butt of his cigarette over the edge of the building, and the Ghost watched it tumble through the air and disappear into the haze of the city. When he looked back, Donovan was brandishing a manila envelope. "Photographs, names, places—everything I've got on the spy."

The Ghost accepted the packet and slid it inside his coat. "Keep in touch, Felix," he said, and then turned and ran toward the edge of the building, leaping up onto the stone lip and propelling himself into the air.

For a moment he was falling again, hurtling toward the street below. Then, seconds later, he was soaring away on twin spikes of flame, up and over the top of the nearby tower blocks, the rush of the wind in his face, adrenaline coursing through his veins.

CHAPTER SIX

He was in hell. He was sure it was hell.

Up there, hanging out of the cockpit of his plane, Gabriel had a view that stretched for miles and miles, right across the undulating landscape, from the rolling hills in the east to the lush farmland in the west. If he craned his neck, ignored the spiraling pillars of black smoke, the remorseless chatter and bark of gunfire from below, he could almost believe he was flying away toward those far-off hills, where the war was a distant concern and the landscape hadn't yet been marred by blood and bullets.

It should have been idyllic, peaceful. But instead, the ground far beneath him roiled with horror.

Muddy trenches had been carved methodically across fields that had once been green, but were now reduced to nothing but brown slurry, churned over and over by mortar fire and peppered with the remains of the dead. People buzzed around in these tunnels like ants navigating their way through a confusing maze, or neurons darting to and fro inside the workings of some ancient, arcane mind.

He wondered if they were, in fact, part of some enormous hive, if there wasn't some greater purpose at play. If that were true, none of those men were fully aware of it or knew exactly what part in it they were serving. All they did was follow orders, rushing headlong toward their deaths, because that was all they *could* do. That was all they knew, the only thing that gave them any purpose. The war had eclipsed everything, like an ink stain on a sheet of blotting paper. It had absorbed these men, turned them into drones for the hive, swallowed their identities and memories and reasons for being, and replaced them with orders and a desire to kill.

Gabriel knew that wasn't entirely true. Nor was it fair. Those men— his friends and comrades—had given their lives for a cause they believed in, to protect their loved ones, their freedom and their country. That was entirely admirable, and it was brave.

Yet Gabriel had learned to hate the war, to hate everything it represented. The war had turned him into a murderer, and while he knew that if he survived this horror, he would return to his country to be heralded a hero, he would never *feel* like a hero. He would only ever feel like a killer, a man who had lost his way. He wondered if he would ever wake up from the numbness that had settled over him. He doubted it.

He'd never intended to be here, in an aircraft high above a killing field. He'd never wanted to see the things he'd seen. Those sights had changed him irreversibly, altered his fundamental view of the world. There was no going back. Even when it was over, for him, the war would last forever.

He looked down upon the battlefield.

Black smoke curled from the blazing wreckage of buildings and vehicles, and lights flashed orange and white as hulking weapons punched explosive round after explosive round toward the enemy encampments. Mud sprayed in massive plumes where the mortar rounds struck the earth, some of them sucking up and spitting out people, too, like miniature tornadoes, striking in a flash, wreaking devastation, and then disappearing again, only to be replaced moments later by another, and then another, and then another.

It was constant, relentless. It was a vast, mindless engine of death, with people as its fuel supply.

From up there, high above the battlefield, Gabriel couldn't tell the difference between the two sides in this terrible game of death, couldn't discern which side was which, so similar were the encampments, the weapons, the uniforms, the tactics.

That was the great irony of all this, he thought. If only they could see themselves from up here, they'd realize how ridiculous it all was, that in truth they were all the same, on the same side. But he knew they were blinded by rage and patriotism, and the killing would simply continue until there was no one left to die.

Gabriel snapped suddenly alert at the *rat-a-tat* of a machine gun and banked sharply to the left, narrowly missing a hail of bullets that had been intended to shred his right wing. He dipped and arced in a loop, spiraling around to face his attacker.

The other plane had come out of nowhere, zipping out from behind the cloud cover as Gabriel had approached. It was a German biplane, armed to the teeth with machine gun emplacements and hungry to bring him down.

Rat-a-tat, rat-a-tat.

Gabriel realized there were two people in the enemy aircraft: a gunman in the rear seat was taking potshots at him while the pilot tried to maneuver them closer for the kill. He was massively outgunned.

Gabriel went into a sharp dive, pushing the flight controls forward as far as they would go, sending the plane hurtling toward the muddy ground below. The propellers groaned and whined as he held his course until, at the last minute, he wrenched back on the controls, pulling the nose up sharply and bringing the plane back into a steady climb.

He could see the enemy aircraft above him now, like a silvery boat hanging in the sky, its belly exposed beneath the water. He raced toward it, his thumbs depressing the buttons that set loose a hail of bullets from the nose-mounted weapons on his own plane.

There was a din of rending metal as the spray of bullets hit home, peppering the fuselage of the German plane with a series of ragged pockmarks. The pilot bucked wildly in his seat but managed to maintain his course.

Seconds later, Gabriel was forced to slew to the left to avoid colliding with the biplane, and he banked around trying desperately to gain height. The German gunman let loose with another shower of bullets, his machine gun roaring, its hot mouth spitting death. This time the gunner's aim was true and the shots caught Gabriel's plane along its left flank, opening a large rent in the thin metal fuselage.

Gabriel breathed a heavy sigh of relief when he realized his fuel tank was still intact and the bullets had narrowly missed his legs, puncturing the area around the cockpit. He could barely hear himself think over the sound of the rushing air and the whine of the rending metal where the side of the plane had been compromised.

He turned the plane in a wide circle, coming about above and behind the German aircraft. He depressed the triggers again, squeezing out another storm of bullets. The enemy biplane swung wildly from side to side, trying to avoid being hit.

For a few moments the two planes danced above the battlefield, ducking and weaving, slewing and banking, diving and looping. All the while, Gabriel maintained his target, mirroring the other pilot's maneuvers, keeping the biplane locked in his sights.

He fired again, roaring in rage and success as he saw the gunner jerk and go suddenly limp. Blood sprayed in a wide arc as the bullets ripped through the man's chest and throat.

Gabriel pressed on with the attack, trying to capitalize on the pilot's fear and disorientation. He swooped down, hovering just above the other plane. He could see the lolling head of the dead gunner as the biplane shook and darted from side to side, trying desperately to shake Gabriel's tail.

Gabriel, however, was too quick. He saw his chance. He took his aim, and fired.

The pilot bucked in his seat, his hands abandoning the controls as he clutched pointlessly at his chest, as if trying to plug the holes where the bullets had punched through his body. He coughed blood, spasmed, and was still.

Gabriel banked sharply and climbed away from the biplane, which, with no pilot at the controls, went into a long spiral as it nosedived toward the muddy battlefield below.

Seconds later, leaning out of his cockpit to watch, he saw the German aircraft plummet into the ground, crumpling with an earth-shattering bang, sending dirt slewing in a tidal wave toward the enemy trenches. There was silence for a moment. Then it exploded with a whoosh of heat and light as the fuel tank went up, causing Gabriel to shield his eyes and look away.

For a moment he allowed himself to feel jubilant. He'd survived. He'd bettered an enemy pilot in a dogfight. Then he remembered the look on the gunner's face as Gabriel's bullets had shredded his torso, the sight of the blood spewing out of the pilot's mouth, the desperate way he had clutched at his chest as if trying to hold himself together.

This was nothing to feel jubilant about. There was no celebration here. He had killed two men.

Gabriel buried those images, suppressing them, locking them in that dark, private place in his mind, that place where all of those horrors resided. He wondered if that was how they all coped, all of the soldiers, locking those thoughts away deep inside their psyches. He wondered if that was why they were all so happy to blithely follow orders like they did. Because it gave them something to focus on, rather than the horrors they would have to face if they ever turned away.

Gabriel pulled back on the controls and the plane soared, rising up through the white, fluffy clouds, until all he could see was a blanket of white and the bright, formless blue of the horizon.

And there, watching him, were the eyes.

Gabriel woke with a start. He sat bolt upright in bed, his chest glistening with sweat. He ran a hand through his hair, feeling disorientated, out of sorts. Where was he? The place seemed unfamiliar.

The walls seemed to resolve around him. A stranger's room? No, the spare room. That was it. He was back in Long Island, back at the house, and he'd spent the night in the guest room because when he'd returned home late from the city, he'd found Ginny curled up asleep on his bed.

Gabriel shook his head, attempting to dislodge the last, clinging vestiges of his dream. It had seemed so real, so vivid. It felt as if he'd actually been back there, in the skies above France, feeling the wind in his hair, his nostrils filled with the heady scent of the engines, hearing nothing above the roaring din of the propellers. And those eyes, those huge, disembodied eyes, staring at him across the void, taunting him, willing him on. Encouraging him to break away, to turn his plane around and soar off into the pale blue skies, to leave that wasteland of death and destruction far behind.

He'd wanted so much to do that, then, to flee from the barking guns, from the corpses of his dead comrades, from the promise of nothing but further death and destruction.

He had stayed, of course, and he had killed, and he had watched everyone he cared about die in those miserable trenches, eking out their last days up to their ankles in filthy rainwater, surrounded by shit and blood and rotting body parts, knowing that any day it would be their turn to die. That they would be next to fall, to become food for the ravens that flocked to the wastelands where their friends and brothers lay still and dead, their unseeing eyes staring all the way up to Heaven.

Constantly, those eyes had watched him, judging him, staring right through to his soul.

Gabriel shuddered. He had never told anyone about what he'd seen up there, in the skies over France. They'd probably tell him he was mad, or that the stress of the war had caused him to hallucinate, to imagine things that weren't really there: a representation of his subconscious mind as it tried to deal with the nightmarish things he had witnessed. That it was the guilt and the paranoia, the thought of being judged for the things he'd had to do, the lives he'd been forced to take. They might even have been right.

Gabriel knew, though, with a clarity that he had rarely known, that what he'd seen up there in the sky had been real. Those strange, shimmering eyes on the horizon, like golden orbs, had been there for him. He had no idea what they were, where they had come from, but nevertheless, he was sure of it. He had seen them time and again when he'd been up there, flying above the clouds.

At first, disturbed, he'd flown toward them, imagining they'd resolve into some feature of the distant landscape, or that he'd realize they were nothing but reflected light in the hazy distance, but no matter what he had done, how he had approached them, they had always remained the same, unblinking, unmoving, just hanging there, watching him, seeing right through him to the core of what he was. He'd never felt so exposed, so open and raw, as when he'd been confronted by those eyes. Not until he'd met Celeste. Celeste had looked at him the same way, as though she'd been able to read his innermost thoughts, as though she understood him better than he understood himself.

Sighing, Gabriel slid out from beneath the eiderdown and padded to the bathroom. He realized when he grabbed for the doorknob that his palms were bleeding from little sickle-shaped cuts where his nails had dug into his flesh. He must have been bunching his fists in his sleep whilst he relived the dogfight.

As he stood under the shower and let the steaming water play over his skin, Gabriel could still see the face of the dead gunner, the slack-jawed expression of surprise, the blood leaking from numerous bullet wounds in his throat.

He hung his head, pressing his palms against the tiled wall.

Gabriel's body was an atlas of scars. Each one told a different story, from the thick, ropy welts that ran all the way from his left breast to the soft flesh beneath his arm, to the gunshot wound in his abdomen, to the tiny puncture marks in his thighs. Women, over the years, had traced these scars with their fingertips, intrigued and appalled, fascinated to discover that this man who had taken them to his bed had more depth than they had ever imagined. Gabriel had *lived*. He had lived more than most people would ever live, and in the course of that life he had been to hell and back. He wasn't proud of what he had done—in fact, in his darker moments he abhorred himself for his actions—but he had learned to live with them. They were like a shadow that he couldn't shake, and the scars were his reminder.

Every day he would look upon his ravaged body in the mirror, and he would remember. Then he would dress and cover himself up. He would slip into the persona of Gabriel Cross and surround himself with people, and once again he would try to forget his past.

Yet Gabriel's mind was also a map of scars, and these were harder to discern, and harder still to disguise.

He wondered sometimes what it was that had caused him to fracture, to wake up one day and decide that the life he was living was nothing but a trivial fantasy, that everything that comprised Gabriel Cross was a lie. That first time, just a few months ago, when he had donned the black suit and trench coat and ventured out into the city had been so liberating, so *real*.

It wasn't power that attracted him, nor the desire to inflict or receive violence. He'd seen enough of that in his short time to last a lifetime. No, it was something else entirely. Something to do with being truthful, with letting the world see everything that those strange floating orbs had once seen, all those years ago in the skies above France. Something to do with accessing that part of his mind he had once closed off and sealed away, swearing he would never reveal it again, not even to himself. Something to do with revealing himself, exposing the real man, the man he had buried in France over a decade earlier. And it was also something to do with the city.

He couldn't bear to watch the city slide into turmoil and corruption without doing something to try to prevent it. Protecting the city gave him a purpose, a reason to be alive. When he was the Ghost, he could *feel* again. The numbness was banished, just for those few hours.

Gabriel stepped out of the shower, dripping all over the bathroom floor. For a few moments he considered going back to bed. It was still early, and he'd been late getting back from the city. But then the scent of cooking eggs and bacon stirred his stomach, and he reached for a towel.

Perhaps he needed the party back? Perhaps that was it. If he surrounded himself with people again, he might feel more alive. But those people couldn't bring back Celeste. Hers was the only face he looked for in the crowds.

At Christmas, the last time he'd thrown open his doors for the interlopers, he had thought for a moment he had seen her there, standing in the doorway of the drawing room, dressed in a glossy red dress that matched her hair, beaming at him, an unfiltered cigarette clutched between the fingers of her right hand.

When he had looked again, she had gone, and in her place stood another of those mindless girls who swished around in their party frocks, searching for oblivion, wishing only for someone to come and take them and fuck them and help them drink until they were sick. Only then would they feel able to tell their friends they'd had a "swinging time" at the party, that the other girls were missing out and that they "really must come along next time, there's a heated pool, you know! Be sure to bring a costume."

Gabriel hadn't been able to look the woman in the eye.

As he dressed, pulling on his usual black suit and white shirt, leaving it open at the collar, Gabriel remembered Ginny.

What had she been doing here, stretched out on his bed when he'd returned from the city? How had she known he would come here after all these weeks?

In her way, Ginny was as damaged as he was. That much had become clear the other day, after the boxing match, when he'd taken her for a drink. It had always been there, of course, but he'd never thought to ask, never even tried to understand her. As far as he'd been concerned, Ginny was just another part of the lie that was Gabriel's life, along with the parties and the fast cars and the booze.

At the time he hadn't seen the truth, hadn't realized what he could have had. Only later had that realization come, and by then it was already too late.

Ginny had tried to know him once, to truly *know* him. Foolishly, he had locked her out, always keeping her at arm's length. She had stuck with him for some months, but after a while, worn down by the constant barriers, she had given up. Whether she'd decided she would never be able to get close to him, or that there was, in fact, nothing beneath that shiny veneer of Gabriel Cross, he didn't know. Whatever the case—one way or another he had lost her because he hadn't allowed her to get close.

Now, though, she was back. Had she seen something different in him, this time? Had he given her a glimmer of hope? He wasn't sure that he wanted that. He certainly didn't want her pity. Yet something inside him wanted her to know he'd been wrong, all those years ago. That much was clear to him: this time there would be no secrets. No lies.

She was still drinking. After the match the other day she'd dragged him to a speakeasy around the corner, a sleazy joint with sticky floors beneath a flower shop, where the barman knew her and had cracked open a bottle before opening time so she could have a drink. She'd polished off nearly a full bottle of gin, drinking it straight over ice, and Gabriel had had to practically manhandle her back to her rented apartment at three in the afternoon.

Now, he could hear her voice drifting up the stairs, chattering away to Henry as he fixed her breakfast. He was probably grateful of the company. He'd been left out here, looking after the old house, while

Gabriel had been living—hiding—in the city. Gabriel had offered to take Henry with him, of course, but the butler was having none of it, preferring to keep to his routines, perhaps knowing that it was only a matter of time before Gabriel deemed it appropriate to return.

Of course, Henry didn't know anything about what had really happened before Christmas, but he knew about Celeste, had even helped Gabriel to bury her in the family mausoleum when he'd proved unable to locate any records of her family.

Henry was a rock, and more than anyone he'd understood the need to give Gabriel space, to allow him to mourn in his own way.

Gabriel didn't know what had made him return to Long Island last night. He'd haunted the rooftops of the city for hours, searching for any sign of the raptors, but in the end had been disappointed. He'd stopped a petty thief from getting away with a shopkeeper's takings around midnight, but other than that the streets had seemed unusually quiet. He supposed Commissioner Montague's advice to remain indoors must have been taken to heart.

Still, he was here now, and he wasn't about to miss out on one of Henry's famous breakfasts. He descended the stairs, listening to the banter coming from the breakfast room. It sounded like Ginny was in good spirits, and Henry was clearly taken with her, just as he had been three years ago when she'd been around all the time, the life and soul of the party.

Gabriel crossed the hall and then, keen not to make too much of an entrance, walked straight into the breakfast room and dropped into a chair at the table, opposite Ginny. "I don't suppose there're any more of those eggs going spare, Henry?" He beamed up at his old friend, who was standing just to the left of Ginny, dressed in his usual immaculate black suit. "And perhaps a side of toast?"

Henry turned to stare at him, a startled expression on his old, careworn face. This soon gave way to a warm smile, however, and he inclined his head in acknowledgment. "Good morning, sir. I'd be only too pleased to rustle something up." He offered Ginny a short, polite bow and then turned and strode off in the direction of the kitchen. Clearly, Gabriel thought, Henry hadn't realized that he'd slipped in during the early hours, and hadn't seen the car parked around the back.

He turned to Ginny, who was leaning back in her chair, a wide grin on her face. She looked perfectly groomed, even for this time in the morning. Her hair was set in a smart bob, and she peered out at him from beneath a severe, but not unattractive, fringe. She was wearing a pink dress that revealed the tops of her arms. It wasn't the same dress she'd been sleeping in the previous night when he'd discovered her on his bed, so, he realized, she must have brought a bag. Sly old Henry, inviting her to spend the night. Gabriel wondered what she'd told him. She was still grinning. "What is it? Why are you grinning like that?"

Ginny emitted a heartfelt laugh and reached for the bloody mary on the table. It was her second of the day—he could tell by the empty glass that Henry had forgotten to clear away in his haste. "I knew it!" she exclaimed, taking a long swig of the drink. "I just knew you'd come back to the house last night!"

Gabriel frowned. Was he really that predictable?

"Why didn't you wake me?" she asked, as if she already knew the answer and was wondering what he would say. She placed her drink back on the table and leaned forward, listening intently.

"I found you asleep on my bed. So I did the gentlemanly thing and slept in the guest room."

Ginny laughed again, and her blue eyes flashed with amusement.

"Oh, Gabriel," her shoulders slumped in mock disappointment, "I didn't want you to be a gentleman."

Gabriel felt himself flush red. He didn't know quite what to say. Thankfully, Ginny stepped in and saved him. "So, how about it?"

"How about what?" For a moment he wondered if she was getting at . . .

"A party, of course! Just like the old times. You know, everyone drunk and dancing and raising cahoots. It'll be fun! What d'ya say?" She seemed so excited by the idea that he didn't have the heart to say no. And, besides, he was relieved the subject had moved on from their bedroom arrangements.

"All right, Ginny. We'll have a party. Tonight, if you like. But first— you still haven't told me why you came back." His head was spinning with all the questions he wanted to ask her, but this seemed like the most important place to start.

Ginny snatched up her bloody mary. "Well . . . I . . ." She was saved by the reappearance of Henry, who shuffled into the room bearing two silver platters, each containing a plate heaped with eggs, bacon and slices of toast.

"Henry!" Ginny almost shouted, the relief evident in her voice. "We're going to have a party! Tonight, right here at the house. Isn't that wonderful?"

Henry issued a heartfelt sigh. "Are we indeed, Miss Gray." He caught Gabriel's eye, a weary expression on his face. But Gabriel could tell he was secretly delighted. The house was going to be full of people again, buzzing with life. Henry thrived on that. For all his complaints, all the work it created, he loved it when the house was full of people. Perhaps, thought Gabriel, the party was what Henry needed, too. Perhaps it was what they all needed.

"Shall I make the necessary arrangements then, sir?" Henry asked, carefully placing the silver tray down before Gabriel.

Gabriel nodded. "I think it would be rather a shame to disappoint Miss Gray, Henry, don't you?"

Henry raised an eyebrow at this. "And may I be so bold as to enquire, sir—are you planning to stay?"

Gabriel speared a forkful of bacon. "I rather think I am, Henry, yes."

CHAPTER SEVEN

The creature in the pit was hungry. That much was clear from the way it was thrashing about, slamming its proboscis against the walls and snapping its many jaws in frustration.

Abraham hated the noises it made when it did that. Sooner or later he'd have to teach it a lesson. If he'd had a more ready supply of the solution he used to control it, slowly withering its tentacled limbs to keep it in check, he'd have done so already. As it was, he'd have to put up with the noise for a while longer, at least until he'd finished making the necessary alterations to his leg. Then he'd be able to give it something to eat.

Abraham was sitting at the back of his makeshift workshop down by the docks, converted from an old boat-builder's hangar. It was cold, drafty and damp, but, Abraham had to admit, his patrons had provided him with everything he needed. For a man in his position, he lived a life of relative comfort. And besides, he was surrounded by his many pets.

Currently, he had his leg up on the workbench before him, peering at it through a large magnifying lens strapped to his head. He'd detached the mechanical limb in order to repair one of the servos in the knee joint, and for the last hour had been having trouble getting the new components to work. He cursed loudly when, after introducing a slight electrical charge, the limb began to spasm, as if operating under its own free will. Nuts and bolts scattered to the floor all around him as Abraham fought to keep the crazed limb under control. After a moment, the spasm subsided. He set about making another adjustment with his screwdriver.

Abraham Took was a leper. This was evident to anyone who saw him from less than a few feet away: his face was blemished by unsightly lesions that had caused his flesh to swell and bloat, leaving him with a permanent, heavy frown and the gnarled, withered look of a man twice his age. However, what people tended to notice first upon encountering Abraham Took was the fact that he was now considerably more machine than he was man.

Abraham Took had spent the last three years slowly, steadily, rebuilding himself. This, in part, was a result of his progressive disease, rather than a simple fashion or fetish with mechanization. It had started with the growing numbness in his left hand as the disease took hold of the appendage, effectively rendering the entire arm useless to him, preventing him from carrying on with his work. For weeks Abraham had struggled on, carrying the limb around like a dead, useless weight, unable even to use it to help him eat, or to hold open doors. Then, one day, whilst assembling the components of one of his raptors, he had struck upon the idea of replacing the limb altogether.

It had seemed like a radical idea at the time, but his work fusing human bone to the metal skeletons of his pets had meant he already had an idea of how to go about achieving his aim. And it gave him hope. The disease was slowly stealing his identity, smothering him, hiding him away inside a body that refused to behave as it was told. This was how he could fight back. This was his means of stealing victory from the arms of defeat.

Abraham had spent the next week constructing the new limb,

improving on his older designs, adding further articulation and precision control, fashioning the hand and fingers to be as close an approximation to the original limb as possible.

It had only occurred to him later that he could actually *improve* on the original human form. At first, he had tried only to emulate it.

The new limb had been magnificent, a triumph of microengineering, and the day after its completion he had pumped his shoulder full of local anesthetic and flayed open the diseased arm, fixing it in a vise and using his good hand to saw through the bone. He'd tied off the artery as quickly as possible, still spilling a tremendous amount of blood on his workshop floor. Then he'd slowly deconstructed the appendage, freeing tendons and hacking away necrotic tissue. After he had finished he had cauterized the exposed flesh of the stump. Then, without any further ado, he had set about attaching the new mechanical arm, fusing the bone to the brass and attaching the tendons. It had taken a number of attempts to get it right, and he'd been forced to sleeve the arm in brass plating to protect the exposed tendons, packing the new limb full of moisturizing jelly to stop them from drying out.

Ten hours later, however, tired but triumphant, Abraham Took had regained the use of his limb.

That had only been the start. Abraham hadn't been able to stop tinkering, making constant improvements to his design. In the end he'd replaced the tendons entirely with a less perishable material, disposing with the need for any organic matter whatsoever.

Next had been his left leg, then his right, and finally parts of his chest and stomach. All of them had been rebuilt, redefined, mechanized as the disease progressed.

It wasn't that he wanted to live forever, that he was attempting to extend his life indefinitely—not at all. It was simply that he wanted to beat the disease. He couldn't let it win, couldn't let it smother him and change him and keep him from his work. So he had continued, altering himself, shedding his soft, diseased body in favor of the new brass components he constructed in his workshop.

Of course, the new appendages were not without their faults, and now, sitting in his workshop trying to reconnect his leg, flustered by the constant shrieking of the creature in the pit, Abraham could almost wish he'd never started. But he knew that was only frustration talking. The mechanization had given him a new lease on life, helping him to live with his disease, and he had learned a few things in the process, things he'd been able to use to make improvements to his pets, the raptors.

He glanced up at them now, watching them scrabbling around among the rafters of the warehouse. They were beautiful. His finest creations. They looked down on him from the shadows, chittering and clicking, and he thought he could see awe in their piercing red eyes. He was their god, their creator. He had given them form and breathed life into them, constructing their bodies from so much lifeless scrap. He was their master, and they obeyed him explicitly.

There were nine of the raptors, plus the two he had sent out into the city and the two he had temporarily decommissioned for repair. Thirteen in all; the perfect quorum. He'd made another six for the senator, of course, but he tended not to think of those orphaned beasts as part of the family.

Abraham had been shocked to find one of them had returned damaged the previous night, its wing torn to ragged shreds by some kind of projectile weapon, but he had patched it up that morning, flaying some fresh skin from one of the corpses and stretching it over the skeletal wing to form a membrane. Within an hour it had been as good as new. He didn't yet know who was responsible for hurting one of his pets, but he intended to find out. When he did, he would make them pay.

Abraham placed the cupped end of his mechanical leg over the fleshy stump of his thigh and gave it a sharp twist. He grunted in satisfaction as it snapped into place. He wiggled the brass digits experimentally to ensure it was working. Then, rising from his chair, his metal feet scraping on the concrete, he turned to survey his work.

The warehouse was cluttered with all manner of bizarre machinery. Electrical components lay strewn across the floor or heaped against the walls. Iron girders were stacked neatly to one side, and electric flood lamps flickered and hummed, illuminating the entire scene in brilliant white light. Rising out of this sea of mechanical detritus were the twin spurs of a great machine, curving like the tusks of some enormous land mammal to form an archway, a doorway, a portal. These spurs were at least twenty feet high, and each was precisely engraved with an array of arcane symbols and ancient pictograms. It had taken Abraham months to etch those markings, carefully tracing the outlines from grainy photographs and line drawings in long-forgotten history books, studiously deciphering their ancient occult significance. Accuracy had been tantamount; any deviation and the machine would fail to work. But Abraham had been careful, and he had not failed.

This, Abraham mused, was his life's work. It was almost complete, almost ready to install in the vessel that waited in the neighboring hangar, ready for its long journey across the ocean. He knew that it worked—the creature in the pit was evidence enough of that. Yet there were more tests still to be run, and before it could be put to use, his raptors had to do their work.

The creature in the pit was still flailing about and screeching, desperate for sustenance. He walked over to it now, looking down over the edge of the hole.

The original purpose of the pit had been to enable the shipbuilders to access the undersides of their vessels, to repair the hulls while the ships were out of the water. But Abraham had found a much better use for it. He'd used it to incarcerate an alien.

The creature was like nothing he had ever imagined, not even in his wildest dreams. It was huge. Its form approximated that of a giant squid, but it was a thousand times more bizarre than anything born of the physical world. The hulking mass of its body was a globular sphere of translucent, glistening flesh, with one large, cyclopean eye at its epicenter. That eye stared up at him now, a sphere of bright, glowing amber, burning with hatred and menace. It had twelve ropy tentacles that served as limbs, formed from the same thick, translucent flesh as its body. Each one terminated in a snapping mouth, lined with razor-sharp teeth, which the creature used to burrow into its prey, extracting the blood that gave it sustenance.

What was more, Abraham had come to realize, it had a very particular taste for human blood.

He looked down at it and sneered. This thing, this alien, had been dragged through his portal from its own dimension. It wasn't really an alien at all, not in the truest sense—it hadn't originated on another world. Rather, it belonged to a dimension of time and space that functioned alongside the one inhabited by the human race, in parallel to it.

These were the creatures that inhabited the nightmares of men, the ghosts on the other side of time. These were the creatures that had known of men since the first primates had dropped down from the trees, that had already been ancient when the dinosaurs had roamed the earth.

This creature and its brethren shared the universe—and the planet—with humanity. Yet the two dimensions were out of sync with one another, only rarely coming into contact. And now Abraham had one of them prisoner in his workshop, by virtue of his creation, his machine that collapsed those dimensions together, creating a gateway between worlds, a doorway into another place.

At first, Abraham had feared the creature, feared everything it represented, feared that it might find the strength to haul itself out of the pit and consume him. The solution he'd developed, however, derived from a sample of blood that he knew to be anathema to the creature, had worked to control it.

He'd perhaps been a little overzealous in his application of the poison at first, accidentally rendering one of its tentacles dead. This had taught the creature a lesson, though, and now Abraham was a little more conservative with its use, applying it only when it was required to force the beast into submission. Consequently, the creature was pockmarked all over its body with patches of decaying, necrotic tissue, much like Abraham himself.

Now, however, Abraham needed more of the solution. He barely had enough to keep the creature in check, and with mounting pressure from his patrons to have the machine fully operational, he'd had to increase the frequency of his raptors' trips to the city. He'd tested over a hundred people now, probably more, and not one of them had resulted in a positive match for the blood type he was searching for. Nevertheless, the rejects had served as a ready food supply for the creature, as exemplified by the random assortment of human bones and articles of discarded clothing that surrounded the thing at the bottom of the pit.

The creature had grown still as it regarded him. Its tentacles curled and writhed, but no longer thrashed against the walls of the pit. *Good*,

Abraham thought. It was finally learning respect. He'd reward it with some food.

Abraham circled the large hole, his metal feet clopping as he walked. He approached the far wall of the warehouse, where three people—a young man and two women—were chained to iron stakes in the ground. He stood over them, trying to decide which of them to throw to the creature first. It had to be the man. He'd proved the most difficult when Abraham had sliced open his arm to test his precious blood, struggling and kicking and trying to break free. Abraham had been forced to employ the raptors to hold him still while he'd worked.

The man was cowering now, however, bound and gagged, a pitiful sight on the warehouse floor. Abraham smiled. He enjoyed the power he commanded over these people. He could choose whether they lived or died. Today, he chose that this man would die.

Abraham hauled the man to his feet, slapping him hard across the face with his mechanical arm to warn him that any insubordination would not be tolerated. The man gave a muffled cry from behind his gag as his cheek split open with the impact. Abraham carefully unclipped the man's wrists from the iron cuffs that bound him to the stake. His wrists were still bound together with twine, as were his ankles, making it impossible for him to flee. If he tried anything, Abraham knew his raptors would make short shrift of him, anyway.

Abraham gave him a short, sharp shove toward the pit. The man stumbled and tried to shuffle away, but Abraham shoved him again, harder this time, and the man fell to his knees. He was crying now, tears streaming down his face, whimpering and moaning. He knew what was coming. He'd seen a woman dropped into the pit the previous day.

Abraham stooped and grabbed the man by his collar. He dragged him forward to the edge of the pit, watching the creature stir again in excitement as it realized what was coming. Without further ado, Abraham pushed the man over the edge, watching him tumble into the slimy folds of the alien's flesh, which blanched under the impact.

"My God, Abraham, do they have to be alive when you throw them in there?"

Abraham turned at the voice of Senator Isambard Banks, who was standing just a few feet away by the spurs of the machine. Abraham hadn't heard him come in. He was surprised the raptors hadn't started up, but he supposed they were used to the senator by now. Abraham smiled. "It likes them better that way," he said, turning back to watch the creature devouring the young man, its multiple mouths burrowing deep into his flesh, drawing the blood out of him. Abraham watched the fluid course along the creature's translucent gullets, dark and red, pooling in its belly. "It's remarkable, isn't it?" he said to Banks, who had drifted over to stand beside him and was looking down, an expression of sheer disgust on his face. "So alien, so deadly. A living nightmare."

"It's barbaric," Banks replied stiffly before averting his eyes to focus on Abraham. "But it's effective. It's exactly what we need."

Abraham grinned. "Yes, it most certainly is," he agreed. He couldn't hide his euphoria at the thought of the part he was playing in the great scheme. His machine, his weapon, would go down in history. Future generations would remember his name. Abraham Took: the leper who had ensured the future of the American nation.

"How are the preparations?" Banks inquired. He looked up toward the rafters, eyeing the flock of raptors as they hopped about, chittering away, watching him intently from above. Abraham saw Banks open and close his fists in a nervous gesture. It was clear he was uncomfortable, even though he knew the raptors were incapable of harming him. That had been one of the conditions the senator had insisted upon when he'd funded their development: the raptors were to accept his command as equal to Abraham's own. It was a simple but effective security measure. Neither of them could order the raptors against the other. Nevertheless, Abraham smiled, enjoying the man's unease. He found people like Banks rarely liked to be reminded how dirty their hands really were.

"The machine is ready. Another day, two at the most, and it'll be fully installed in the transporter. But we still lack the necessary supplies to properly operate it."

"The solution?" Banks asked, frowning.

Abraham nodded. "No matter how many of these idiots I test, none of them have the blood type I need." He indicated the two women with a wave of his hand. They were watching him, wide-eyed and terrified.

Banks shuddered. "Can't you just synthesize some more from the batch you already have?"

Abraham resisted the urge to cuff the senator around the side of his head for his naïveté. "I've told you before, Senator, it's not that simple," he said, through gritted teeth. "If I can get enough blood I can dilute it, slowly, to create a vat of the stuff. But I need the base material to do it."

Banks exhaled slowly. He reached inside his coat for his cigar case and then stopped at a severe look from Abraham, who had told him before that there was to be no smoking inside his workshop. "Then you'll just have to step up the program, Abraham. More testing."

Abraham frowned. "We're already snatching three, sometimes four people a day, Senator. It hasn't gone unnoticed. Have you seen the newspapers? It's all over the front pages. And one of my raptors returned damaged last night, as if it had been in a firefight. If we increase the frequency of the abductions, we risk exposing ourselves."

Banks shook his head. "You let me worry about that, Abraham. I have the police in check. That transport is leaving for London in three days' time."

"Three days!" Abraham almost spat the words. "That's impossible!"

Banks took a step forward, looming over the half-mechanical man. Above, the chattering of the raptors increased significantly in pitch. "Three days. Things are moving, Abraham. Events have dictated that we need to bring forward our plans. That vessel will be leaving whether you have the solution or not."

"But that's lunacy!" Abraham nearly screamed in the senator's face. "You can't be serious! Those things won't stop, you know, once they run out of people to devour on that tiny island. Not unless we can control them, or destroy them. They'll come for us, too!"

"Then you'd better make sure you do as I say, Abraham, and increase the frequency of the testing. Get them all out there tonight, the whole flock of them." Banks took a step back, straightening his back and pointing up at the raptors. He fixed Abraham with a firm stare. "Remember what you're doing here is in the interests of the nation. Remember that, Abraham. Whatever it takes."

Abraham gave a curt nod. Whatever the senator said, it would be madness to unleash those things on the world without the proper measures in place to prevent them from rampaging all over the globe. Yet something about the look in Banks's eye told him the issue was not up for discussion.

It seemed his raptors were going to be very busy indeed.

Abraham watched the senator's back as the man crossed the warehouse floor and disappeared through the door. Sighing, he turned back to the creature, watching with a smile as it discarded the now-exsanguinated corpse of the man and slumped back against the wall, momentarily sated.

CHAPTER EIGHT

The party was in full swing.

Gabriel rocked back in his chair and watched a group of men and women cavorting on the lawn. It was cold, and their breaths fogged in the crisp evening air. He could overhear a little of their conversation, just snatches and fragments here and there: "Oh, John, you *do* say the most peculiar things . . ." and "What made him decide to throw a party *tonight*? Tonight of all nights!"

Gabriel couldn't help but laugh. It was as if they somehow felt obliged to be there, to flock to his never-ending party because, whatever else they chose to do, *not* being there was worse.

The house was buzzing with people, faces he hadn't seen for weeks. He didn't even know most of their names. This was *Gabriel's* life, not his. He felt detached from it, like a guest in his own existence.

He watched the partygoers as they moved unconsciously in circles through the house and grounds. They were all dressed up, sparkling dresses and sharp suits, peacock feathers and silk ties. They swanned around his property like they owned the place, draping themselves over the furniture, trying to make themselves look beautiful. Trying to find meaning, to prove their worth.

That was the thing that struck Gabriel most of all, as he sat there in his favorite armchair, smoking and observing; that it wasn't escape they were searching for. He'd always thought that was the reason they came, that they were looking for distraction, trying to find a way out of the mundane, an escape from their ordinary lives. But, he thought now, watching a couple kissing furtively in the shadows of an oak tree on the lawn, he'd been wrong. They weren't looking for distraction at all. They were trying to find their place in the world.

He thought he could understand that.

For all her talk, Ginny seemed content to hang back and observe the revelers just as he did. She'd traded pleasantries with people, of course, but now, with the party under way, she was perched on the arm of his chair, her hand on his shoulder, drinking gin and watching the party go on around her.

He wondered if this was what she'd intended. Was she disappointed? Perhaps she'd pushed for it because she'd thought it would make him happy. Or perhaps she was just searching for normality, too, like all the others. For *her* place in the world.

He didn't know where things were going with Ginny. He still didn't know why she'd come back, what she wanted from him. For now, though, he was content to let things unfold at whatever pace she needed them to. He would find out soon enough. He hoped that by then he might have made some sense out of his own conflicted feelings for the woman.

She'd certainly made an effort to doll herself up for the party tonight. He had to admit she looked stunning in her low-cut silvery dress and high heels. Whatever she lacked in grace she more than made up for in gumption.

Gabriel felt a tap on his shoulder and tore his gaze away from the window to see Henry standing beside him, a worried expression on his face. "What's wrong, Henry?" He had to shout to be heard over the music.

"A call on the holotube, sir. It's a policeman. He says it's urgent."

Gabriel glanced at Ginny, whose face creased in concern. "Is everything all right?"

"I'm sure everything's fine," Gabriel said, rising from his armchair. "Henry, where can I take the call?"

"In your bedroom, sir. I think it should be quiet enough up there for you to hear." Henry motioned toward the door.

"I'll be back in a moment," Gabriel said to Ginny, patting her reassuringly on the arm. She nodded, reaching for a cigarette.

As he'd expected, Gabriel found Donovan's face staring out at him from the mirrored cavity of the holotube terminal when he made his way up to his bedroom a few moments later. It was a bad signal, and the inspector's face shimmered and fractured as he leaned in close to the transmitter at the other end.

Gabriel lowered himself onto the edge of his bed so the other man could see him.

"Ah, Gabriel, you're there," Donovan said in hushed tones, as if trying to avoid being overheard by someone off camera.

"Is everything all right, Felix?" Gabriel prompted when Donovan didn't continue. It was unusual for the detective to risk calling him at home. Usually he left cryptic messages for Gabriel at his Manhattan apartment. Still, at least Gabriel would be able to assuage Henry's fears by telling him it was related to the mugging the other night, the one Henry had made him report to Donovan the prior day.

"We've found a body, Gabriel, down in Greenwich Village," said Donovan.

"Left by the raptors?"

"No. In a run-down apartment building. I think it might be related to that . . . British problem we talked about. Can you meet me there?" Donovan glanced at something behind him. "Yeah, I'm on my way, Mullins," he called to the sergeant.

Gabriel glanced at his watch. Nine-thirty p.m. "I can be there in a couple of hours."

Donovan frowned in frustration. "No sooner?"

Gabriel shrugged. "I'm out at Long Island, Felix."

"Okay, okay. Two hours. Look, here's the address. I'll get rid of everyone else."

Gabriel scrawled the address on his cigarette packet, the only scrap of paper he had to hand. "I'm on my way," he said, reaching for the switch that would cut the connection. Then, hesitating, he caught Donovan by the eye. "Be careful, Felix. This thing you're getting us mixed up in—you don't know how big it could be."

Donovan nodded, and then the connection went dead.

Ginny was waiting for him at the bottom of the stairs when he returned to the party a few moments later. She took a long draw on her cigarette and eyed him through the ensuing haze of smoke. For a moment he felt disconcerted; it seemed as though her eyes were disembodied, floating there in the hallway, watching him. "Do you have to go?" she said, and he couldn't read what she was thinking.

"Yes, I have to go."

"Are you in trouble?"

Gabriel laughed. "No. No, Ginny, I'm not in trouble. Someone needs my help."

She gave him a coquettish grin. "Can I come?"

Gabriel shook his head. "I don't think that's a good idea. It might be dangerous."

Ginny stepped forward, pressing herself up against him. "I'm in the market for a little danger, Gabriel."

"You're drunk, Ginny."

She smiled. "Not drunk enough." She grabbed him by the lapel of his jacket and leaned in, kissing him lightly on the lips. "You can't leave me here, Gabriel. You simply can't."

Gabriel didn't know what to say. The party was still raging around them. Henry was nowhere to be seen.

"Where are we going?"

Gabriel sighed. "*I'm* going to Manhattan. Ginny, look, it wouldn't be fair . . ." He stopped short as she pushed him away, glowering at him. He could see the hurt in her eyes, and suddenly it brought it all back, all the lies and the tears and the mistakes he'd made. No, it really wouldn't be fair, not to do that to her again.

No lies. No secrets. He'd promised himself that. He owed it to her. She'd meant so much to him before, and he'd never told her. He'd allowed her to think he was just a drunken playboy, allowed himself to push her away, keeping the real Gabriel hidden beneath layers of secrets and lies, protective barriers. This time it would be different. This time he had to trust her. He took a deep breath, lowered his voice to a whisper. He realized he was trembling. "Have you heard of a man called 'the Ghost,' Ginny?"

She nodded, unsure where this was heading. "Yes. The crime fighter.

The vigilante. I've read about him in the *Globe*. But what's he got to do with it?"

Gabriel put his hand on her arm.

"Well, there's something I need to tell you. . . ."

—•—

"One of the neighbors reported gunfire, so a couple of the boys from uniform came down to check it out. They were expecting to find some kids playing around with a handgun. They weren't expecting this." Donovan said this as he led the Ghost along the hallway to the door of the apartment where the body had been discovered.

The apartment block was a dingy sort of place, probably inhabited by more rats than humans. What was more, it stank. The Ghost had to cover his mouth and nose as he picked his way along behind Donovan, trying not to step in any of the heaps of discarded trash that had gathered in the stairwells or lobbies. It didn't fit at all with his mental image of the sort of place a foreign spy would set up shop. He supposed that was precisely the point.

He'd left Ginny in the car, keeping watch on the door. He still wasn't entirely sure if he'd done the right thing telling her about his double life. She'd seemed to find the whole thing terribly exciting, bombarding him with questions in the car all the way to Manhattan. He'd tried to impress upon her the gravity of the situation, the need to maintain the secrecy of his separate identities—the risk he'd taken by letting her in on his secret.

He'd also explained to her why he'd done it. Why he'd felt the need to be honest with her about it, about who he really was. At this she'd gone quiet, serious, circumspect.

Later, she'd watched in awe as he'd stripped in his apartment on Fifth Avenue, running her fingers over his scars, silent as he'd donned his black trench coat and fastened his buckles, collecting weapons from his armory in the back. She'd helped him to strap his fléchette gun in place, watched as he'd loaded pistols and secreted knives in hidden sheaths all over his body.

When they'd returned to the car to drive down to Greenwich Village, to the address Donovan had given him on the holotube, something had changed between them. Some slight alteration in the way she was acting. He wasn't quite sure what it was, but she'd looked at him differently. He'd wondered if she was judging him, if by telling her the truth he'd made a terrible mistake. Had he simply caused the rift between them to widen? When he'd sat behind the wheel, she'd looked over at him as if she didn't recognize him anymore. It went deeper than the change in appearance, too. She seemed to be seeing him for the first time.

He hadn't known how to respond, so he'd started the engine and the car had hissed away from the curb, trails of soot belching from its exhaust funnels. The way she'd looked at him—it was as if she'd seen into the core of him. It was as if the lines between Gabriel and the Ghost were blurring, merging, and he didn't know who he was any longer. The two halves of his life had collided, and the resulting confusion had been too much to deal with. So he'd buried all thoughts of it while he focused on helping Donovan, and he'd told Ginny to wait in the car, despite her protests. He'd put her in enough danger simply by bringing her along. He'd never forgive himself if something happened to her.

Donovan had been waiting for him in the lobby. He'd shut the lights off and ushered the Ghost in quietly, trying to remain inconspicuous. Then he'd led the way to the dead man and the apartment, where, it seemed, the British spy had based all of his operations.

The corpse was lying in the hallway, just behind the door. He'd clearly been there for a while—a day, at least—and if the pool of sticky blood beneath him wasn't testament enough to the damage that had been inflicted upon him, the butt of the penknife jutting out of his left eye socket was.

The Ghost dropped to his haunches so he could take a closer look. The dead man had clearly been well built, and, judging by the thin white scar running along the line of his jaw, he hadn't been a stranger to violence. The man's left eye had putrefied and dribbled out of the socket, leaving a terrible, gaping hole, caked in blood around the handle of the knife. The knife itself was buried all the way to the hilt. The killer had struck with considerable force, driving the blade right through the eye and piercing the brain behind it, killing the man instantly.

It wasn't a precision killing. Of that much the Ghost was sure. It looked more like the dead man had disturbed someone who'd panicked and used whatever weapon they had available. The dead man had been the one who'd fired the shots, it seemed—he had powder burns around his right wrist, and his corpse was still clutching the handgun.

"Have you checked his pockets?" the Ghost asked Donovan, who was standing behind him, regarding the corpse through narrowed eyes.

"Not personally," Donovan replied, "although the men who found him said they were empty."

"Completely empty?" The Ghost dug into the man's jacket pockets. When he found nothing, he turned out the pockets of the man's pants, too. Donovan was right—they were completely devoid of any belongings.

"Either he was a pro, a killer sent out to find our man, or the British agent stripped his pockets after he killed him." Donovan stepped back to give the Ghost room to stand.

"I suppose either is possible," said the Ghost, but I'd wager he's a government agent. That would explain what he was doing here. He probably tracked the spy back here and tried to take him out.

He glanced around, taking in the rest of the apartment. It was functional, to say the least. It didn't look as if anyone had actually lived here, but rather used it as a safe house, a place to hide away anything suspicious that might otherwise endanger his position. From what he knew about this spy, he'd managed to successfully infiltrate some impressive New York political circles, and that would have brought with it a high risk of exposure. He probably kept another apartment somewhere in the city, too.

The Ghost walked through to the bedroom, where it was immediately clear there'd been a struggle. The bed was mussed up and there was a pockmark in the wall where a gunshot had blown away a fragment of plaster. On the floor by the side of the bed was a shot-up holotube transmitter, still wired into a socket in the wall.

"I left everything as we found it," Donovan said, framed in the doorway, watching the Ghost as he paced back and forth, taking it all in. "Looks like the spy was trying to make a call when he was disturbed."

The Ghost nodded. "That adds more credence to my theory about the dead man," he said. "If they were trying to get to him before he passed his information back to London, or wherever, they'd have had people trailing his every move. If the dead guy had picked up his trail and followed him here, found him in the middle of making a call . . . well, it seems like he soon put an end to that, possibly at the expense of his own life."

"How so?"

"He spent two shots disabling the holotube transmitter. He must have missed the spy with his first shot, here, on the wall," he pointed out the pockmark to Donovan, "but then took the time to put two shots in the machine before going after the spy himself, giving the spy chance to find a weapon." He rubbed a hand over his chin, thoughtfully. "My guess is the call had already connected and the dead man didn't want the person on the other end hearing anything of what was going on. Either that or he was worried the spy would call out some code word or something, immediately alerting the person at the other end."

Donovan frowned. "But still . . . if they heard the shots after the call had already connected, surely they'd want to know what was going on? Especially if they couldn't raise the spy again afterward."

The Ghost shrugged. "You've got me there." He crossed to where Donovan was standing in the doorway. "Anything else of note?"

"Oh yes," Donovan said with a smile. "It's like your place. A veritable armory back there."

He led the Ghost into the back room, stepping carefully over the corpse in the hallway. It was like walking into the incident room of a police investigation. The walls were plastered with photographs, maps, notes, schematics. Half of these had been torn off, some of them left where they fell, others clearly missing. The windows had been blacked out with thick paint, and there was nothing but an overturned chair and a small table by way of functional furniture. Folders and files had been flung all over the floor, a spray of multicolored paperwork, and three large, wooden chests lay open in the middle of the room.

The Ghost approached the chests with interest. They were full of weapons. One appeared to contain knives and blades of all possible shapes and sizes, another handguns and pistols, the third explosives, grenades and what looked like a portable rocket launcher. He turned to Donovan. "Someone clearly left in a hurry. And if the contents of these chests are anything to go by, he's armed to the teeth."

Donovan nodded gravely. "I had the same thought. If these are the weapons he chose to leave behind . . ."

The Ghost turned to study the wall. There was a large, scale map of Manhattan, upon which a series of locations had been marked out in thick, black ink. They all appeared to be residential properties. Beside each of these the spy had pinned photographs of well-known politicians, businessmen and public servants. The Ghost stepped forward and tapped one of these photographs with his gloved fingertip. "Senator Isambard Banks," he said, glancing over his shoulder at Donovan.

"Indeed. But have you seen what's even more interesting?" Donovan came to join him, pointing to one of the photographs attached to a residence on the Upper East Side, right by Central Park.

"Commissioner Montague," the Ghost said in surprise. "You think these are the people involved in whatever this spy got himself mixed up in? One of the 'circles' he'd infiltrated?"

Donovan shook his head. "I don't know. Perhaps. Maybe they're targets. They're all high-profile public figures. If he was here to cause trouble and sow seeds of terror, these are the people he'd hit. With that arsenal . . . perhaps he was here to assassinate one of them. Maybe more?"

"Perhaps," the Ghost replied, noncommittally. He didn't want to press the point with Donovan, not yet, but it seemed far too much of a coincidence to him that two of the people implicated by this web of conspiracy were the very same people who had—rather irregularly— charged Donovan with finding the spy.

The Ghost continued to examine the wall. There was a patch of bare plaster where something had very obviously been removed in a hurry, torn from its place so that little shreds of paper still clung to the pins. Beside that was the schematic of an enormous airship, a blueprint for its construction. It was one of the huge transatlantic vessels that regularly ferried passengers—or at least those of them fortunate enough to be able to afford it—back and forth between Europe and America. It was weeks faster than steamship, and, the Ghost was led to be believe, significantly more luxurious.

While it was true that the cold war had caused movements between Britain and America to become very restricted, London was still one of the world's centers of commerce, and many American people had valid business there, or in Brussels, Paris, Berlin. Business had been booming for the airship providers, and as their routes around the world had grown in ambition, so had their vessels grown in size and scope.

"I can see you're as baffled as I am by that one, Gabriel. What would a British spy be doing with the construction plans of a transatlantic passenger-class airship?" Donovan said this as though to suggest he'd already deciphered the meaning behind it.

"Go on," said the Ghost.

"Look at those crates of weapons, Gabriel. I think he might be planning to make a strike against one of these passenger ships."

The Ghost shook his head. "No. It doesn't fit. What would be the purpose of it?"

"Assassination? Terror? To ignite a war between America and the British Empire?" Donovan spread his hands.

"None of that makes sense. If that was his aim, he could do that more effectively by picking off the people on this chart, one by one, just as you suggested. And if it's war they're looking for, why trigger it like that? Why give us the chance to muster our forces? Surely the most effective way to start a war is to invade?"

Donovan shrugged. "I don't know what to make of it," he said, reaching for his cigarettes. He offered them to the Ghost, who shook his head. "And we're missing a big piece of the puzzle." He waved his cigarette to indicate the empty space on the wall where the spy had torn down part of his collage.

"I think the most interesting thing here is perhaps the least obvious, Felix," the Ghost said, pointing to a small, grainy black-and-white photograph pinned to the wall, just beside the map of Manhattan. It was crumpled, as though the spy had attempted to tear it free and then given up, changing his mind in his haste to get away. Donovan came closer, peering at it myopically, trying to make out what was in the picture.

"Is that what I think it is?" he said. He didn't even try to disguise the surprise in his voice.

"Yes," the Ghost replied, reaching up and plucking the photograph from the wall. It was blurred, but its subject was clear. It was one of the raptors, perched on the top of a building, surveying the street below with its glowing red eyes.

"Good God," said Donovan. "If there's a connection . . ."

The Ghost slipped the photograph inside his pocket. "I think it's time I checked on Senator Banks, don't you?"

Donovan nodded. "But be careful, Gabriel. He's a dangerous man to find yourself on the wrong side of."

"I rather think that's the point, Felix. But anyway, I need to get Ginny back to her apartment first."

"Ginny?" Donovan asked inquisitively.

A smile curled at the edges of the Ghost's mouth. "She's a friend."

"And you brought her here?" Donovan queried, incredulous. "Does she know . . . ?"

"She knows."

The inspector gave a plaintive sigh. "You're playing a dangerous game, Gabriel," he said. He left the next sentence unsaid, but the Ghost caught his meaning. *Remember what happened to Celeste.*

"Don't worry, Felix. I left her in the car, and she's going straight back to her apartment."

Donovan nodded, but the skepticism was clear on his face.

"I take it you'll preserve all of this?" the Ghost said, changing the subject. He tapped the wall with his hand, indicating the spread of remaining documents. "That list of names and addresses might prove useful."

"We'll take it all back to the station in the morning," Donovan said between drags on his cigarette. "The body's being collected in an hour. Then Mullins will start going through the files."

The Ghost started toward the door. "I like Mullins. I think he shows promise."

Donovan laughed. "Get out of here, Gabriel. I have work to do."

—•—

Outside, the cold had set in, and the Ghost felt the chill even through the thick fabric of his jacket and coat. He could see across the street to where Ginny was still sitting in the passenger seat of his car, huddled up against the cold, puffing on a cigarette. Her red cloche was pulled down right over her head, and she'd brought her knees up to her chest. She looked up and waved when she saw him coming.

He was just about to raise his hand to wave in response when he heard a chittering sound from somewhere above. He looked up to see two of the raptors gliding across the canopy of the night sky, their long, membranous wings outstretched, their propellers whirring as they cut a swath across the rooftops.

It took only seconds for the Ghost to respond. He flicked his wrist and heard the satisfying crank of his fléchette gun snapping around on its ratchet. He palmed the pneumatic bulb and dropped to one knee, raising his arm to the sky and squeezing off a staccato volley of shots. The raptors screeched in fury as the tiny metal blades drummed against their underbellies or pierced the fleshy membrane of their wings.

They both turned, parting in midformation, one darting left, the other right. The Ghost tried to keep them both in view, but lost track of the one on the right as it glided off across the rooftops. He concentrated on the one he could see, squeezing off another shower of fléchettes. He aimed for its wings, hoping to disable it so he could bring it down. On the ground he stood a much better chance of beating it in a fight, and if he could ground it, he could pull it apart and find out what made it tick.

The Ghost snapped his head around at the sound of the car door clicking open. Ginny was halfway out of the vehicle, one foot already on the tarmac. "Get back in the car, now!" he bellowed. He turned back to the raptor, but he'd taken his eyes off it for too long.

The mechanical creature, diving at him from upward of twenty feet, collided with him at full force. The blow sent him reeling, and the raptor's talons raked his chest as it made a grab for him, trying to drag him away into the air. He twisted, desperately slapping at its brass legs as it pulled him along the ground.

With an almighty effort he managed to wrench himself free of one of the claws, but he was forced to keep both hands on it to hold it at bay. The claws flexed and scrabbled, searching for purchase as the creature tried to reassert its hold.

The raptor screeched again, dragging him along the road. It lifted him a few feet and then dropped him again, one of its talons still buried in his chest. His head slammed against the tarmac as he came down, and the raptor repeated the motion, trying to daze him, or worse, to split his skull against the road.

Half-delirious, lolling in the raptor's grip, he caught sight of the second one, now circling in the sky high above, like carrion attracted to a kill.

He looked up into the strange, skull-like face of the one that had hold of him. There was malice behind those glowing red eyes— dark, inhuman malice. It was if something intelligent was haunting the machine, as if some malign spirit had somehow gotten inside it, inhabiting the brass shell. The thought didn't offer a lot of comfort, as the raptor shook him from side to side and slammed him down against the ground once again, doing its utmost to knock him unconscious.

The Ghost tried to free his right hand, to bring the barrel of his fléchette gun around to give him a clear shot, but the raptor was waiting, and as soon as he released his grip on its other limb, the claws were digging into his chest, and the raptor was turning, lifting him into the air in a slow spiral.

He knew what was coming next. The creatures weren't likely to take him back to their lair. Not after he'd shot at them. It was going to try dropping him from a height.

Together, the Ghost and the raptor continued their spiral climb. His chest felt like it was on fire, and he could feel blood oozing from multiple puncture wounds beneath his jacket. The back of his head was throbbing, too, where it had repeatedly struck the tarmac. He realized that, once again, he'd lost his hat at some point in the chaos.

As they climbed higher and higher, the Ghost felt himself beginning to swoon. The pain in his chest and his head were threatening to overwhelm him, to put his body into shock. He fought against the tide of blackness, shook his head to clear the syrupy fog that was clouding his vision.

And then someone was shooting.

The raptor reeled and shrieked, spinning in the air as a bullet tore through its left wing. The Ghost craned his neck, trying to see what was going on as the raptor beat its damaged wing and whirled and spun, trying to maintain altitude. He caught sight of Ginny far below, standing on the sidewalk beside the car, two of his pistols in her hands, taking drunken potshots at the mechanical beast.

What was she doing! She risked being attacked by the other raptor, or worse, hitting the Ghost himself if one of her shots went wide. She moved slowly, both of her arms outstretched, tracking the struggling raptor across the sky.

She fired again, and her aim was perfect. The Ghost felt the raptor buck and thrash as twin bullets tore through its other wing.

And then he was falling, tossed away by the desperate creature, tumbling over and over in the air as he hurtled toward the ground.

A strange sense of serenity passed over the Ghost. He felt the cool wind rushing around him as he fell, felt as if the world had suddenly slowed. He felt peaceful.

Then he caught sight of the second raptor, diving toward Ginny, and his heart stopped.

He reached inside his trench coat, grappling with the pull string that would ignite his ankle rockets. His chest screamed in pain with every movement. He gave the cord a sharp tug, and then he was hurtling upward again with no sense of direction or control.

The Ghost fought to right himself, to make sense of what was happening. The first raptor—the one that had attacked him—was still attempting to right itself in midair, screeching and flapping in desperate abandon. Ginny was still shooting, and the other raptor was descending on her, its vicious talons raking the air before it.

Ginny didn't have the Ghost's physique, nor his combat skills or protective suit. The raptor would rip her to shreds in seconds.

The Ghost twisted in the air, bringing his legs together and folding his arms across his chest. He went into a steep dive, matching the raptor's trajectory, hurtling toward Ginny and the sidewalk.

The two figures streaked out of the sky like falling comets, mirror images of one another, plummeting toward the stricken Ginny. The Ghost was a dark blur riding a plume of searing orange flame, the raptor his gleaming opposite, its brass fame shimmering in the reflected moonlight.

Ginny screamed, and the sound was shrill and piercing in the empty street. She fired indiscriminately at the onrushing raptor, emptying the chambers of both guns, forgoing all sense of aim or purpose to simply shower the thing with as many bullets as she had left. They bounced off its brass chassis like pebbles pinging off a lover's window.

The Ghost could hardly breathe as he swooped low, only a few feet from the ground, and made a grab for the woman. He collided with her, bowling her off of her feet, but somehow managed to wrap his arms around her protectively, sweeping her away from the raptor. He clutched her to him triumphantly, holding her close as he spiraled up into the air, feeling her gasp in fear and amazement as they soared away into the frigid night. The wounds in his chest screamed for attention.

The raptor shrieked in frustration, its talons raking the ground in a shower of sparks where only seconds before its prey had stood rooted to the spot.

Ginny clung on to the Ghost tightly as they wound their way up and up through the sky, heading for the rooftops. He was trying to put some distance between them and the baying mechanical beasts.

The two raptors were circling now, watching to see what the Ghost would do next. The one with the damaged wings had managed to right itself, and while it was clearly struggling to maintain altitude it still posed a significant threat.

The Ghost knew he couldn't stay airborne for long, not like this. Here, he was exposed, and the extra weight of Ginny would slow him down, limiting his options. He angled his body, skimming across the rooftops of the nearby buildings, looking for a place to set Ginny down. The roof of the apartment building—the one in which he and Donovan had been standing over the body of the murdered man just a few moments earlier—looked as if it might provide some limited cover. For whatever that would be worth.

He pulled Ginny closer. "Pull that cord!" he called out to her, as they shot over the rooftop, rolling in midair to narrowly avoid slamming into a large, squat water tower.

"What? Which cord?" she shouted back in confusion. He could feel her warm breath on his cheek, smell the residue of the gin she had consumed at the party.

"By your right hand!" he said, desperately. "Just inside my coat."

Ginny struggled in his grip, trying to free her arms. "This one?" she replied, yanking hard on the dangling cord.

The spurs of flame from the Ghost's ankle boosters guttered and died, and the Ghost held Ginny tight as they careened across the rooftop, dropping out of the sky and bouncing across the paving slabs like a stone being skipped across the surface of a lake.

The Ghost pushed Ginny's face into his shoulder to protect her head as they rolled and rebounded. His right shoulder jarred painfully against the edge of a roof light, and then they were coming to rest, inches from the edge of the building itself.

The Ghost gasped as his body lit up in pain. He'd taken a series of knocks as they'd come down, skidding to a stop by using his elbows as brakes. His trench coat was shredded, as was the fabric of his jacket beneath. But he was okay. He could live with bruises. If the raptors didn't get to him first, that was. . . .

He looked down at Ginny, who was limp in his arms. "Are you all right?" he breathed. There was no reply. He felt suddenly hollow, as if the bottom had just been pulled out of his world. "Ginny! Are you all right?"

She stirred beneath him, looked up into his face. Their eyes met. "Yes," she said breathlessly. "Yes, I'm all right." Her eyes widened suddenly, and the Ghost felt her stiffen in his grip. She'd seen something over his shoulder. The raptors were coming.

The Ghost rolled again, taking Ginny with him. As he went over onto his back, he scanned the sky above them, getting a measure of the situation. The raptors were coming right for them. There wasn't going to be time. . . .

"I'm sorry," he said to Ginny, softly. "I'm so sorry. . . ."

The second raptor—the one whose wings were still intact—was heading right for them, its talons flashing. Any second now . . .

The Ghost thrust Ginny away from him, flinging her forcefully across the rooftop, putting all of his momentum and weight behind it. She squealed in shock, striking the flagstones hard. The Ghost, on his back, raised his arm, a hopeless last gesture of defense against the mechanical monster.

There was a crack of gunfire, and the raptor suddenly changed its course, swinging around and climbing, two perfect round holes in its wing. The Ghost glanced at Ginny to find her lying on her back, two smoking pistols in her fists. His hands went instinctively to his belt, and he couldn't help but grin. She'd pulled them from his holsters while he'd been on top of her.

He scrambled to his feet, ran over to her and helped her up.

"Thanks . . . " he started, but Ginny shook her head.

"No time," she said curtly, nodding over his shoulder. The raptor was coming in for another attack. She raised the guns and snapped out another round of shots. But this time the raptor wasn't going to be dissuaded.

Behind her, the Ghost saw the other raptor—the one with the ragged wings that had dragged him across the ground, drop to a roof a few feet away. The things were trying to pin them in place.

"Get behind me!" he barked, and she did as he said, pressing her shoulders against his so that they stood back-to-back, each of them facing one of the oncoming raptors. "Concentrate your fire on its wings," he shouted, and he felt her nod in acknowledgment. But he knew that would only work for so long. And so did the raptors.

Once they were on the rooftop, they didn't need their wings.

The Ghost palmed the trigger of his fléchette gun and released a hail of silver shards. The raptor, the one that had landed on the roof and was marching menacingly toward him with its clawed hands extended, continued undeterred. The tattered remnants of its wings fluttered in the wind, semitranslucent in the moonlight. Its red eyes glowed like the burning embers of hell.

Ginny followed his lead and started shooting again. He didn't dare take his eyes off the metal creature charging toward him, but he feared Ginny's shots would have little or no effect on the other raptor.

He couldn't fight them both at once. He couldn't protect her. But he couldn't let it happen again. He couldn't see another person he cared for torn apart because of him, because of who he was. He roared as he unleashed everything he had at the raptor, filling the sky with a snowstorm of a thousand razor-sharp fléchettes.

There was a whooshing sound from somewhere across the other side of the rooftop. Suddenly, everything was on fire. Ginny was screaming, and the Ghost's ears were ringing with the echo of an almighty explosion.

He fell to the ground, bowled over by the force of the explosion, as if a hand had shoved him firmly in the small of his back. He felt the patter of tiny, burning fragments showering down upon him and realized that the raptor—Ginny's raptor—had exploded. He was facedown in the gravel. He blinked, spitting dust.

The Ghost glanced up, suddenly remembering the other raptor. It had also been bowled over by the force of the blow, but was already picking itself up, chittering insanely as it leered at him.

The Ghost followed suit, pulling himself to his feet. His body groaned in protest. He risked a glance behind him to see Ginny on her knees, still covering her eyes with the crook of her arm. The sky was alight with a rain of burning components, and he watched them tumbling over the precipice of the building, twinkling stars falling to the sidewalk far below. Thick, black smoke curled from the ruins of the machine's torso, discarded a few feet from Ginny.

"What did you do?" he said, urgently.

Ginny peered up at him, as if only just realizing that she wasn't dead. "What? I didn't . . ."

Realization struck, and the Ghost swung round to catch sight of Donovan on the far side of the roof, standing over a tripod, upon which sat the stocky cylinder of the British spy's portable rocket launcher. He must have heard the commotion and come to their aid. The Ghost was just thankful he'd had the foresight to make use of the weapon cache they'd uncovered. He wondered if anything less than the explosive mortar would be enough to take one of the raptors down. He was about to find out.

The raptor leaped at him from at least ten feet away, the propellers mounted on its shoulders roaring with power as they drove it forward.

The Ghost sidestepped to avoid a swipe from its left arm, but wasn't quick enough to dodge the one that followed from the right, striking him on his upper arm and drawing blood through the ragged remains of his costume.

He struck out in response, punching it hard in the face, but his fist rebounded painfully from the brass skull and the raptor hardly seemed to notice. It let out another chittering cry and thrashed at him with both claws.

The Ghost brought his arms up, parrying the blows, and kicked out at the thing, striking it in the midriff, just below the rib cage. It staggered back under the force of the blow, but it was barely enough to halt its attack, and in seconds it was on him again, its claws scratching at his face, the bony remains of its wings beating him back.

Desperately he caught it by the arms, trying to pin it in place, but this only aided the creature, providing it with a pivot, which it used to swing its legs up so it could bury its talons in his belly. He felt the daggers tear through the thick fabric of his jacket, and he staggered back, trying to hold it at bay.

Again, the raptor capitalized on this, its propellers roaring, forcing him farther back, unable to stop his boots from sliding on the ground, unable to prevent himself from being forced farther and farther toward the edge of the roof.

He heard Donovan shouting his name, but he paid the inspector no heed, remaining focused on the raptor, on using every ounce of strength he had to push back against it, to keep its talons from rending his flesh.

He took a step back and felt the lip of the building with his heel. He only had to hold on a little longer. Just a little longer . . .

The raptor shrieked as it strained against him. Its engines were whining with the pressure, the blades beating at the air with a steady roar. He gazed into the creature's eyes. *Creature* was the right word for it. This was no simple machine.

The Ghost still gripped the raptor's brass, skeletal arms in his gloved fists. Its feet were wedged against his belly. He took a deep breath and stepped over the edge of the building.

He heard Ginny scream as he toppled backward, pulling the raptor down with him. The creature screeched as its shredded wings beat ineffectually at the air, trying to slow their descent. He clutched it tight, using his momentum to somersault in the air, twisting so that the raptor was beneath him.

Almost serenely, the Ghost freed one hand, allowing the raptor's free hand to rake at his chest. He reached inside his coat, his fingers closing around the ignition cord. He pulled it sharply and his rocket boosters fired, kicking them both forward, pushing them on toward the ground.

The raptor thrashed and bucked, trying to regain control, but it was trapped, its talons lodged in the fabric of the Ghost's jacket, one of its arms still clutched tightly in his left fist. Without its wings, its propellers alone were no match for the momentum and the downward thrust of his rockets.

The tarmac was fast approaching. Gritting his teeth, the Ghost released his grip on the creature's other arm, grabbing for its ankles and wrenching its talons free from his midriff. He let go, bringing his arms up and twisting his body away from the ground.

He almost miscalculated, and for a moment he thought he was going to be dashed across the street, but at the last minute he managed to pull up, the thrust of his rockets carrying him in a sharp arc across the ground and then up again, hurtling back into the sky.

The damaged raptor, however, wasn't so lucky. Freed with only seconds to spare, with no time to try to right itself and unable to spread its now-defunct wings as a brake, it slammed into the road with a terrific crash.

The Ghost veered away into the night sky, gasping for breath. He felt light-headed with the exertion; tasted the gritty, metallic tang of adrenaline on the back of his tongue. His heart was pounding in his ears.

Twisting his body, he swooped low, drifting over the site of the impact, scanning the road for any signs of the raptor.

The shattered remains of it lay scattered all over the street below: in the road, on the sidewalk, in the gutter. The raptor had fractured with the impact, spilling cogs and bits of engine housing, broken limbs and the tattered remnants of its wings. The Ghost felt relief wash over him.

He descended slowly in a plume of orange flame, still wary, still tensed and ready for whatever might happen next. Beneath him, on the sidewalk, the broken torso of the raptor still twitched and jerked maniacally, as if in the throes of death. The Ghost set himself down beside it, cutting the fuel line to his rocket canisters with a sharp pull on the cord inside his jacket.

It had been utterly smashed, dashed across the tarmac by the tremendous force of the fall. One gangly brass arm now hung limply from the aperture of its shoulder, clicking and tapping against the paving slabs with every spasm. The other limb had been lost entirely, scattered somewhere across the road. Likewise, both of its legs and one wing, reduced now to stumps and gaskets, cracked pistons and fragments of claw. The engine casings housing the turbines on its shoulders had both split apart, although one propeller still turned, futilely churning the air as if trying, ineffectually, to drag the creature away.

The Ghost dropped to his haunches, staring into the creature's upturned face. The red lights behind its glassy eyes glowed with vehemence. Its head turned slowly toward him and its broken left arm twitched. He could sense it was still trying to get at him, even now, reduced to this. Whatever malign force was motivating it was utterly relentless.

He studied its chest plate more closely. It was largely intact, even after the fall. It was fashioned to resemble a human rib cage, with thick, brass ribs that curved round to protect the delicate machinery inside. Through the gaps between the ribs he could see whirring cogs and coiled springs, ticking levers and tiny golden chains. The machinery of life; the engine that animated this monstrous thing.

There was a small panel in its chest, too—an ornately inlaid door right above where a human heart would reside. Cautiously, the Ghost ran his fingers over the engraving, tracing the pictograms with his gloved fingers. They were unusual, and he could tell they were ancient in origin, like the symbols he had seen on the Roman's marble gateway at the Metropolitan Museum, before everything had turned to shit, before Celeste . . .

The Ghost could see no handle, no obvious way of opening the little door. He applied pressure, and the panel depressed, clicking open and folding back to reveal the cavity behind. The raptor emitted a shriek of rage, and its torso went into spasms again as it protested at his invasion, but there was little it could do to prevent him.

The Ghost leaned forward and peered inside the compartment and almost recoiled at what he saw. A bird—a blackbird, still twitching and writhing against its terrible bonds—had been trapped inside the cavity, its wings pinned to a panel within a carefully painted red circle. Its head bobbed nervously and it opened its beak, but no sound was forthcoming. Its once-black feathers were now dowdy and gray.

Around the outside of the red circle, esoteric runes and pictograms had been etched in intricate detail, tooled with precision into the brass backing plate. By the bird's feet, which lung limply, as if its legs had been broken, was a yellowing paper scroll, tightly wound and bound with coarse string. It, too, was pinned to the hardwood panel.

The shell of the raptor jerked again, and the creature emitted a throaty shriek.

The Ghost reached inside the cavity, took the bird's head between his thumb and index finger, and with a sharp gesture, snapped its neck. It was the only peace he could offer the creature.

The raptor's torso jerked again in response. Rocking back on his haunches, the Ghost watched with interest as the once-burning lights in the raptor's eyes now dimmed and flickered out. The head dropped to the sidewalk with a clang, and the remains of the brass creature lay motionless.

The Ghost reached for the scroll and withdrew it from the raptor's chest. He untied the string and unfurled the yellowing paper. It seemed old, and one edge was ragged, as if it had been torn from an old book. It contained more diabolic symbols: a pentagram scratched crazily in thick, black ink. The signs of the zodiac, rendered in immaculate, intricate detail in a wheel all around the five-pointed star. The page was covered, too, in mathematical equations, numbers written in haphazard fashion at each point of the star or scrawled in the margins in a thin, spidery hand. These had been added later; they were not original to the book from which the page had been removed.

Frowning, he slipped the scroll into the pocket of his trench coat. Were the raptors really powered by some sort of terrible, demonic enslavement? Was it somehow eking away the bird's life force as a kind of fuel, taking it for its own? He didn't know. He was prepared to believe it, though. These days, he mused, he was prepared to believe almost anything.

The Ghost turned at the sound of footsteps on the sidewalk behind him, moving at a run. Ginny, and Donovan. Both of them were panting for breath. They must have taken the stairs down from the roof.

The Ghost stood and smiled at Donovan, clapping him on the shoulder as the inspector bent double, trying to catch his breath. "You're alive, then," Donovan said between gasping breaths, as if he'd expected to find quite a different sight waiting for him at the foot of the apartment building.

The Ghost laughed. " More or less," he said. He helped the other man upright. "Some good shooting up there, Felix."

Donovan nodded, chuckling between sharp intakes of breath.

Ginny stepped forward, still clutching the Ghost's twin pistols, allowing them to hang nonchalantly from her fingers. She moved closer, pressing herself against him, looking up at him as she slipped the firearms back into the holsters on either side of his waist. The Ghost met her gaze. Something—he wasn't sure exactly what—passed between them. Understanding, respect . . . he didn't know. Something. She held him in a clinch.

"Not quite the party I was expecting this evening," she said brightly, "but all the same, I've had a swell time." There was a gleam in her eye, and she couldn't contain her laughter. The Ghost wondered if it was as much relief that had made her giddy—elation that the whole thing was over. But he suspected not. Ginny was too savvy for that, too worldly. To her, the entire episode had probably seemed like one big adventure.

The Ghost leaned forward and kissed her gently on the forehead and then spun her around to face Donovan, holding her by the shoulders. The fur collar of her coat was soft and springy beneath his gloves. "Felix, this is Ginny Gray."

Donovan, standing with his hands on his hips, burst out laughing with sheer incredulity. "I thought you said she was staying in the car!"

"She was," he replied, his hands still on her shoulders.

Ginny offered Donovan a wry smile.

"Anyway, we already met," said Donovan, still grinning. "While you were taking the short way down, Miss Gray and I had plenty of time to get acquainted."

The Ghost smiled. He'd never intended for Ginny to get mixed up in all of this. Had he simply been showing off? He knew he should have left her behind at Long Island, at the party. He'd put her right in the line of fire. He didn't even know what she was doing there—why she'd come back, or why he'd felt the need to have her along. Yes, she'd talked him into it. But he'd allowed it to happen, and if he was honest with himself, he'd wanted it, too.

In the end, he supposed, he was glad she *had* been there. If it hadn't been for her sharpshooting, he'd probably be dead, lying in the gutter across the street, torn apart by the raptors.

"My God!"

The Ghost turned to see Donovan standing over the shell of the ruined raptor.

"Is that . . . ?"

"Yes. It's a bird," the Ghost replied levelly. "It was still alive when I found it. I snapped its neck to put it out of its misery."

"And the raptor?"

"The fall broke its body, but it didn't kill it. It only powered down when I broke the bird's neck."

Donovan frowned. "What are you saying? That the bird was somehow keeping it alive? Are you suggesting there's some sort of occult business going on here?" He almost spat the words with sheer distaste. "I thought they were just machines. If there's more to it than that . . ." He trailed off, his point made.

The Ghost shrugged. "I don't know, Felix," he replied noncommittally, but he could feel the pressure building in his chest, the horror of the situation creeping over him. *Not again . . .*

Donovan turned the raptor's head with the edge of his boot. It lolled to one side on its damaged neck brace. "Vicious-looking thing," he said, his voice low.

The Ghost laughed. "I'll say." He met Donovan's eye.

"Are we *any* closer, Gabriel? Have we learned anything that might help us to discover who's responsible for these . . . *abominations*?"

The Ghost shook his head slowly. "Nothing. Whoever's employing these things has been very careful to cover their tracks. There's nothing here that could be used to trace it back to its source. Unless I can figure out a way to follow one of them, we're out of luck."

He turned to glance at Ginny, who had lit a cigarette and was standing watching them, her head cocked slightly to one side, smoke riffling from her nostrils. "We'll have to study it properly, of course," he continued, indicating the scattered remains on the ground. "It may be that something shows up under scrutiny, some component or part that we can trace back to its origin. But there's nothing obvious in the wreckage, nothing to even indicate what its real purpose might be."

Donovan shook his head. His exasperation was clearly evident by the manner in which he screwed up his face. "Or what it has to do with British spies," he said, sighing. "I'll have it all taken back to the station for Mullins to go over."

"British spies?" chirped Ginny quizzically, glancing from one man to another, "Now this really *is* getting exciting." She flashed a smile at the Ghost.

"I'll tell you in the car," he replied with a heartfelt sigh.

By now, the sound of the explosion had begun to draw interest from the people living in the surrounding tenement blocks, and civilians were beginning to spill out onto the street, crowding around doorways, whispering in excited tones.

Donovan's face creased in concern. "Gabriel, you'd better make yourself scarce. I'll look after things here." He put a hand on the Ghost's shoulder, a gesture of friendship and solidarity.

The Ghost nodded. "Ginny?" He took her by the hand, leading her toward the parked car. He looked back at Donovan as he opened the door to climb into the driver's seat. "Until tomorrow."

Donovan gave a brief nod of his head in acknowledgment.

The Ghost slammed the door shut behind him, gunned the throttle and eased the car off into the road. With a roar of the engine, they shot off into the night.

CHAPTER NINE

Rutherford sat in the uncomfortable wooden chair and stared out the window at the teeming city below. He enjoyed watching the city come to life, the people slowly blinking their way out into the sunlight of a new day, the hiss of morning traffic, tires slick with the kiss of tarmac.

New York wasn't so different from London, not really. People behaved the same the world over. That was something he'd learned over the years, throughout all his travels. Human beings were fundamentally the same. They had different quirks, yes, different personalities, but that was all gloss. Scratch it, and beneath it all, people were just people.

Perhaps, if there was anything different about the New Yorkers, it was their boundless sense of optimism, their hubris, and their belief that anything—absolutely anything—was possible. To them, it seemed, the world was wondrous and new, there for the taking. London, on the other hand, was so heavy with the weight of its own history that sometimes it seemed overbearing. To Rutherford it seemed that the people carried that weight around with them, right there on their shoulders. It was clear in the way in which they went about their business, heads down, avoiding contact with their fellow men. New Yorkers, in sharp contrast, walked around with their heads held high, as if anxious to face the day, as if they hadn't yet been worn smooth and morose by centuries of grinding history.

America, to Rutherford, was such a young nation. Not simply in terms of its national history, but in terms of its outlook. This, he had decided, after years of living there, was absolutely a good thing. Yes, perhaps the people were a little naïve at times, but they still had enthusiasm for the world, a fundamental belief in humanity. Londoners, in Rutherford's experience, had given up on that long ago.

Despite all of that, though, Rutherford loved his country, and he missed it dearly. He missed the winding, cobbled streets of the metropolis, the leaning buildings, the bustle of the markets. He missed the ramshackle old manor houses, ancient farms and country lanes of the Home Counties. He missed the lush green countryside and the River Thames. He missed home. He had adopted America as his second home, but—and it was clear from the results of his encounter at the apartment the prior day—America had not adopted him.

In the end, it mattered little. Whatever the case, he wasn't about to let a small group of egoists and madmen start a war between these two great nations. He might be working for the British government, and he would do whatever was necessary—but he was also working for the people out there, on the street below, the people who went about in blissful ignorance, their heads held high. He would not let them be worn down by another war, a needless war. He would fight that with every reserve of strength he had left.

He turned to glance at the geisha girl on the bed. He had spent the night here, in a whorehouse, renting a room from the overbearing, odious madam below stairs. His options had been limited, and he'd needed somewhere he could keep a roof over his head without giving a name, without being asked any difficult questions. Of course, he'd had to rent a girl, too. But that was not something that had ever interested him.

He glanced over at the bed. The clockwork geisha lay draped across the silky sheets, propped up on the scattered pillows and clad only in a lace negligee, its metal legs curled beneath it like those of a cat.

It was a bizarre creation: an automaton, its brass skeleton sheathed in supple leather to offer the illusion of flesh, its body shaped to resemble the curves of an Oriental woman. It was programmed for only one purpose—the pleasure of men—and although it gave every indication of life, it was, in truth, nothing but a lifeless machine, devoid of personality or intelligence. It operated, as far as Rutherford had been able to tell, on a repetitive cycle, trapped in an endless loop of depravity and manufactured desire.

Its blank, porcelain face turned toward him as he looked on, and it beckoned to him with a single languorous gesture of its finger, calling him to its mechanical embrace. This . . . routine had gone on for hours. But of course, he had left her—it—there on the bed and had taken the chair by the window instead.

Rutherford couldn't see what other men could possibly find attractive in these strange dolls. It wasn't even a real woman—and he had never had much interest in those, either. At least not in *that* way.

More than anything, though, the sight of the thing filled him with a deep sense of sadness. It might not have been alive, but it was still a slave, still something that had been brought into the world to serve the needs of others in the worst possible way.

Nevertheless, it was difficult not to admire the artifice that had gone into the creation of the nameless machine. It moved with a fluidity and grace that belied its true nature, giving the impression of life, if not the thing itself. If only such a creation could have been put to a better use. At least, he supposed, it wasn't a real girl who'd be pressed into such dreadful servitude.

But the face—the blank, porcelain face. It haunted him: emotionless, terrifying, as if it reflected the emptiness within. He'd been unable to look upon it for long, unable to stop himself imagining the face of a real woman behind it, trying desperately to scream. And so he had sat by the window, holding vigil throughout the night, tired, weary, and alone. He must have slept at some point, he thought, but if he did, it could not have been for very long. He could feel the lethargy in his very bones, but he knew he had to keep moving, to stay alert, to watch every shadow or doorway. They were onto him now—that much was clear from the incident in Greenwich Village and the man he had regretfully been required to dispatch back at his apartment.

He had been running through various scenarios in his mind, contemplating his next move. There was always the safe house in Brooklyn. He'd considered, after what had happened, jumping aboard one of the pneumatic trains and disappearing, becoming somebody else for a while. He could even scrape together enough money to purchase a booth aboard an airship under an assumed identity, although that, in itself, presented its own risks. He knew it wasn't really an option, though. What use would it be to save his own hide if it meant everything he held dear was put at risk? Even worse, if it resulted in the outbreak of war?

But what else could he do? There was little chance he'd be able to deliver his message to London in time, now. A holotube call wouldn't be secure, unless it was from the embassy building, but it was beginning to look increasingly necessary. It would most likely mean the end for him. If the operator was screening calls for the police, they'd be on him in moments. It wasn't so much that he was afraid to sacrifice himself for the cause—he'd crossed that line many times before and always been lucky. No, it was more that he wanted his sacrifice to be worthwhile, and if he gave himself away now, he'd be no use to anyone.

If only he could find his way into the embassy. He knew the staff there would be too scared to speak to him now, though, and in all likelihood they were being observed, too. Any clandestine meeting he might be able to arrange would only lead the American agents straight to him, and worse, could endanger his colleagues and countrymen. Either way, he'd be playing right into their hands, and the outcome could be only one thing: war.

Even if he could get a message to London, there was very little they could realistically do to prevent the planned attack from taking place. If they went in with guns blazing they'd be giving the Americans exactly what they wanted—or at least that small group of dissident Americans who had engineered this whole situation with such meticulous precision. At least they'd be ready for it, however, able to mount some sort of defense. And at least they'd understand that the attack had not been sanctioned by the president, but plotted by a splinter group of sour-faced politicians anxious only to line their own pockets with the spoils of war.

What Rutherford needed was an ally, someone who could make the call on his behalf, who wouldn't be suspected. That would then leave Rutherford free to act, to be the man on the ground, to attempt to prevent the attack from ever taking place.

Then it struck him: Arthur Wolfe, a curator at the Metropolitan Museum of Art, an Englishman living in exile in New York. One of the few. They'd met on occasion, at first by coincidence, but more recently by design.

Wolfe knew Rutherford only as Jerry Robertson, the philanthropist from Boston, but perhaps now was the time for Rutherford to show his hand. Could he trust Wolfe to take his message to the embassy? He didn't know the man well enough to be sure, and it was a hell of a risk. Whatever he was, though, Wolfe wasn't a traitor. Rutherford had established that much during their brief interactions at the museum. Through careful questions disguised as idle chitchat—the skilled work of a spy—Rutherford had come to understand that Wolfe still loved his country. Perhaps now he could be coaxed into helping to save it.

A plan resolved in Rutherford's mind. He would wait here, with the geisha girl, until the museum opened for the day. Then he would settle his account with the madam and be on his way. After that . . . well, he still hadn't quite decided. If he could get out of this alive, then at least he'd be free to act. He knew the players involved in this dangerous game—the people he had spent the last few months in the company of, winning their confidence, pretending to be someone and something he was not. He could start there. If, of course, Arthur Wolfe would be prepared to help.

—•—

The Metropolitan Museum of Art was a remarkable edifice, an imposing mausoleum filled with all the many wonders of the dead. It sat squat on Fifth Avenue, overlooking Central Park, and while Rutherford had always admired the institution, he couldn't help thinking its classical columns and monumental facade looked somehow misplaced among the teeming streets and towering apartment blocks of the metropolis, more like something out of Regency London than New York City.

Nevertheless, he'd found the place both a haven and an inspiration during his time in the city, and while its collection didn't quite, for him, live up to that of the other, similar institution that was so close to his heart—the British Museum—it was still quite remarkable.

He found the ticket hall empty, and his footsteps echoed as he pushed his way through the heavy wooden door. It was still early, and the bustle of tourists had yet to emerge, bleary-eyed, from their hotel room beds. Rutherford crossed to the sales desk, where a young woman—pretty, he supposed, but somewhat marred by a sour-looking expression—greeted him with all the enthusiasm he had come to expect. She gazed vacantly up at him, as if warning him not to make her life any more difficult than it already was.

"One-day pass?"

"Please," Rutherford responded politely, folding a few dollar bills out of his wallet and placing them on the counter before her.

She slid the bills toward her and pulled the stub of a ticket from the machine, passing it over with a contrived smile. "Thank you. Have a good day."

Rutherford nodded and took the ticket, dropping it into his pocket. Then, folding his overcoat over his arm, he turned and crossed the lobby toward the Roman exhibit in search of Arthur.

The Roman collection, he knew, had been somewhat diminished following the events of the prior month. Rutherford wasn't privy to all of the details—and Arthur had been cagey at best about what had really occurred—but he gathered there had been some sort of confrontation between the mob and the police, resulting in a firefight that had destroyed almost half of the exhibits. Consequently the Roman wing had been closed for two weeks while the mess was cleared up, and when it had reopened, many of the exhibits had been missing, damaged and being repaired, or destroyed.

Arthur had been busy, trying to sort through the wreckage to ascertain what could be salvaged and what could not. He'd also—he'd told Rutherford in a rare moment of candor—been provided with a significant budget by the museum's curator to replace as many of the artifacts as possible, or to find suitable alternatives in the bustling auction houses of Europe. He was planning to make a trip home the following month, back to England, before going on to Paris and Rome, his pockets stuffed with the museum's dollars.

Rutherford nodded to the impeccably dressed security guard as he passed from the lobby into the Roman wing, his footsteps ringing out in the cavernous space. The place was deserted, occupied only by the ghosts of yesteryear.

Rutherford paced around, taking in the exhibits. The blank faces stared at him from across the millennia. The faces of the dead, the remnants of an empire long gone, reduced to dust by the weight of history. Rutherford feared that if he couldn't somehow stop the planned attack on London, the British Empire would end up the same way.

He supposed that was inevitable, eventually. The empire wouldn't—couldn't—last forever. The people behind this scheme to ignite the tensions between the empire and the United States were aiming to accelerate that decline, however, to bring matters to a head, to engage the empire in all-out war. If they were successful, whatever the outcome of that war, it would set the British back decades, if not longer.

Even if they proved victorious, it would only be a matter of time before the entropy set in. The expense of another full-blown conflict—in terms of men as well as arms and commodities—would stretch the empire beyond its breaking point. No longer able to police their borders, and most likely facing revolt as a consequence of the ensuing rise in crime, violence and political unrest, the British would soon lose their hold on their colonies. After that . . . well, they'd be laying themselves open to an attack from any number of potential suitors, not least their former cuckolds, the Americans.

Whatever the case, what the empire couldn't withstand was the fallout that would result from another war, and Rutherford was, he realized with a frisson of fear, the only man on the ground who could do anything about it. Well, him and Arthur Wolfe, if the haughty expatriate could be persuaded to help him.

Rutherford knew it was a waiting game now. Arthur would be along shortly, as he always was, and he would stop to pass the time of day with his acquaintance, Jerry Robertson. It was then that Rutherford would have to show his hand, and hope to God that Arthur didn't lose his cool.

In the event it was only a matter of a few minutes before the gangly curator came bustling through the exhibit carrying a cardboard box. His glasses were balanced precariously on the end of his nose—a little jauntily—and he looked hassled, as if the day were already throwing up insurmountable problems. He stopped, however, his expression changing, when he saw Rutherford standing by a glass case filled with Roman coins.

"Hello, Jerry. A little early in the day for you, isn't it?" Arthur said in his bright British accent.

Rutherford smiled. When he spoke, it was with the thick New England accent he'd spent so long practicing during the last few months. "You know what they say about the early bird, Arthur," he said, grinning. "I was hoping to have a word."

Arthur looked a little taken aback, but nodded. "Of course. Why don't you come with me while I find a home for this box? Another fragment, I'm afraid. Not much use to anyone anymore."

Rutherford smiled, then followed Arthur across the hall toward a small office hidden in the far corner. The door was inset with opaque glass. Arthur handed Rutherford the box while he unlocked the door, and Rutherford was surprised by how heavy it was. "My office is upstairs, tucked out of the way. This is just a storeroom. We're using it to store all of the fragments while I see what we can save." He held the door open and Rutherford stepped inside, sliding the box onto a wooden workbench that ran the length of the left-hand wall. The room was small and overflowing with fragments of broken statues, pottery and cardboard boxes. Disconcertingly, a woman's head, carved exquisitely from white marble, lay on the floor just by his feet.

"So, what was it you wanted to talk to me about, Jerry?" Arthur ventured, still standing in the doorway, propping the door open with his foot.

Rutherford cleared his throat. He fixed the other Englishman with a serious expression. "Step in and close the door, if you will, Arthur," he said, dropping the accent and allowing Arthur to hear his real voice for the first time.

Arthur's expression changed immediately from one of interest to one of suspicion. "What's going on, Jerry?" he said, remaining steadfastly where he was. He looked back over his shoulder, as if to see where the security guard was placed.

"My name isn't Jerry," Rutherford said, quietly. "It's Peter Rutherford. I'm an Englishman working for the British government, and I'm here to ask for your help."

Arthur stared at him, his eyes wide with incredulity. "So you've been lying to me all this time? Pretending to show an interest in my work, so you could . . . what? *Recruit* me?"

"No, it's not like that, Arthur. Please believe me." Rutherford wanted to grab the other man by the collar and shake him, tell him to shut up and listen, that he was the only one who could help. But instead, he kept his tone calm, measured. "Please, step inside. We need to talk."

Arthur glowered at him, but did as he said, and Rutherford breathed a short sigh of relief. So, he was willing to listen. "I'm sorry I deceived you, Arthur, but I'd ask you to believe me when I say I was trying only to maintain my cover. I've been working in New York for some months, infiltrating a small group of powerful men who are planning to try to start a war between the United States and the British Empire." He paused for a moment, allowing his words to sink in. "There's an airship leaving for London in a few days, ostensibly disguised as a passenger liner, but in reality carrying some sort of superweapon that it will attempt to deploy when it arrives. The men behind this attack believe the British government will see this as a preemptive strike from a country with which they have been locked in a cold war for the last decade and will advise the queen to commit to a full retaliation. By that time, however, half of London will have been destroyed, and the war will already have been lost."

Arthur shook his head in apparent disbelief. "This is madness. You're telling me the US government is about to lay siege to London?"

Rutherford shook his head. "No, not quite. It's a splinter group, nine men with enough money and motivation behind them to engineer the attack. But if they succeed it'll be enough to ignite the conflict and bring everything to a head. The British will have no choice but to respond, and then the US government will order in their troops. It'll be a bloodbath."

"And why come to me with this? I work in a museum, for God's sake! What can I do?"

"I need you to take a message to the British embassy. That's all. Just walk in there and hand them a note. That way they'll know what's going on and they can get a warning to London. They have a secure line, directly to the Minister for Foreign Affairs." Rutherford rubbed a hand across his face. This was it. This was crunch time.

"If it's such a simple task, why can't you perform it yourself?" Arthur asked, clearly wishing he were somewhere else. "Why involve me?"

"Because the embassy is being watched, and they know who I am. I'd never even get through the door. You, on the other hand—no one will suspect a museum curator of being involved, especially as you're planning a trip home."

Arthur shook his head. He made to reach for the door handle. "Look, I'll have no part in your ridiculous war games, Rutherford—or whatever your real name is. I think you need to leave."

"Arthur, you're missing the point! I'm trying to *prevent* a war! Can't you see? If this attack is allowed to go ahead, the British won't hesitate to authorize a full-blown retaliation. Queen Alberta is spoiling for a fight. Things will escalate, and before we know it there'll be another conflict, this time on a scale none of us can even imagine. Millions of people will die. It's in your power to help me put a stop to it." He paused, searching the other man's face. "Please, will you do it?"

Arthur was wearing a pained expression. "I won't be a pawn, Rutherford. I won't be misled into getting involved in something above my head. Something dangerous."

Rutherford sighed. "I won't lie to you, Arthur, not anymore. It might be dangerous. But if you don't help me, it's likely I'll die trying to make that call." He met the other man's gaze. "I might well die anyway, but at least that way I'll die trying to make a difference. Trying to stop that airship from ever leaving New York. If you can take this message to the embassy"—he reached into his pocket and pulled out a sheaf of paper, holding it out to the other man—"then even if I fail, at least they can be ready. At least they can try to defend themselves." He searched Arthur's face. "If I'm wrong, what's the worst that can happen? You make a fool of yourself taking a scrap of paper to the embassy and telling them a spy came to see you at the museum and handed you this note."

Arthur eyed the folded piece of paper in his hand. He seemed about to reach out for it, and then hesitated. "How do I know I can trust you?" he asked.

Rutherford shrugged. "What have I possibly got to gain? I've been through one war, Arthur, and it damn near ruined me. I've seen what it can do to a man. I've seen better men than me perish in their thousands. I won't allow that to happen again. This isn't what the American people want, and it isn't want the British want, either, despite what Queen Alberta might say."

Arthur nodded, and then reached forward and plucked the note from Rutherford's hand. "All right, I'll do it. I'll do it because I can't risk not taking you at your word. Because if I didn't do it and all those people died, I couldn't live with that. I'll do it to prevent a war."

Rutherford nodded. "Then you have my undying thanks, Arthur. Act quickly, as soon as you possibly can. The earlier we get the message to London, the better. It's all in the note."

"What will you do now?" Arthur said, a concerned expression on his face.

"Whatever it takes, Arthur," Rutherford replied levelly. He'd been mulling it over as he'd been talking, and a plan had slowly begun to resolve in his mind. He knew who was responsible for this mess, the man who had originally conceived the plan to attack London, the man who the others in that small cabal of statesmen and politicians all looked to for their lead: Senator Isambard Banks. That was his best lead. He was the man on the ground, and he had to act. Arthur would get the warning to the embassy, and from there they would transmit it to London. Now it was up to Rutherford to see if he could prevent the attack from happening at all. "I'm going to try to stop a war," he said determinedly.

He reached out and took the curator's hand in his own, shaking it briskly. "Thank you, Arthur. And good luck."

Arthur gave him a wry smile. "Don't go and get yourself killed, Jerry—Peter," he said, tucking the scrap of paper into his shirt pocket.

Rutherford grinned. Getting himself killed was absolutely the last thing on his mind.

CHAPTER TEN

The hangar was immense.

It squatted like some vast, metallic growth by the docks, all steel cladding and heavy iron girders—a huge, shining limpet in the heart of a gray industrial landscape. It had been erected six months earlier along with its twin, which sat squarely beside it, identical in almost every way. The buildings had been commissioned by the state of New York and, as such, had actually been funded by taxpayers, although if asked, most tax-paying New Yorkers wouldn't have known anything about them. If anyone *had* cared to look, they would have been able to trace the paperwork all the way back to the state senator himself, Isambard Banks.

Inside the hangar was suspended a enormous airship, a transatlantic liner that had been adapted, altered and otherwise transformed into a military behemoth of a sort never before conceived. Weapon clusters bristled from wide gashes in its silvery, reflective skin—machine guns, grenade launchers, even cannons—and it bore no livery or marking of any kind.

The maiden voyage of this particular vessel would be its one and only crossing of the ocean. No air traffic controller in London was expecting to receive it at a berthing field on the outskirts of the city. No wives or children impatiently awaited the return of their menfolk who had been away on business. No, the purpose of this particular vessel—which Abraham had taken it upon himself to name *Goliath*—was singular and devastating.

Goliath was designed with only one purpose in mind: to deliver a weapon to the heart of the British Empire, a weapon so powerful and unique that it would bring the empire to its knees.

Within days of *Goliath*'s arrival in London there would be a new world order. Buckingham Palace would have been utterly destroyed, and with it, Queen Alberta and her legions of cronies. The war would be over before it had even begun, and the victors—the great republic of America—would reap the spoils. What was more, it was down to him, Abraham, that such a thing could even be conceived.

Abraham shivered with delight at the thought. In his hands he held the power to change the world. He had discovered and built the device that would win the war. Now he was fitting it inside the ship that would deliver it to its final destination. His chest swelled with pride.

Of course, all of this was colored by Abraham's concern that, by rushing him in such a way, the senator was effectively dooming them all. The man was arrogant—an egomaniac, even—and while his belief in the American ideal was to be applauded, his zeal also spoke to Abraham of a certain ignorance. He seemed to think that faith alone would be enough to protect them, no matter what they unleashed on their enemies. He clearly thought they'd be able to control the creatures, once the weapon had been activated and they had spilled hundreds, if not thousands of the things upon the unsuspecting British.

Abraham, however, knew differently. He knew this because he had tested a whole plethora of weapons against the creature he had trapped in the other hangar, and it had proved impervious to them all. Something about its extradimensional origin meant that it didn't react to terrestrial matter in expected ways. He had managed to harm it eventually, of course, but that was only because it was weakened by his continued ministrations of the poison. He kept it that way, just on the verge of death, just to be sure. Nevertheless, it had proved incredibly resilient. Even if it managed to escape in its current condition it would put up a hell of a fight. Without the solution—without the blood with which to make it—even the might of the American military would be as nothing against an army of these alien things.

The weapon was a Pandora's box: once it had been opened it would be near impossible to close it again. That was the price they would have to pay for victory and dominance, and the risk they would run for their haste.

Abraham rocked back on his mechanical legs, admiring his handiwork. The cavernous interior of the hangar bay in the lower section of *Goliath* was filled with a vast array of mechanical and electrical components: a bank of six miniature Tesla coils which, when powered up, would generate enough electrical current to force open the dimensional rent; thick, snaking cables tied in tight bundles; pneumatic pistons that would open the loading doors and release the creatures once they had begun to pass through the rift.

Then, at the center of it all, his crowning achievement: the gateway itself. It was like some bizarre fusion of the ancient and the modern: a large archway formed out of shaped iron girders and steel cladding, but etched with an array of incomparably ancient runes and symbols, some of them so intensely *alien* that Abraham couldn't even look at them for more than a few moments before being overcome with a strange giddiness.

It had taken him weeks to etch them onto the framework, and longer still to prepare himself to test it. He'd known what to expect, of course—during his time working for the Roman he'd become more than familiar with the procedure used to birth the creatures through the interdimensional rift, but procedure was one thing, and he had not been present when the Roman had finally managed to lure one of the creatures through. He was glad of that, in retrospect—the procedure had evidently gone horribly wrong and the Roman had been killed in the process, along with pretty much everyone else who'd been present.

Of course, Abraham's attempt to test his machine had been far more successful, and had given rise to the creature now trapped in the pit in the neighboring hangar.

The Roman had been almost as zealous as Senator Banks, Abraham mused, and that, he supposed, was why everything had gone wrong. It was an object lesson in caution, and one Abraham had been quick to learn. He certainly believed in letting others make all the mistakes first.

Abraham had been employed by the Roman ostensibly to build the crime boss an army of artificial mobsters—golems created from earth and clay, built on a subframe of brass. They'd been effective, in their way, but inelegant and rather unwieldy. Nevertheless, they'd inspired Abraham to develop the raptors, using the techniques he had learned creating the moss men, drawing on the occult sciences and marrying those ancient methods with more modern techniques. The results had been quite astounding.

Abraham wondered how his flock was getting along. He'd taken a huge risk that evening, sending them all out at once on Senator Banks's instruction. He supposed he'd had little choice. He needed to find a ready supply of the right blood if he was to have any hope of making enough of the solution to pacify or destroy the creatures that would be deployed by *Goliath*, and with Banks accelerating the timeframe of the whole venture—well, he'd had to do it, of course.

He cringed when he considered the gaggle of pathetic, mewling creatures that would be waiting for him back at the other hangar—assuming, of course, that his raptors had done their work.

Abraham had never intended to become an executioner, and the role didn't really sit well with him. The occasional death here and there—well, that was inevitable in his line of work, and he'd reconciled himself to that long ago. Even more recently, he'd enjoyed watching some of the people brought back by the raptors—the rejects from his experiments—begging for their lives before being pushed into the pit to be consumed by the alien creature. But it was all a matter of scale.

It wasn't because he was squeamish, nor because he had any qualms about ending those people's pathetic lives. No, it was because, he considered, he would have to deal with them all while they were still *alive*. At the end of the day, Abraham simply wasn't cut out for dealing with people. He hated interaction with others, abhorred the way people stared at his strange, mismatched body, and worst of all, couldn't bear the way they would do anything—anything at all—just to hold on to their ridiculous lives. As if any of them had anything worth living for. Nevertheless, as his old mom had always told him, you couldn't make an omelet without breaking some eggs.

Abraham surveyed his work one last time. It was nearing completion. He'd had to work through most of the night, and would have to do so again the following day, but the *Goliath* would be ready for its maiden voyage on time.

He ran a hand through his hair and sighed. He couldn't put it off any longer. If the raptors had brought him a plentiful bounty of potential donors, he would need to start processing them immediately. It was a quick enough test to carry out—he need only draw off a vial of their blood and allow a few droplets of it to fall on the creature in the pit to identify whether he had a match or not. It would only take him an hour, and if he was quick, he could dispose of the unnecessary donors immediately. He didn't want to wake to such an onerous task in the morning.

Abraham rose stiffly on his piston-powered legs, straightening his back. He left his tools where they lay—he'd need them again in the morning—and quit the belly of *Goliath*, hopping down the loading ramp and out into the hangar beyond.

Outside, the city was freezing, glossing over with a layer of sparkling ice. He could see it reflecting in the moonlight on the top of the nearby buildings. He hurried across the concourse to the neighboring hangar, anxious to get out of the cold. Even though he was now more machine than flesh, Abraham still felt the chill.

He'd locked the door to the other hangar behind him when he'd left earlier that evening, knowing that the raptors would find their way in through the hatch in the roof. He fished in his pocket for the key, now, smiling at the sounds he could hear coming from the other side of the door. The raptors had returned, and with them, they had brought their prey.

Abraham turned the key in the lock and pushed the door open, slipping quietly inside. The scene that greeted him was one of utter pandemonium. The raptors were playing, toying with the ragtag assortment of waifs and strays they had plucked from the streets. There were at least eight or nine people running around, screaming and wailing, as the raptors tormented them, slashing at them with their talons, hissing and shrieking, shrilling and chattering in delight.

The raptors seemed to get some measure of enjoyment out of this torture, making the humans rush about in blind panic, herding them like animals. They were like cats toying with captured rodents, always stopping short of dealing the killing blow.

Occasionally, after a particularly good haul like tonight, Abraham would toss a few of the rejected donors to the raptors instead of throwing them in the pit. The creature had a ready supply of warm bodies—much to his frustration—and it gave his pets pleasure to actually be allowed to shred one of the captives for a change. He would do that for them tonight. First, though, he needed to run his tests.

"That's enough, children!" he called, and the raptors immediately ceased their antics and turned, as one, to regard him. They had only a rudimentary intelligence, but it was enough to recognize a handful of commands, and to recognize their master. "Tie them up with the others," he said, and the raptors did as he commanded, shepherding their protesting flock to the shackles that awaited them at the rear of the hangar.

Abraham waited until the raptors had finished securing the prisoners and had taken once more to the rafters, where they sat on their haunches, chattering and hissing at one another. He counted them off quickly and realized that two of them were missing. Had they simply not returned yet? Or had something happened to them? He felt a slight twinge of panic at the thought that they might have come to harm. He'd *told* the senator it wasn't safe to send them all out at once. After one of them had returned with a damaged wing the previous day . . .

Still, it would have to wait. There was still a chance they could return. In the meantime, Abraham thought, rolling his sleeves up, he had work to do.

CHAPTER ELEVEN

The eyes had continued to haunt him.

All throughout the war, all throughout those long months of bloodshed, mortar shells, engine oil and death. Every time he'd gone up in his aircraft, every time he'd looked to the skies, the eyes had been there, watching him, judging him.

Gabriel had retreated into himself. He had prosecuted his missions with an increasing sense of dislocation. He felt as if his mind was disengaging. What was real? What was not? Had reality somehow fractured? Or was it simply his mind creating figments, ethereal ghosts, unable to cope with the atrocities he had seen, with the knowledge of what he was doing every time he depressed the trigger to set loose another shell. Was it simply the war, doing this to him? He didn't know, and soon enough even that question was lost as he drifted through the fog of those months, unable, in truth, to engage with anything or anyone other than what was strictly necessary for him to get through the ordeal as quickly as possible.

Life became a series of stuttering moments, repeating over and over: eating, sleeping, shitting, flying, eating, shitting . . . The borders of his universe had shrunk, and he was hemmed in. Only the war in France existed. Nothing more. He felt as if he were being eroded by it, as if soon, that shrinking universe would close in on him completely and he would simply blink out of existence, forgotten, like all the others left for dead on the fields of battle.

Throughout it all, the eyes had remained a constant, unwavering companion. They reminded him of his duty. Not his duty to his captain, or his country, but his duty to himself. His duty to protect the core of what he was, of *who* he was. He knew this conflict would change him, and everyone around him, utterly. Yet somehow the eyes reminded him to preserve what he could of Gabriel Cross, to bury it, to leave it untouched by the madness, and the violence, and the horror.

So Gabriel had done just that. He had taken that small kernel, what was left of *him*, and he had buried it somewhere over France. It wasn't until years later, in New York City, that he had even been able to conceive of unearthing it again. By then he had changed beyond all comprehension.

Of course, the horrors had continued. While Gabriel had become desensitized to the loss of human life—a notion he still found horrific to this day—the things he had seen during his crash, in those few lucid moments before delirium and his injuries had overwhelmed him, had perhaps done more to alter his perception of the world than anything that human beings could do to one another.

He barely remembered the moments leading up to the crash. Just the sensation of hurtling through the sky, out of control, of thinking, *Finally, this is it. This is where I die.*

Silence and motion. The blur of speed, of the world sliding past the toughened glass of the cockpit. Black smoke smudging the sky, peacefulness. These were the impressions he was left with. And then . . . nothing.

When he'd come to, he had been on his side. The noise and the pain had returned with a startling ferocity, assaulting his every sense, filling his head with confusion. It had taken him a few minutes to realize what had actually occurred, to catch his breath and calm his nerves enough that he could think. He remembered pinching himself, disbelieving that he could truly be still alive. Then the world had resolved around him, suddenly snapping back into sharp focus. He'd glanced around, trying to get his bearings.

His plane had saved his life—a metal cocoon that had protected him from the worst of the impact. He'd lost a wing in the crash, and the other, damaged beyond repair, had been pointing up at the sky like an accusatory finger, jutting proudly from the wreckage. The plane had clearly rotated onto its side as it struck the ground.

Still strapped into his seat and hanging limply out of the shattered cockpit, Gabriel had been able to tell from the churned earth that surrounded him that the fuselage had gouged a long rent in the muddy loam, like a crazed plow, turning over the landscape as it came to rest.

In the distance dark smoke rose in long spirals, and he'd heard the sharp whine of engines overhead: his brothers-in-arms, still intent on smiting the enemy, on avenging him, their dead, fallen comrade who had been blasted out of the sky by enemy fire. He'd known they would not come looking for him. No one survived a crash such as the one he had experienced. No one. To his friends and fellow pilots, he was already dead. Dead the minute the enemy weapon had burst open his engine housing and sent him careening toward the ground.

Gabriel had fought to free himself from his webbing, and had cried out at the lancing pain the movement stirred in his leg. He hadn't been entirely unscathed, after all. Nevertheless, he'd known the danger of staying too close to the wreckage. The engine could have gone up at any moment if a stray spark found an exposed fuel line or spillage from a split tank. He'd seen it happen to other downed planes, even discussed it with the other pilots, explained how he saw it as a fitting end for a dead pilot, to be cremated along with his vehicle. Better that, surely, than being left to be picked over by scavenging animals? At least this way there was some dignity left for the dead man, something to be claimed from the horror of what had become of him.

He'd never even considered before that some of those pilots might still have been alive.

Taking all of the strain in his upper arms, Gabriel had heaved himself out of the cockpit and slumped onto the wet, clinging mud below. He'd lain there on his back for a while, watching the sky. And surely enough, up there, in the distance, that pair of eyes had stared back at him, unblinking.

It had been after this, after he had freed himself from the carcass of his downed plane and stumbled, near delirious, toward a farmhouse in a neighboring field, that he had first encountered the creature that would change his life.

The farmhouse had been long-abandoned, its occupants most likely fleeing in the face of the oncoming conflict, the tide of violence and death that was sweeping across their country. But something else had taken up residence in the dilapidated building.

Gabriel had practically fallen in through the door, desperately in search of help. His leg had been mangled in the crash, and he'd been barely able to support himself as he'd stumbled toward the building in the hope of salvation. It had taken every ounce of his remaining strength. With hindsight, he'd been able to see how foolish he'd been to expect to find any help in that crumbling old wreck of a home. Of course there would be no one there, in the middle of a war zone. They would have been evacuated months earlier, their home given over to the soldiers or left abandoned, target practice for the enemy bombers.

Nevertheless, he had pressed on, fixated on the idea that if he could only get to safety, to the haven of that farmhouse, everything would be all right.

Instead of the hoped-for assistance, however, instead of the kindly French farmer he'd imagined in his half-hallucinatory state, he'd found something else there, lurking in the dark. Something that should never have existed. Something that shifted and stirred in the shadows, that unfurled itself as he'd crept into that blackened shell of a building, readying itself to feast on his broken, exhausted body.

It was an alien thing, a monster, a creature derived from his very worst nightmares, spawned from the depths of hell itself. It had reached out for him with its thick, ropy tentacles, its pink flesh glistening in the half-light, dripping with syrupy mucus.

He'd thought then that he was probably insane, that this thing, this figment, had been born out of his waking dreams, just like the eyes that haunted him from above. He'd tried to convince himself it was a hallucination, a creation of his damaged mind. Others had said the same, too, when—a day later—they had picked him up, stumbling across the fields, still fleeing the unbelievable creature he claimed to have encountered near the wreckage of his plane.

Of course, the crash site had been located and the farmhouse had been explored, and nothing had been found to corroborate his story. It had been dismissed as the ravings of an injured man, driven temporarily mad by the shock.

He'd held on to that notion after he'd recovered, after he'd been invalided home back to Long Island to have his leg treated. The dreams had continued to torment him, of course, but those strange, all-seeing eyes had remained in France, as had the beast. And so he came to accept that theory as the truth—that of course such things could never exist, that the creature he had seen had been nothing but the product of his unconscious mind, the means by which his mind had coped with the horror of his ordeal, an externalization of the pain. He'd listened to the doctors and had come to believe what they told him. He had followed their advice, and he had slipped back into his mundane, ordinary existence. The eternal party had once again come to define him.

Yet somewhere, deep inside that kernel of himself that he had buried so long ago, he knew that in his complicity, in his readiness to believe in the mind-fever, he was deceiving not only the doctors, but also himself. A part of him recognized the truth, but he kept it hidden, terrified to admit it even to himself. Because in acknowledging the truth—that everything he had seen had been real—he would be admitting that either he had, truly, been driven insane, or else that there were such horrors in the universe that knowledge of them might amount to exactly the same thing.

He had kept such thoughts buried for years, even when he had first donned the black suit of the Ghost. And then, just scant weeks earlier, he had seen another of the creatures, here in New York City, in the basement of the Roman's mansion, thrashing about as it hauled itself through the gateway from its own world into his.

It was perhaps one of the most terrifying, and yet liberating, experiences of his life. After all this time, all those years of repressing the truth, he had finally allowed himself to recognize that he had been right all along. In doing so, he had blurred the boundaries between the twin halves of his life.

Gabriel—or the Ghost—had fought the beast, and it had taken from him the woman he had loved. Only Celeste had been able to stop it. Celeste. Remarkable, beautiful Celeste. She had known the truth all along, had known of the existence of such things, and had known also that her blood was anathema to it. She had killed it by sacrificing herself, and in doing so she had saved him, Donovan and the city.

In doing so she had offered him hope—hope that those things could be stopped—but at a price he could barely stand to consider. Her loss was like a burning poker in his chest. When he thought of her, he found it difficult to breathe. The pain was still so acute, so pointed, so fresh.

But now he knew beyond a shadow of a doubt that the monsters in the darkness did exist. This was the burden he carried. One of the many.

Gabriel woke with a start, thrashing his way through layers of unconsciousness.

Had he called out to her? To Celeste? He thought perhaps he had.

He sensed movement, and turned to see Ginny stumbling through the doorway of his bedroom, blinking into the early-morning light like a vampire emerging into the dawn. He watched her for a moment, trying to remember where he was, what had happened, why she was there.

Yes, that was right. They were in Manhattan, in his apartment on Fifth Avenue. He'd spent the night in an armchair, giving his bed up for the girl. Judging by the light streaming in through the window, it was already well past dawn.

His body ached. He stretched wearily, feeling a sharp pull in his shoulder. That was where the raptor's claw had bitten into his flesh. He cycled through the events of the previous night—the party, the trip into town, the apartment and the dead agent, the fight with the raptors. Ginny and his two pistols. It came back to him in a cascade of stuttering images.

Ginny eyed him as she crossed toward the kitchenette. Had she heard him calling out? Is that what had roused her and brought her out, blinking into the morning light? Most probably. But then Ginny knew what it was to have bad dreams. She was broken, just like him. Only instead of donning a black suit and traversing the rooftops by night, searching for penitence, for someone to take it all out on, she handled her demons in a different way. She found solace at the bottom of a bottle. The thing was, he just didn't know why.

"God, I need a drink," she said, rummaging in the cupboards for a glass. Her voice was still groggy with sleep.

"Isn't it a bit early for that?"

"Gabriel, my dear, that's precisely the point." She smiled coquettishly and ran a hand through her mop of unruly hair. Her red, glossy lipstick was smeared across her cheek. She still looked pretty, Gabriel considered. Devastatingly so, perhaps more so because of her rumpled state, her lack of perfection, her humanity. Why, then, had he chosen to sleep in the armchair, alone?

He felt strangely reluctant to acknowledge his feelings for the woman, as confused as they were. What was it that was holding him back? Was it because she reminded him of a past he'd thought he'd left behind, a part of his life he'd sooner forget? Was it because he suspected her of something underhanded, for walking so brazenly back into his life without any sort of explanation as to why? Or perhaps it was loyalty to the memory of Celeste, who had died only a few weeks earlier? Even fear that it might happen again—that if he allowed himself to fall for this girl once more, she might disappear again, or worse, that he might lead her unwittingly to her demise?

He didn't know. But one thing was sure—he wanted to be around her. He wanted her close. And perhaps that was enough for him, for now.

Ginny sauntered over, drink in hand, ice cubes clicking in the glass. She folded herself smoothly into the armchair opposite him, crossing her knees. She was wearing his long, silk dressing gown, and it looked faintly ridiculous on her, billowing around her like some oversized kimono.

Gabriel, on the other hand, was still wearing the accoutrements of the previous night: the coat and jacket of the Ghost. He'd unclipped the long barrel of his fléchette gun and dropped it on the floor beside his chair. Likewise the canisters of his rocket propellers, which he had unstrapped from his ankles and cast across the room. His hat was resting on the coffee table. He'd need to bathe before facing the day.

He studied Ginny as she sipped at her drink. "Why did you come back, Ginny?" he asked her, his voice low.

She watched him for a moment, searching his face for any clue as to the tenor of his question. When he didn't give anything away, she shrugged. "To see you," she said, and reached for his discarded packet of cigarettes on the coffee table. She drew one out of the packet with her long, white fingers and pulled the ignition tab. It flared briefly, and she placed it, a little shakily, between her lips.

"It's been a long time."

"Yes, I know. But I simply knew I needed to see you. I was thinking about old times, about old friends. That's all." She smiled, but her eyes told the real story. *I needed to see if you could fix me.*

Gabriel would have laughed, if it wouldn't have seemed so heartless. He hadn't been able to fix himself, let alone someone else. "I'm dangerous, Ginny. Dangerous to be around. You'd be better off finding someone else with whom to dredge up the past."

"Perhaps," she replied airily. "But it isn't about the past, is it, Gabriel? It's about the present. About the here and now. You and me, and whatever's going on out there, with those raptors. And besides"—

she flicked the ash from the tip of her cigarette into a half-empty coffee mug—"it beats swanning around the apartment all day getting drunk."

Gabriel couldn't repress his smile. "What happened to you?" he asked, and then immediately regretted it. Was it too much?

She shrugged. "Life. That's what happened. Cold, hard reality. It's a terrible world out there, Gabriel," she said, as if that was enough, as if that told him everything he needed to know about her. That she had faced reality, and it had proved too much to bear. He thought there had to be something more to it than that.

Ginny could see he was bemused by her answer. He could tell that from the wry expression on her face, the slightly wonky smile on her lips as she deftly turned the question back on him. "And what about you? About that . . . *suit*?" She waved her hand to indicate the apparel he was wearing.

Gabriel didn't meet her gaze. What about the suit? He'd done it to preserve his identity, to separate himself from the persona that everyone knew, the Gabriel Cross that lived in Long Island and threw parties and didn't care about anything but himself. He'd done it to keep the people he cared about safe. And where had that gotten him?

"It's . . . a disguise, I suppose," he said, and he knew it was much more than that. It was another life, another attempt to cope with the world. It was a fresh start.

Ginny laughed. "We all have masks of one kind or another, Gabriel," she replied cryptically, and downed the rest of the bourbon in her tumbler. Gabriel watched her shiver as the alcohol hit her palate. She cocked her head, her eyes suddenly bright. "So, what now?" She asked this as though it was a given, as if the events of the previous evening and her knowledge of his secret life meant that she was now inextricably involved in whatever would happen next. Her smile told him that she knew he wouldn't be able to resist.

Gabriel glanced out of the window. The sun was coming up over the city. Birds wheeled over the rooftops. In the distance, dirigibles stirred the clouds, and biplanes dragged vapor trails across the sky. At least the fog had begun to lift.

He looked back toward Ginny, who was watching him expectantly. "I don't know," he said, his voice hard, firm. "I'm hoping Donovan can turn up something regarding the dead man we found in that apartment. As for the raptors . . . well, we're no closer to knowing what it is they're up to."

"What about the bird and the things you found inside that one you destroyed last night?"

Gabriel shrugged. "All that tells us is that we're dealing with someone very dangerous indeed. Someone who has a notion of how to marry science with the dark arts. We've still no real idea of what it is they're up to, or why they're abducting people from the streets."

Ginny took a long draw on her cigarette. "Then we need to come up with a way to find out," she said determinedly. "If only we were able to talk to one of the victims, to find out where they were being taken. As I see it, the abductees are the only ones who know the truth." She flicked the ash from the end of her cigarette, and it was at that moment that a plan began to take shape in the back of Gabriel's mind.

CHAPTER TWELVE

Donovan hulked behind his desk, brooding. It was too early: he needed more coffee. He dragged at the butt of his cigarette, sucking the harsh fumes down into his lungs, enjoying the sensation of the nicotine flooding into his bloodstream. Around him, the precinct was already buzzing with life.

Donovan had hardly slept. When he'd finally arrived home after the encounter with the raptors—and after staying on to brief Mullins regarding his plans for the apartment that had belonged to the missing British spy—he'd found Flora asleep on the sofa. She'd waited up for him. His dinner was in the oven, now burnt and dry.

He had gently woken her, slipped his arms beneath her and carried her up the stairs to their bedroom.

Then, unable to sleep, he had crept back down to the kitchen, where he had sat with a packet of cigarettes and a bottle of bourbon to consider everything that had occurred. It was only hours later, just before dawn, that he had climbed into bed, groggy from the tiredness and alcohol, for what amounted to a couple of hours of unsatisfactory unconsciousness.

There would be no berating from Flora when he eventually saw her later that day, however—he had left her still asleep in bed that morning, creeping out of the apartment so as not to disturb her. She had learned long ago that the life of a policeman's wife was an extraordinary one—

or at least that she would have to learn to deal with an extraordinary amount of disappointment—as, when engaged with a case, Donovan was very much the absentee from the marriage.

It pained him, he thought, more than it did Flora. Not that she didn't care, but more that she had resigned herself to it, and that she accepted her husband for who and what he was—a police inspector in one of the busiest cities in the world. She was proud of him, she reminded him regularly, for standing up for what was right, for upholding justice in this most unjust of times. He loved her for that, for that unqualified faith she had in him, for seeing the goodness in him, even when he couldn't see it himself.

For his part, all Donovan wanted to do was be a better husband. He couldn't always see that, to Flora, that meant something different than simply being around. Because if he was, if he gave up everything he believed in to be by her side, he would be a lesser man in her eyes.

She'd told him that the day before their wedding, all those years ago, when he'd taken her to one side and explained that he was thinking of leaving the force. She'd taken his hand and resolutely told him that she loved him and that he had to do what he thought was right—and that she would continue to love him even when he wasn't around.

She'd been true to her word. For all those years, she'd stood by him and supported him, and never once mentioned the ruined dinners or missed dates, the late nights or the injuries. One day, she maintained, he would be done with the police force, with chasing criminals and catching serial killers. And when that day came, then they would make up for lost time. In the meantime, he was to continue to help people the best way he knew how. And if that meant she had to grow used to the disappointments, well, that was what being a policeman's wife was all about. She'd known that before she'd ever accepted his ring.

Nevertheless, it didn't stop Donovan struggling with pangs of guilt. He supposed it never would.

Donovan stared at the clock. All through the night he'd been racking his brain for that sudden flash of inspiration, that insight he needed to get the breakthrough in the case he was searching for. He was clearly missing something. Something that should have been obvious to him, but was, for the time being, remaining elusive. Some fact or implication, some link he just couldn't see.

This Jerry Robertson, the British spy he was supposedly trying to locate—there was a bigger story behind that, Donovan was sure of it. Why had the man had photographs of the state senator, the commissioner and other businessmen and politicians on his wall? Was he planning to execute them? Is that why Senator Banks was involved? Clearly he and the commissioner knew more about the situation than they were prepared to divulge. And what of the raptors? Were they somehow linked? It seemed unlikely . . . but then the spy had also had a picture of one of those, too, stuck to his wall.

Whatever the raptors were, Donovan needed to rid the city of them. They were a scourge, a diabolical plague upon the populace, and he shuddered at the thought of what they might be doing to the innocent citizens they continued to pluck so brazenly from the streets. Even the Ghost was having trouble getting to the bottom of the matter, with the raptors dancing rings around him or putting up too much of a fight. Now, finally, they'd managed to destroy one—the remains of which were still stashed in the trunk of his car—but they were still no closer to having an answer.

Donovan stared at the paperwork on his desk. The words meant nothing to him, just a jumble of tics and scratches on the page—more of the endless bureaucratic nonsense he had to deal with instead of real police work. He rubbed his eyes. His lids were heavy and he needed sleep. But he knew he wouldn't be able to rest, even if he could get away. Perhaps, he thought reluctantly, he just needed caffeine and more cigarettes. Wasn't that the story of his life.

He looked up at the sound of footsteps approaching his desk. Mullins was looming over him, a dark expression on his face. The portly young man was flushed and sweating, with dark rings beneath his eyes, and he pulled nervously at his collar. He looked tired, too. Something had gone on.

"You look as if you've been up all night," said Donovan, empathizing with the other man.

"I have," Mullins replied warily, as if waiting for Donovan to make some further comment or judgment. Instead, he simply shrugged and waited for the sergeant to continue. "I have bad news for you, sir," said Mullins gingerly.

"Just what I need," Donovan sighed heavily. "What's happened? Further abductions? A murder? Someone run off with the commissioner's pussycat?"

Mullins didn't raise a smile, and Donovan felt a sinking feeling spreading throughout his chest. No, this really was bad news.

"No, sir. None of that. It's about the apartment you asked me to deal with last night, the one in Greenwich Village. Someone burned it to the ground before we were able to finish removing the contents."

Donovan fixed Mullins with a confused stare. "Burned it to the ground? But it was on the third floor."

"Yes, sir. They took the whole apartment block. Razed it completely. At least twelve people perished in the flames." Mullins swallowed, clearly affected by the news he was imparting. "Inspector Anderson is down there now, attempting to establish exactly what happened. But one thing is clear—the fire was started in the very apartment you were interested in."

Donovan allowed a long whistle to escape from between his teeth. *Twelve people.* Twelve people, all for the sake of some papers and a collage on the wall. As well as, perhaps, the corpse of a dead American agent. That was quite a price someone was prepared to pay. He'd been right—there was definitely more to this than he'd been allowed to know about so far.

"So we lost everything?"

Mullins shook his head. "Ah, well, there's perhaps one small bit of good news, sir. We managed to extract the corpse before the arsonist was able to make his move. None of the files, none of the photographs you wanted, but we have the body in the police morgue."

"Well, at least that's something, Mullins, although it's hardly much consolation when it's about to find itself accompanied by twelve others. Did anyone survive?"

Mullins shook his head. "Not so far as we're aware, sir. It was the middle of the night. They'd have found themselves trapped in their apartments by the flames. The first most of them would have known about it, it would already have been too late. It seems the arsonist started a secondary fire in the basement, just to be sure." He dabbed ineffectually at his forehead with a handkerchief. "One thing's clear though, sir. The dead man wasn't a government agent."

Donovan frowned. He realized the butt of his cigarette had burned down to the filter and had gone out. He flicked the remains of it into the ashtray on his desk, scattering plumes of gray ash. He reached inside his jacket for another. "Not an agent?" he asked quizzically. "Go on."

"We managed to get a positive identification for the man from our records, sir. He never worked for the government in any official capacity. He was hired muscle by the name of Paulo Lucarotti. He had a connection to the mob. What's more, he'd been in custody at a state penitentiary until two months ago, at which point he was given an early pardon and released." Mullins stood back, evidently pleased with himself. But, Donovan noted, the haunted expression had not left his eyes.

"That's unusual," Donovan replied, frowning. "So you're telling me a mob heavy gets released from jail early in order to go after a British spy, winds up dead, and then the scene of the crime gets torched, killing twelve innocent people in the process."

"That's about the size of it, sir, yes," said Mullins. "There's one other thing, too."

"What's that, Mullins?"

Mullins placed his hands on Donovan's desk and leaned forward, glancing from side to side before he spoke. When he did, his voice had dropped to a whisper, so that Donovan had to lean forward in his chair to hear. "Commissioner Montague himself is the signatory on the release papers." He stood back, rubbing the base of his spine, as if leaning forward had unbalanced him and caused his creaking bones to grate.

Donovan exhaled smoke thoughtfully from the corner of his mouth. "The commissioner . . . Now that really *is* interesting, Mullins."

"I thought so, sir."

Donovan studied the sergeant's face but could see no trace of irony there. "Good work, Sergeant. Very good work indeed." He leaned back in his chair. "I think it's time I went for a little chat with the commissioner, to update him on our progress." He jammed his cigarette between his teeth and spoke around it. "Be a good man, Mullins—get the coffee on. You look like you could use it as much as I could."

For the first time that morning, Mullins smiled.

—•—

Donovan felt suddenly imbued with nervous energy as he mounted the stairs to the commissioner's office. He didn't know if it was the caffeine finally starting to take effect, or more a sense of trepidation at what he might be about to uncover. What had the commissioner gone and gotten himself involved in? First Senator Banks, and now this . . . irregularity. Why was the commissioner getting personally involved in the early release of a mob heavy? Had he been leaned on? Donovan thought that unlikely—he'd never had Montague down as a mob man. Was it some half-baked attempt to send a hit man after the British spy? That would make more sense, but it was hardly above board, and clearly unlikely to succeed. He wondered if the dead man was actually their last resort—if they'd tried everything else already in their attempts to locate the spy.

More to the point, however, Donovan wasn't sure what he would do if he *did* discover the commissioner was involved in something murky. Who the hell would he go to with *that*? The commissioner was involved in state politics at the highest level, and had friends in all sorts of places. He probably thought he could do whatever he wanted, and he wouldn't have been far wrong. Short of being caught with his hand in the money pot, or around the throat of a whore, Montague was pretty much untouchable. Especially when one factored in the consideration that he was working closely with a state senator. With Banks there beside him, Montague could be confident that pretty much nothing would stick.

Donovan rapped on the door of the commissioner's office with a heavy heart. He knew that whatever happened here, he was in for a rough ride. The commissioner would want to know why Donovan wasn't any closer to bringing in the spy, and would probably even berate him about the arson attack on the apartment building. The commissioner would have to deal with the public relations nightmare that would arise from the death of twelve innocent civilians, and that would put him in a bad mood for days. And, Donovan suspected, the man wasn't likely to take kindly to being questioned about his conduct by a junior officer.

"Come." The command was a muffled bark from within the room. Donovan reached for the doorknob, turned it in his clammy palm, and stepped into the room.

It took him a moment to pick out the commissioner from among all the furniture that dressed his ostentatious lair. He was propped in an armchair by the window, a fat cigar clamped between his teeth, wreathed in gray-blue smoke. He was wearing a smart pinstriped suit and a burgundy cravat. Donovan wondered if he'd just come from an important meeting.

"Ah, Donovan! Come in," Montague said, waving for Donovan to come closer. "I hope you come bearing good news."

Donovan cleared his throat. "Well . . ."

The commissioner's demeanor changed almost immediately. "Sit down, Donovan." He grabbed his cigar between his thumb and his index finger like a pencil, withdrew it from between his teeth, examined the now-sodden end, and then pushed it back into his mouth. Then, grasping the arms of his chair, he leaned forward, eyeing Donovan as he lowered himself into one of the chairs. It was comfortable—far *too* comfortable in Donovan's eyes—more like something from a high-end hotel than an office.

"It's a simple job, Donovan. Find the man and bring him in. That's all I ask. Manhattan Island is not that big a place. Anyone would think I'd asked you to find the proverbial needle in a haystack."

Donovan swallowed, biting back not fear, but anger at the man's recriminations. What the hell would he know about it? He measured his next words very carefully. "By your own admission, Commissioner, this man is trained to be an expert in subterfuge and espionage. He's dangerous, and he knows how to lose himself in a conurbation. Without any leads—"

"You *had* a lead!" the commissioner snapped. "And a damn good one. Mullins tells me you managed to stumble across his hideout, full of all the leads you'd ever need, as well as a damn corpse! What more do you need?"

"Well, sir, it's really not that simple," said Donovan in a conciliatory fashion.

"No," the commissioner replied sullenly, shaking his head, "it never is." He chewed on the end of his cigar for a moment. Then, as if deciding Donovan had been given enough of a dressing down, his tone altered. "So, what—someone torched the place?"

"That's about the size of it, Commissioner," said Donovan, echoing Mullins's earlier words, "before we'd had the chance to strip it of anything useful. The walls were covered in maps, schematics, photographs—it was a treasure trove. Whoever torched the place was clearly trying to prevent us from getting hold of it."

"Hmmm,' said the commissioner. "I'd have thought that much was obvious, Donovan, even to you." Donovan winced, but the commissioner's tone lacked malice. "Did you get *anything*?"

Donovan shrugged. "Just the corpse."

The commissioner was frowning, staring into the middle distance.

"I'd wager . . ." he trailed off and then turned to Donovan, seeming to snap out of whatever reverie had momentarily distracted him. "I'd wager it was this spy himself who torched the place. Realized you were on to him, took his opportunity while your back was turned. You shouldn't have let your attention wander, Donovan. You shouldn't have left it all to Mullins."

Donovan nodded. Perhaps the commissioner was right about that. Perhaps he had put too much on the sergeant's shoulders. But Mullins was the only one he trusted, and he had to stand up for him. "He's a good man, Commissioner. He'll make a fine inspector one day."

Commissioner Montague frowned. "I don't doubt it, Donovan. But that doesn't mean he's ready to take on something this big. He's inexperienced. He'll miss things you might see."

"I hardly—"

The commissioner waved him silent. "Excuses," he said, and his bristly eyebrows raised, as if challenging Donovan to go against him.

Donovan realized he was bunching his fists by his sides, and he made a conscious effort to relax.

"So you got the corpse, then."

"Yes, and Mullins identified the dead man this morning." He let that hang for a moment, studying the commissioner, watching for any response. "A mob man by the name of Paulo Lucarotti. Does that mean anything to you, sir?"

The commissioner's eyes went wide in surprise. The timbre of his voice raised an entire octave. "Me? Why in God's name would it mean anything to me?"

Donovan smiled inwardly. He could tell by the man's reaction that he was either deeply offended, or else deeply concerned. He couldn't tell which. "Lucarotti was released from state custody two months ago, sir, by a special order. He's a known criminal, held up on charges of attempted murder and grievous bodily harm."

"What's that got to do with me?" the commissioner asked, and this time Donovan was sure the man had something to hide. He was protesting just that little bit too strenuously. Donovan studied his careworn, liver-spotted face.

"Because you signed the release papers, sir," he said in reply.

"What? I . . . well, no, I don't know him," he stuttered in response. "I sign hundreds of those ruddy things. The desk sergeant brings them up, puts them in front of me. I sign them on recommendation, he returns and takes them away again, end of story. I don't doubt the man's release papers have my signature on them. Half the time I don't even look at their names anymore. You know what it's like, Donovan. You have to file reports. Don't tell me you always go over the fine details."

Donovan nodded slowly in response. Now it seemed as if Montague was appealing to him to turn a blind eye, to brush it under the carpet. But he recognized the commissioner's explanation for the bullshit it was—the last time Montague had openly signed any release papers was at least two years earlier, and then only under considerable pressure from the diplomats involved in a particularly sensitive peace treaty with the Japanese. There was much more to it than that.

Donovan considered pressing on with the questions. Why had the commissioner's photograph been on the wall of the spy's apartment alongside that of Senator Banks and a gaggle of other powerful men from the city? What exactly was the spy threatening to do?

For now, though, Donovan considered it best to let the situation slide, to let the commissioner think that he'd successfully managed to brush the situation under the carpet. It wouldn't do to have the man breathing down his neck any more than he already was, and perhaps this way, Donovan would have the chance to get to the bottom of the situation. On top of that, he didn't suppose the particular line of questioning he had in mind would get him anywhere. The commissioner would simply clam up, and that would be the end of the interview. Donovan would leave with his card marked, his position compromised. Perhaps even worse. He didn't yet know how far the commissioner was involved. Had he had anything to do with the fire at the apartment? Was the commissioner trying to prevent Donovan from discovering the truth about what he was up to with the senator? Ask too many of the wrong questions and Dononvan might find himself on the receiving end of an arson attack.

Whatever the case, however outlandish that might be, he was feeling particularly uneasy. If he'd been suspicious earlier, now he was sure. Commissioner Montague was hiding *something*.

The commissioner, seemingly relaxed once again, had leaned back in his chair and was puffing thoughtfully on the end of his cigar. "It sounds to me, Donovan, like this mob fellow had a bone to pick with our British spy. Perhaps he was working on behalf of the mob; perhaps it was a more personal affair. Whatever the case, he confronted this Jerry Robertson and went and got himself killed. I wouldn't waste any more time on him. A man like that, well, we're better off with him six feet under, don't you think?" Donovan didn't like where this was going, the dismissive nature of the commissioner's tone. It was as if he was being warned off. "No," the commissioner continued, "get on with the case in hand. Damn shame that apartment block went up in flames. A *damn* shame. But that tells us the spy can't have been very far away. He's still here in the city. He must have been watching the place and saw you arrive, for him to know that you were on to him. And that means one of two things is about to happen. Either he's about to go deeper undercover to try to throw you off the scent, to lose himself in the slums, or he's going to get desperate and show his hand. If I were a betting man"— he extracted his cigar and allowed the smoke to plume lazily from his nostrils, a wide grin cracking his face—"then I'd wager the latter was true. Otherwise, why would he have torched the place, unless he was nearing his endgame?" He pointed at Donovan with the burning tip of his cigar. When Donovan didn't speak, he shrugged and continued. "Whatever the case, you need to be ready. Don't want you ending up like that Luca-whatshisface, Donovan."

Donovan couldn't argue with the commissioner's logic. He'd been thinking pretty much the same thing himself—that the spy was either going to make a play for it, or was already halfway across the Atlantic—although he wasn't as ready to accept the notion that the spy was responsible for the arson attack as the commissioner appeared to be. There were other people who might benefit from the loss of the material at that apartment, possibly the very same people who had hired Paulo Lucarotti to go after the spy. Possibly, even Senator Banks and the commissioner himself. Either they were targets, or they were responsible for whatever it was the spy was attempting to investigate. Whatever it was, Donovan was sure it wasn't worth the lives of twelve innocent people.

Without the evidence of those photographs, however, there was no way of implicating anyone else in the whole sordid business. Donovan supposed that was exactly the point.

He nodded, keen to get away from the commissioner's office, to give himself space to think. "Very good, sir. I'll get on it right away."

"See that you do, Donovan," came the considered reply, "see that you do. Senator Banks is breathing down my neck. This goes all the way to the top, Felix. There's a great deal at stake. I hope you're not going to let me down."

"Oh, I won't allow that to happen, Commissioner," Donovan replied drily. "I'll do what's right for the city, and for my country."

Commissioner Montague stood and clapped a hand on Donovan's shoulder. "Delighted to hear that, Felix. Truly I am. Now"—he gestured to the door—"go and bring me the head of that British spy."

Donovan nodded and made for the door. Once outside, he gave a long, deep sigh, but it did little to relieve the tension he could feel bunching in his neck and shoulders. This really did go all the way to the top, and Donovan wanted no part of it. He would not be a cog in their machine. He would not idly sit by while twelve or more innocent people were allowed to perish uncommented, simply to save the reputation of a handful of rich old men. No, he would do exactly what was needed, whatever the cost. That was what Flora had meant when she had married him, when she had whispered to him all those years ago about making a difference. He would fight this corruption for all he was worth.

He took the stairs two at a time. He needed to make a call.

Donovan didn't stop to collect his coat, nor did he acknowledge Mullins, whom he saw frantically trying to get his attention across the precinct floor, as he marched straight toward the exit. Outside it was brisk and cold, but Donovan walked with intent, weaving his way through the press of pedestrians bustling on the sidewalk.

Two blocks later he made a sharp left and ducked inside a small store. The legend above the door read KOWALSKI'S GENERAL GOODS. Outside, racks of fruit and vegetables were lined up, trying to tempt any passersby. Cured meats hung in the windows.

Inside, Donovan stamped his feet to shake himself free of the cold. The shopkeeper—a small, broad, balding man in his late fifties—

looked up from behind the counter and caught Donovan's attention. "Morning, Inspector."

"Morning, Chuck. I need to make a call."

The shopkeeper jabbed his thumb over his shoulder. "You know where it is, Felix. Go help yourself."

Donovan smiled and patted the older man on the shoulder as he made his way out the back. There, among the heaped boxes of stock and stacks of brown paper wrap was a holotube terminal. It was an illegal device, connected to the network but tampered with so as to be virtually untraceable. Donovan had used it many times before for just this reason—to call someone who didn't want to be traced.

Donovan made directly for the device, flicked the switch to the "call" position and dialed a number from memory. A moment later a familiar face began to resolve in the mirrored cavity.

"Gabriel," said Donovan, not even waiting until the image had fully resolved, "we need to meet."

CHAPTER THIRTEEN

To him, the rooftops of Manhattan were like a second home. He thought this as he drifted lazily above them, the rocket canisters at his ankles blazing with furious orange light. His breath formed ghostly shapes in the frigid air as he twisted and turned, taking it all in, and he found himself absorbed by the wintry canopy, high above the avenues and streets below.

Frost lined the rooftops. Icicles dripped from lintels and overhangs, and the noses and wingtips of bizarre, gargoylish forms. Electric light glowed bright and harsh and yellow in the windows of apartment blocks, or through pyramidal roof lights that crested those same buildings. Steam gushed from standing pipes and vents like the exhalations of giant predators, looming in the darkness. The tall buildings of Manhattan reached up for the stars like the icy fingertips of the world.

Up here, above the city proper, everything was cold and quiet. Below, the city throbbed with life, pedestrians and vehicles ebbing through the streets as if they were its very lifeblood, and the Ghost, on his way to meet Donovan, its lone protector.

High above the city, the moon was low and gibbous, and framed against a canopy of frozen gray fog. It had descended again during the afternoon to choke the city, and ice particles glistened in the air, reflecting the shimmering light of his rockets. Even the dirigibles overhead—the police craft—seemed like nothing but indistinct blurs, buzzing around like insects, their searchlights flickering like long, incandescent legs.

There was something else up there, too, something that the Ghost had not expected to find here, in New York. Something that he'd thought he'd left in France long ago, which had returned to him recently in his dreams: a pair of eyes, stark and bright against the freezing night. They peered at him across the rooftops of the city, asexual, ominous.

The Ghost pirouetted in the sky, crossing his arms over his chest and spinning past a water tower, rocketing low and fast across the rooftop of an office block. He dipped low, ducking into the top of an alleyway between the office block and the building opposite, coming out again on the other side, twisting through the air. Still they were there, the eyes, unwavering, unblinking, unmoving.

Why now? Why had they returned now? First in his dreams, and now here, high above the city. What did it all mean? Was it a symptom of his recent encounter with one of the creatures? Was it the past finally catching up with him, his moment of judgment, his time to atone for the terrible crimes of his past? Or perhaps it was the stress of what had happened to Celeste, the onset of a nervous breakdown, a mental fever? Was it all in his head, just as it could have been all those years ago, just as the army doctors had told him before they'd invalided him out of the force? He didn't think so. Nevertheless, he felt something stirring deep within him.

These last few days, it had been as if Gabriel Cross and the Ghost had somehow been merging, as if his fractured personalities had been collapsing in on each other once more, the lines between them blurring. It was as if, ever since Ginny had walked back into his life, ever since he'd taken her into his confidence, shown her this other component of his life, the barriers between those twin existences had been breaking down. Ever since he'd returned from the war, the Gabriel Cross he had been, the Gabriel Cross everyone had known—the aristocratic playboy, the dilettante who threw the most amazing, drunken parties at his Long Island home—had been a lie. That kernel of himself, buried so long ago as a defense mechanism, a means of protecting himself from the horrors of the war, was it now once more coming to the fore? Had Ginny inadvertently woken something within him? Something that had lain dormant for so very long.

The thought unnerved him, more than he wished to admit. He felt suddenly vulnerable, as if everything he had come to stand for was at risk, as if now, here, at this very moment, with those piercing, heavy-lidded eyes watching him, he was nothing but a tiny man in a black suit, riding on the zephyrs like a fragile bird. The Ghost was a vigilante, a killer, a liar, a cheat. He was insignificant against the immensity of the city and everything it stood for, against those striking blue eyes. They diminished him. They saw to the core of his being, saw that he was no one but Gabriel Cross, that his personas were simply that—disguises he could shed, masks he could hide behind. But the eyes knew the truth. The eyes were Gabriel's eyes, staring back at him in the mirror. They *were* the truth. Everything else—*everything*—was just fiction.

The Ghost howled in frustration and rage, circling in the air and sending himself spinning down toward the asphalt below. Would it be easier to simply end it now than to keep on going, to drive himself into the sidewalk, there to be found in the morning by an unsuspecting man walking his dog, or a mailman, or a bank clerk? All he could see was the street below; all he could feel was the rush of cold air in his face as he hurtled toward the ground. . . .

And then he was twisting, turning himself around, swinging his legs out beneath him and rocketing up into the air again. He startled a flock of crows, sending them cawing away into the frigid night.

No, that was not the way. He had a duty to the city. To himself. The eyes reminded him of that, just as they had in the burning skies above France. Whatever the truth, whoever Gabriel Cross really was, he was not this. He was not this weak.

The Ghost sucked in his breath. He had a job to do. That was how he would prove his worth, to himself, and to anyone who was watching. He tucked his chin into his chest against the cold, and pressed on, toward Donovan and the precinct.

—•—

The police precinct building was dramatically picked out against the night sky by the crisscrossing searchlights of the hovering dirigibles tethered to its roof. Even here, even stationary, they continued to probe the streets around the police headquarters with their long fingers of light, both, the Ghost knew, for security, and as a warning. He was aware that many people saw the precinct building as a kind of bastion, a fortress against the criminal elements of the city, a sanctuary for those on the right side of the law; but he, in truth, knew it for what it was: a place of administration and a haven for the criminals who knew how to work within the law. Inside its impressive, towering walls, it was simply an office filled with yes men and uniformed criminals taking their wage from both the state and the mob.

The police were in the pocket of the government, and the government was in the pocket of the mob. The Ghost knew of only a handful of men who did not pander to this regime: Donovan, for one, and his sergeant, Mullins, for another. Because of it, they shone out like beacons, as bright as any searchlight, against the overwhelming tide of despondency and corruption.

The Ghost sailed up toward the top of the building, his rocket boosters flaring as he darted around the shimmering beams of the searchlights. It wouldn't do to let anyone know he was here—anyone, of course, except the man he had come to meet.

Dipping over the lip of the building, the Ghost reached inside his trench coat, righted himself, and pulled the cord that cut the fuel line to the rocket canisters strapped to his ankles. The flames guttered, spat and blinked out, and the Ghost dropped easily to his feet. Around his boots, the hoary rime of frost that caked the top of the building began to melt with the residual heat.

He glanced from side to side and caught sight of the glowing tip of a cigarette flaring in the darkness by the fire escape. He smiled. "Come on out, Felix," he called, careful to keep his voice low.

He watched as Donovan emerged into the dim half-light of the city night, silhouetted against the horizon. Manhattan was never truly dark. There were too many people, too much light. Even in the freezing fog, the city under-lit the sky like a vast, gray canopy, a canvas awaiting the strokes of an artist's brush.

Donovan was shivering, even wrapped in a thick overcoat, a scarf around his throat. He exhaled nicotine fumes through his nostrils and stamped his feet. "I'm sure we can think of somewhere warmer to meet, Gabriel."

The Ghost laughed. "You're right. Next time I'll use the front door."

Donovan shook his head, but he was smiling. "Don't be so bloody sarcastic." He looked back at the fire escape, the door of which was propped open. "And somewhere with fewer stairs to climb, too, while we're at it."

The two men lapsed into silence for a moment, each regarding the other in the gloom. "So, what news?" said the Ghost, causing Donovan to frown deeply.

"I don't know, Gabriel. I get the sense there's something bigger going on here, and we're only party to a small part of it."

This was new. Perhaps Donovan did have something useful, then. "Go on," the Ghost prompted.

"That apartment block in Greenwich Village, the one where we found the body," said Donovan.

"Yes?"

"It was torched. After we left last night. The whole block reduced to nothing but cinders and ash. Whoever's responsible was taking no chances—the neighboring apartments all burned, too. Twelve people died in the fire."

"My God . . ." The Ghost didn't know what else to say. He clenched his fists beside him. Twelve innocent lives. Whoever started that fire was going to pay for every single one of them.

"Everything on that wall, all those photographs, papers, maps— everything. All gone. Someone clearly thought we were getting too close to the truth, or else they wanted to cover their tracks."

The Ghost shrugged. "Then we've reached yet another dead end. We've lost our best and only lead."

"Not necessarily," Donovan replied darkly. "Mullins managed to retrieve the corpse before the flames took hold." Donovan took a long draw on his cigarette and exhaled before continuing. "And what's more, Mullins has been able to provide us with a positive ID."

"I told you Mullins showed promise," the Ghost said, smiling.

Donovan grinned. "It makes interesting reading though, Gabriel. The dead man wasn't an agent of the American government as we suspected. That much is very clear."

The Ghost frowned. "So, who was he?"

"Hired muscle by the name of Paulo Lucarotti," said Donovan. "He had ties to the mob, and what's more, he'd been in custody until recently, serving time in a state penitentiary for roughing people up. He has a rap sheet as long as my arm: trafficking illegal liquor, grievous bodily harm, burglary. A very unsavory character."

"So how did he end up dead in the apartment of a British spy?" said the Ghost.

"That's where it gets really interesting," said Donovan, taking a final draw on his cigarette before flicking the butt away across the rooftop, scattering a spray of hot, glowing ash across the frosted paving slabs. "The release order was signed by Commissioner Montague himself."

The Ghost frowned. "The commissioner signing release papers?"

"Precisely," said Donovan. "Of course, I went to quiz him about it."

"Allow me to guess," the Ghost sighed. "He clammed up."

Donovan nodded. "In a manner of speaking. He told me to drop it, that it was insignificant and that I should stick to the case in hand. That I needed to redouble my efforts to find the spy."

"Did you mention the photographs we saw on the wall of the apartment? Montague, Banks and the others?" All sorts of things were running through the Ghost's mind as he asked the question. The potential implications of what Donovan was saying were huge.

Donovan shook his head. He rubbed his hands together to stave off the cold. "No. I thought it prudent not to press him any further, especially when he started spouting all-too-convenient theories about how the spy had obviously started the fire himself, and that we didn't really need to delve any deeper into what had occurred. Regardless of the fact there are twelve fresh corpses in the morgue."

"So you're saying that you think Commissioner Montague is mixed up in something he shouldn't be?" asked the Ghost. He could feel a burning rage beginning to well up inside him at the thought that the commissioner could so easily dismiss so many lives.

Donovan shrugged. "No . . . well . . . perhaps," he said, with a gesture that clearly showed he was struggling to come to terms with what his instincts were telling him. "It's hard to refute the evidence. He's clearly got something to hide. But if the commissioner is mixed up in this—well, where does it stop? What the hell can we do about it?"

A moment of silence passed between them. Donovan was right. It felt as if the two of them were standing on a precipice, about to lift the lid of a veritable Pandora's box of intrigue and deception. The fallout from any such action would be tremendous, but that wasn't reason enough not to do it. They couldn't put their own safety above that of the city and its people.

If the commissioner was involved in a cover-up, if he'd been leaned on to provide hired muscle to search out this spy—or worse, he was implicated in some political or possibly even criminal scheme that had led him to arrange the torching of the spy's apartment building in order to maintain his secrecy, well, he was as bad as any mob boss or murderer the Ghost had yet encountered. Perhaps worse, given that he hid behind a veneer of respectability, supposedly responsible for the safety of all the citizens that inhabited the city below.

"The frustrating thing," said Donovan morosely, "is that we're out of leads. We've got nothing, other than a half-baked notion that Commissioner Montague and Senator Banks are involved in something untoward. The only person who could possibly begin to help us understand what's going on is the British spy, and his motives are questionable at best. Plus he covers his tracks well. We don't even know where to start looking for him." Donovan sighed. "Then there's this business with the raptors. It's a bloody mess, Gabriel."

The Ghost put his hand on Donovan's shoulder, trying to offer him some reassurance that they were doing the right thing. They needed to stay focused. "Do you think there's some connection? Between the raptors and what's going on with Banks, Montague and this spy? The photographs we saw at the apartment, they surely can't have been coincidental."

Donovan shrugged. He was still shivering with the cold. "Possibly. Possibly not. Although it seems odd that our British spy would show an interest in something so localized if it were entirely unrelated."

"My thoughts exactly," said the Ghost.

Donovan looked up at him, searching his face with tired eyes. "How the hell are we going to get to the bottom of this, Gabriel? Are you going to try to catch another of those things?"

The Ghost shook his head. "No, I've got a better plan. I need to find out where they're taking them, all those people they're abducting. What they're using them for."

"But you've tried following them before. You said they were too quick."

The Ghost smiled. "Yes. But this time I'm going to let *them* do all the work."

"What do you mean?" Donovan gave him a confused look.

The Ghost's grin grew suddenly wider. "Tomorrow night, Felix, Gabriel Cross is going to get himself abducted."

CHAPTER FOURTEEN

"You're what?"

Donovan had hardly been able to believe what he was hearing. He knew that Gabriel could be reckless, but this new plan, to go and get himself abducted by one of the raptors, elevated things to an entirely new extreme. "Have you got a death wish?" he'd asked drily, only half joking.

The Ghost had met his eye, a grave expression on his face, his trench coat billowing up around him in a sudden, wintry gust. "Can you think of a better way to get to the bottom of this, Felix?" he'd replied, and Donovan had faltered, unable to find a response. Truthfully, he really couldn't think of a better way of locating the raptors' lair.

They still didn't, after all, have any idea of what the raptors were really up to, where they were taking the people they abducted, or what they were doing with them. There was a chance the whole business was mixed up with the British spy and whatever the commissioner was involved in. Nevertheless, it still didn't sit well with Donovan. The risks were manifold and immense.

"Look, I'll need someone to follow me. I can slow it down, give you time to follow behind in your car. I'll be delivered right into its nest, and you and Ginny—"

"Hold on! Are you insane, Gabriel?" It was this that had really set

Donovan's alarm bells ringing. "I can't bring that girl with me on an errand like that. If you want to put yourself at risk, well, that's up to you. I'll even allow you to take risks with *my* life, if they're strictly necessary. But Ginny? We've made those mistakes before, Gabriel. Can't you remember?" Almost immediately after saying this he felt guilty for what he considered to be a cheap shot. But the point still stood.

The Ghost had looked away, glancing off over the rooftops for a moment and refusing to meet Donovan's eye. When he'd spoken again, his voice had taken on a stern, measured edge. "Of course I remember. But don't think for a minute that this is in any way the same situation. You've seen Ginny handle herself, Felix. She's no shrinking violet. And besides, you'll need someone to spot for you while you drive. She can call out directions."

Donovan had sighed. "Fine," he'd said, but his tone had made it clear it was anything but . . . and yet here he was, sitting behind the wheel of his car, the girl Ginny beside him, both of them watching the figure on the ledge high above. Now, Donovan wished he had argued harder. He was worried he'd allowed it to happen because he wanted company out here, tonight. Stakeouts like this always passed much more quickly with someone else around, and the Ghost had been right—when the time came he would need someone to spot for him while he tried to maneuver through the streets in pursuit of the raptor, trying desperately not to mow anyone down.

And who else was there? It wasn't as if he could bring Mullins. He, like the rest of the men at the precinct, saw the Ghost as some sort of radical, a criminal gone crazy, out to get even with the mob. Yes, they were happy to turn a blind eye when the Ghost was making their lives easier, breaking protection rackets and weeding out contract killers. Either that or they were too afraid to take him on themselves, either because they believed the superstitions and thought him to be some kind of superpowered monster, or else they were up to their eyeballs in the stink of their own corruption and were terrified he'd find them out.

It was a shame Mullins had fallen in with those idiots. He had the potential to be a great cop. But he was young and impressionable and hadn't yet learned the lessons that Donovan had—to always think for himself. That was the key to successful police work, Donovan had found—ignoring the received wisdom of others and taking a fresh look at anything and everything. That, in his opinion, was where so many others failed.

Mullins was learning, though. He had great intuition, but he hadn't yet learned to question policy and rhetoric. Until he had, he'd never be able to recognize someone like the Ghost for what he really was: the best hope the city had of ridding itself of the criminal blight under which it was now in sway.

The Ghost was unconventional, yes; free and easy with the law, certainly. Yet Donovan knew that Gabriel's heart was in the right place. The Ghost wanted only to do what was right for the people of the city, and frustrated by the bureaucracy and corruption that plagued the police force, he had taken it upon himself to act. Donovan could respect that. In some ways, he wished he could do the same.

It wasn't that he didn't have his doubts about the Ghost on occasion, of course. He sometimes wondered if Gabriel's desire for vengeance stemmed not only from frustration, but also from something darker inside of the man, a need to lash out at the world. What was it that Gabriel was fighting? Yes, of course, he could give it a name in the shape of the crime bosses and corrupt politicians, the serial killers and pimps. Donovan couldn't help thinking, though, that it was somehow more abstract than that, something more innate. He supposed he'd never know, wasn't sure that he wanted to. Gabriel had become a good friend to him, and the Ghost was a useful tool for them both. As long as he stayed on the right side, not of the law, but of Donovan's moral code, then he would continue to cover for him and keep his neck off the chopping block at the precinct.

Mullins, the commissioner, the other men at the precinct—none of those others would ever understand that. All they could see was a violent criminal operating outside of the law. If Donovan's association with the vigilante were ever to come to light, all they would see there, too, was his complicity.

Well, increasingly, Donovan was beginning to think it was Commissioner Montague who was complicit. Throughout the day he'd observed the comings and goings of the man and his visitors. He'd been surprised to see Senator Isambard Banks return for an interview that lasted over an hour, although this time Donovan had not been summoned to pay lip service to the man. Nevertheless, it did much to confirm Donovan's suspicions that the commissioner was mixed up in something he shouldn't have been.

There'd been more abductions, too, during the night. And even now Mullins was on the trail of those missing people, interviewing the family and friends, tracing their last known movements. Donovan knew it would be no use, though. If the raptors had taken them—which undoubtedly they had—the poor bastards would most likely already be dead. He'd know soon enough, anyway, if Gabriel's plan worked.

He'd had to call Mullins off the whole Lucarotti matter that morning. The commissioner had shut it down following their conversation the previous day. Mullins had informed Donovan upon his arrival at the precinct that morning that the decree had come during the night: all investigations into the background of Paulo Lucarotti were to be considered a waste of police resources and were to be immediately dropped. They should be focusing on finding the missing British spy, or quelling the fears of the population regarding the persistent rash of abductions, the commissioner had said.

This, to Donovan's eyes, was as good as an admission of guilt. There was now no doubt in his mind that the commissioner was involved in the whole affair. First, Montague's signature had inexplicitly featured on the man's release papers, and now this.

The whole thing made him utterly furious. The commissioner had traded in the press on his stance regarding bribery and corruption. He pledged honesty and openness. His entire tenure as commissioner had been built on those tenets. He'd spent years weeding out the corrupt elements in the force, stifling the reach of the mob. He claimed his dream was an untouchable police force, free from bribery and the fingers of organized crime. Yet it seemed now he was as guilty as any of the men he'd put away for such crimes. Worse, though, it made him a liar and a cheat, a hypocrite. And Donovan despised hypocrisy.

If the commissioner proved to be involved in the deaths of those twelve people and worse, if he had sold his sold to Isambard Banks, involving himself in a plot that sanctioned the creation of the raptors and the recent spate of abductions, Donovan would expose him. He would bring it to an end. The commissioner would rot in an uncomfortable cell, much smaller and less opulent than his office. He might even find himself in a box, six feet under the ground.

For now, though, Donovan had a very different job to do. Gabriel was up there on a ledge waiting for the raptors. Donovan had to keep him alive. He had to be ready for when the raptors swooped.

Tonight they would flush the diabolical things out of their nest. They would discover the truth about what had been going on, the reason for the abductions. And, with any luck, they would still be alive in the morning.

—•—

Gabriel stood on the ledge atop the building and looked out over the city below. The freezing fog of the previous night had cleared somewhat, and here and there between the thick, yellow clouds were windows to the starry night beyond.

It was cold, chilling him to the core, and his legs felt leaden with exertion. He'd had to climb his way here via the conventional route: taking the stairs. The elevators had been out of order. Perhaps now, he smiled to himself, he had a little bit more sympathy for Donovan.

He'd decided not to equip himself with the Ghost's many accoutrements this evening. It wasn't so much that he felt he didn't need them—he would probably need them more than ever—but more that he couldn't risk being recognized by the raptors. He had no notion of whether the things had any real sense of intelligence, or whether they even *could* recognize him from their previous encounters, but if they did, the whole enterprise would fall to pieces.

So, instead, he'd come dressed as a civilian, as Gabriel Cross, and he hoped that this would be enough to lure them in. He would make himself seem like easy pickings, offering himself up to the brass flock.

Gabriel had upon him a number of concealed weapons, of course, including the long barrel of his fléchette gun, hidden in the arm of his pinstripe suit. He hefted it now, feeling comforted by its weight, by the feel of the rubber trigger bulb in his palm.

The wind whipped Gabriel's hair about his face. He felt naked, disadvantaged, without his night vision goggles or his black trench coat and rocket boosters. It was as if, up here, awaiting these demonic, shining golems, he had come without his protective mask, and the feeling unnerved him. Perhaps Ginny had been right. The Ghost was no more than a simple disguise to hide behind.

Tonight he was not *Gabriel Cross*, the playboy millionaire, the ex-soldier. Nor was he simply the Ghost in plain clothes. Tonight, this was the real Gabriel, standing there, vulnerable on the rooftop. The thought terrified him. For the first time in years he was revealing himself to the world. The lines were blurring. One man was becoming the other.

Gabriel closed his eyes and held his arms out at his sides, feeling the crosswinds here at the top of Fifth Avenue buffet him gently, rocking him back and forth on the ledge. The previous night, Donovan had asked him if he had a death wish, and he'd been unable to answer the question directly. He'd pondered on it afterward. He certainly wasn't scared of death, but nor did he welcome it. What terrified him most of all was how quickly it could come. It wasn't so much the abstract concept—the notion that one day he would simply cease to exist—but more how swiftly a life could be extinguished, how quickly all of those hard-won experiences, all of those innermost thoughts and emotions could blink off like a light. He'd seen it a hundred times, a *thousand* times, during the war, and he'd seen it since. He'd been responsible for dealing killing blows himself, and it was the look in the eyes of those dying men that haunted him—the sudden shock, the surprise of it all, the knowledge that everything you are or could ever be was about to cease to exist.

It was a lonely thought, but then Gabriel's was a cruel, lonely world. Perhaps he deserved to die? Perhaps the universe was seeking to redress the balance, to take an eye for an eye? Perhaps that was it. That would suggest there was some greater design in the emptiness of the universe, however, and Gabriel didn't believe in that, either.

No, he didn't want to die. He wasn't looking for release, wasn't driven by a desire to find solace in a box, six feet beneath the earth. He wanted only to protect the city he cared for and the people who lived within its walls. He wanted to protect his way of life, to uphold the freedom of the citizens below, to weed out those elements that would see that dream crushed for their own gain.

Gabriel sighed. He could barely feel his extremities with the cold. He'd been there for over an hour, nearer to two. Another hour longer and he'd have to give up, assume the raptors weren't coming, or that they were hunting further afield that night. He'd picked this place— on the roof of his own apartment building—because the police reports suggested a number of abductions had taken place the area in recent days.

A case of hypothermia wouldn't get him anywhere, though. He'd hold out for a little while longer, and then he'd have to call it a night.

Gabriel reached inside his overcoat and withdrew a packet of cigarettes, hoping that he might be able to eke some warmth from smoking one of them. His hand was shaking as he withdrew it from the packet, put it to his lips and pulled the self-lighting tab. He sucked hungrily at the nicotine, dragging it down into his lungs.

He glanced down at the sounds of a passing police siren and caught sight of the sleek, black vehicle careening along the avenue, flashing past his building, bell ringing loudly to warn any pedestrians to get out of the way. Across the street, Donovan's car—an almost identical model, all black curves and sweeping lines—was parked alongside the curb. Donovan would be behind the wheel, ready, he knew. He could tell the car engine was already running by the black, oily fumes that were issuing from the exhaust funnel at the rear of the vehicle, coiling into the night sky like genies escaping from a lamp.

Ginny was leaning out of the passenger window, staring up at him, seemingly oblivious to the cold. She was wearing a pink cloche hat studded with glass beads, and they reflected the moonlight back at him, glinting as she moved her head. He couldn't make out her expression from so high up. He didn't want to. He'd had a blazing row with her that afternoon, too, when he'd outlined his intentions. Of course, unlike Donovan she'd insisted on accompanying him, but not, as he had intended, as a navigator for Donovan. No, Ginny, perhaps fearful that she risked missing out on all the fun, had declared her intent to accompany him on the rooftop, to get herself abducted by the raptors too. She'd strenuously put across her case that he was not to be left to the mercy of the raptors alone, and that she should come with him back to their nest for added protection.

Gabriel had laughed, and kissed her then, full and firmly on the lips. But she had slapped him away, berating him for his dismissal and for trying to dissuade her with sentiment. She was wrong, though. That hadn't been it at all. More than anything, it had been her drive, her ambition, her unfaltering sense of loyalty, her need for adventure that had caused him to sweep her up in his arms. For all that she was a drunk, for all that she had fallen out of love with life, she lived it with exuberance, inhabiting every single second of it, embracing every experience. More than anything, then, Gabriel had wanted to take her by the hand and promise her she could come with him. But, of course, he had not, because he knew that exuberance would get her killed, and that, he would not be responsible for. Not again.

So instead, now, she was hanging out of Donovan's car window, searching the skies for the oncoming raptors, keeping a dutiful eye on him.

He'd smoked the cigarette down to the butt already, and he flicked it away, watching it tumble over the side of the building until it disappeared from view. It was then that he noticed something glinting in the distance. It was too far off to make out what it was, and at first he dismissed it as a biplane, circling the city, having launched from one of the far-off rooftops on a spike of rocket flame. As he watched, however, he saw that there was no exhaust or spike of flame. He studied it intently. No, this was something else. There were more of them, occupying the same region of the sky, shining brightly in the moonlight. A flock of them. This was it. Five raptors, and they were coming his way.

Gabriel took a deep breath and tried to shake some blood into his fingertips. He could feel his chest tightening in anticipation, feel the muscles around his neck and shoulders bunching as he prepared himself for what was to come. He raised his arms, holding them out by his side, allowing the wind to buffet him once more. All the while, he kept his eyes fixed on the oncoming storm of brass.

Would they even see him? Would they care? He hoped he would look to them like easy pickings. Bait.

A quick glance down at the car told him Ginny had seen the raptors too. She was speaking frantically to Donovan, who was out of sight in the shadows, and pointing frantically up at the sky.

A moment later, Gabriel became aware of the thrum of the raptor's propellers and the incessant chitter-chatter they made as they swarmed out of the darkness toward him, their eyes glowing red, their talons extended.

They were flying in an arrowhead formation, swooping low over the rooftops, searching for prey. For a moment he thought they were simply going to ignore him, to flash swiftly overhead and dart away toward the relative seclusion of Central Park, but then he saw one of them—the one on the left at the rear of the formation—cock its head toward him. Its burning eyes fixed him with a menacing glare, and he knew then that there was no backing out. It was coming for him.

Gabriel braced himself as the raptor broke formation, baying loudly. Its long wings extended, stretching their thin skein of flesh, and the rotors of its engines roared as they churned the air.

Gabriel closed his eyes and sucked at the cold air. One way or another, he was about to discover what was really going on.

—•—

Rutherford knew all too well where Senator Isambard Banks had taken up residence since moving to Manhattan from Brooklyn twelve months earlier: the Plaza Hotel on 59th Street, perhaps the most resplendent, and decadent, of all New York hotels.

Rutherford had even visited the senator's apartment on occasion in his guise as Jerry Robertson, being wined and dined and taken into the senator's rather overbearing confidence. He'd been forced to sit for hours listening to the man pontificate on his radical policies, his opinions of the British, his dream that one day the American people could have an empire just as extensive and powerful as that of Queen Alberta. He couldn't see how ridiculous it made him sound, how much of an egomaniac he had become. America already had an empire as extensive as the British: the United States. Rutherford loved the country almost as much as his own, and it saddened him to hear such radical views expressed by someone who had the potential to wield such power.

Rutherford, of course, had long ago learned how to play the political game, and had fed the man's ego, expressing confluent views, testing the water with his own falsified opinions, egging the man on until, months later, he'd been invited back to the apartment on an almost weekly basis to discuss the senator's plans for igniting the war.

Now, Rutherford could see the silhouette of the senator moving about in the apartment through the gossamer curtains that flapped at the open window. It was icy cold outside, but the senator was not a slim man, and given the amount of pacing back and forth he was doing, Rutherford imagined he'd opened the window in order to cool down.

The apartment itself was a sumptuous affair, almost as grotesque to Rutherford's tastes as the senator himself. He supposed it was a reflection of the senator's personality that he needed to be surrounded by gilded things, most of which, Rutherford had realized upon closer inspection, were in fact cheap decorative copies, glamorized and disguised as priceless objets d'art. That, in itself, told Rutherford much about the senator's personality and his outlook on life: he was more concerned with outward appearances than he was with substance and depth. His policies, Rutherford knew, were only as well-thought-out and robust as his collection of art, there only to empower him and his cronies, to make him feel important, to offer him the illusion of grandeur. It was this that he craved above all else: fame, and a place in the history books. He saw the means to achieve this goal in his plans to lead the country to glory through a war with the British. It was his intention to be the man remembered for bringing a new golden age to the glorious empire of America.

Rutherford shivered. His fingers were growing numb now with the cold, clutching the steering wheel of the stolen car. He'd taken it earlier from a side street, cracking the lock and hotwiring the engine. He'd been reluctant to steal, of course, but he'd needed transport, especially if he was going to successfully tail the senator. His breath was fogging the windows, and he rubbed at the glass ineffectually with his sleeve and then leaned over and rolled down the passenger window, allowing the frigid air to swirl in. He'd been there for hours, and he was freezing cold, but it wasn't as if he had anywhere else to go.

Rutherford could barely believe that all those months of undercover work, of living as someone else in the company of all those rich and powerful statesmen, had come to this. It wasn't that he feared acting against those people, or even putting his own life at risk for the greater good of his country, but more that this was not at all how he had planned for the endgame to play out.

All those months spent winning Banks's confidence, getting the man to trust him, becoming his confidant and working his way into the inner circle, had allowed him to build a picture of what was going on, an understanding of what this cabal of men were planning.

They were secretly building a superweapon that they planned to unleash on London. He didn't know exactly what it was, or where it was being built—other than the fact the engineer responsible had designed it to be housed inside a huge transatlantic airship—but he knew from the conversations he'd overheard that it was incredibly dangerous, without parallel in modern warfare. They were worried about being able to control it once it was fully activated.

The only member of the cabal of politicians and businessmen behind the scheme who knew where to find the device was Senator Banks, their unelected leader. Banks was the driving force behind the entire project. He was the key to all of this. His radical politics, his sheer force of will, had won over those other men. Weak-willed and hungry for power, they had flocked like magpies to his cause and his extraordinary promises of the bright new future to come, the bright new future in which they would all play significant roles on the world stage.

It went right to the top, too. Governors, bankers—even the police commissioner was involved, all easing the way, all smoothing things so that Banks's policies and plans could be put into practice. For a while, Rutherford—posing as Jerry Robertson—had been a part of that, and he had seen firsthand how easy it must have been for those others to get swept up in Banks's world. The man was a trickster, a showman: charismatic, charming and strong-willed. He was a natural leader, and a very dangerous man indeed. And Rutherford knew that at some point in the coming hours, he was going to have to kill him.

The thought did not sit well with the British spy. He'd killed too many people already in his short life. He'd always acted in the line of duty, of course—during the war, and more recently as a means of self-preservation. Assassinations never sat easily with him, though. There was something too cold and calculated about them. Killing someone during a fight, or to protect himself—well, he'd had to learn to live with that, and at least the victim typically brought it upon themselves. This, however, would be nothing but cold, hard murder.

There was no question, of course. He'd have to do it. If he didn't, tens of thousands, perhaps more, of his countrymen would die. He wouldn't feel sorry for Banks—the man deserved to die—but more for himself, for the little bit of him that died alongside every person he'd had to murder in this way. It was as if Rutherford himself became a little less human with every violent act he was forced to commit.

First, though, he needed Banks to lead him to the weapon. Simply taking out Banks was not enough. He could do that here, now—and had been sorely tempted to do just that, to slow everything in its tracks and buy some time. But it was risky. It left the possibility that the others could continue Banks's work. He knew Banks was a meticulous man, never doing anything without careful planning. While he'd been careful to keep the exact details and location of the weapon to himself, Rutherford was sure that he would also have organized a failsafe.

Banks was obsessed with his pursuit of power and fame, and he wasn't about to let a little thing like death get in the way of his place in the history books. He would have doubtless found a way to ensure it. Someone else would be ready to step in and act in his name.

The silhouette by the window had gone and the lights in Banks's rooms had blinked off. Rutherford clutched at the steering wheel and forced himself to breathe. His heart was hammering in his chest. This was it; this was his chance. Wherever Banks went now, Rutherford had to follow. He had to stay on the man's tail until, eventually, Banks gave himself away. Only then could Rutherford make his move.

The car was shuddering gently around him, the engine idling, smoke coiling from the exhaust funnels. He hoped he'd parked far enough from the building so that when Banks emerged, Rutherford wouldn't draw his attention. He knew he was playing a dangerous game. Banks knew Rutherford for what he was, now—no longer the political activist from Boston, but the spy from across the Atlantic. If the senator caught even a glimpse of him, the game would be up.

Moments later, the revolving door of the hotel turned, and Banks appeared on the sidewalk. He was wrapped up against the chill in a gray woolen overcoat, a porkpie hat perched on his head. But Rutherford knew beyond a shadow of a doubt it was him.

Seconds later a sleek black car appeared at the intersection up ahead, pulled into the street and purred to a stop in front of the hotel. Another man, a driver, climbed out and circled around the back of the vehicle to hold the passenger door open for the senator, who slipped quietly inside. The driver then returned to his seat, and the car slid silently away.

Rutherford fixed its taillights in his sights, released the handbrake of his own, stolen vehicle, and moved away in pursuit.

CHAPTER FIFTEEN

Donovan watched in horror as the raptor at the rear of the formation broke away from the rest of its flock and swept down to snatch Gabriel off the rooftop. It shrieked loudly in what Donovan could only assume was glee.

Ginny had produced Gabriel's twin pistols from her belt and was now brandishing them out of the window, one in each fist. For a moment Donovan thought she was going to open fire, but she held her nerve, keeping the barrels of the weapons trained on the mechanical beast as it plucked Gabriel from his perch. The raptor spiraled higher again, fanning its wings as it climbed, while the rest of its flock chattered off into the frozen night, baying for further victims.

Donovan had to admire Gabriel for what he was doing, as crazy as it was. His plan had worked; the raptors had taken his bait, and now this was their best chance yet of finding their lair and getting to the bottom of what was going on. Assuming, of course, Gabriel didn't go and get himself killed in the process.

Now, in the grip of the mechanical monster, Gabriel looked to Donovan like a tiny rag doll clutched in the hand of a child, limp and lifeless. The raptor circled once, issued another of its strangled cries, and then darted off across the rooftops, heading in the opposite direction to its brethren.

Donovan realized that Ginny was shouting something, barking commands. He grabbed for the steering wheel and slammed his foot on the accelerator.

"South! It's heading south," she called, leaning out of the passenger window, her guns still trained on the sky.

Donovan swore loudly and grappled with the machine. He spun the wheel, slewing the vehicle around into the road and half mounting the sidewalk in the process. A quick glance up at the sky told him that the raptor was barely encumbered at all by its new payload, and for all Gabriel's plans to attempt to slow it, he still appeared to be hanging limp and unconscious from its claws.

"Move, Donovan!" Ginny bellowed, and Donovan jammed his foot to the floor in response. Tires screeched again the frost-covered asphalt, and the engine groaned in protest as he pushed it for all it was worth. The intersection ahead meant he had to make a left and then cross two blocks before he could turn about and get them onto an avenue heading in the right direction.

"Keep your eyes on it!" he shouted across to Ginny as he spun the wheel, twisting the car around in a tight circle, ignoring the oncoming traffic and careening out dangerously into the road. The vehicle tilted to the right, two of its wheels lifting momentarily from the tarmac, before Donovan managed to get it under control once more and they were away again.

"We're heading in the wrong direction!" Ginny exclaimed, and Donovan glanced over at her, fearful that she would tumble out of the window if she leaned out any farther.

"I know! I know! Stay with it!" he called back. The car shot across the two blocks, around the next corner and out onto the next avenue, this time heading downtown. Donovan could still see the mechanical beast, a tiny speck on the skyline, glinting in the moonlight. They were still on its tail. Now, he just had to keep it in his sights.

His mouth felt dry and he could hardly breathe. The consequences of getting this wrong, of losing sight of the raptor—well, he'd tried to warn Gabriel what might happen. But Donovan was in it, now, up to his eyeballs, and all he could think about was how much he was looking forward to a cigarette when all of this was over.

"It's getting away," Ginny called in exasperation. "We're too slow!"

There was little Donovan could do. He was pushing the vehicle as much as he dared, his foot pressed to the floor. The traffic here was heavy, and he found himself having to swerve and slow down in order to avoid a collision. It wouldn't do any of them any good—Gabriel included—if he managed to wrap his car around another vehicle in the process.

He considered firing up the siren but decided not to risk it, in case it alerted the raptor to their pursuit; he and Gabriel had discussed it earlier and dismissed the idea, hopeful that it wouldn't prove necessary. If the raptor was panicked it might drop Gabriel in order to get away more swiftly.

"Hold on!" Donovan shouted as he leaned heavily to the left, throwing the car out wide and weaving around a large, black lorry, the driver of which was forced to slam on his brakes to avoid colliding with a taxicab. The man blared his horn loudly in annoyance, but Donovan had already shot past, leaving the near miss and a wave of incensed drivers far behind.

Donovan continued to dip in and out of the traffic, ignoring the risks to not only himself and Ginny, but the other drivers. All that mattered at that moment was the fact that Gabriel was up there. That's all he could think about right now. Gabriel was in the clutches of one of those horrifying, mechanical beasts, and it was Donovan's job to ensure the thing didn't rip him to pieces.

He caught sight of it then, dipping low above the skeletal frame of girders and scaffolds that marked a new hotel that was being constructed here. For a moment he thought it was going to drop inside this half-finished shell, and he wondered if this was where the things had established their nest, but then it banked sharply to the left and continued on, making its way toward Lower Manhattan.

Up ahead he could see a stoplight had turned red. Private cars and taxi cars alike had pulled up in a long line. Ginny was bellowing at them from the window, demanding that they get out of the way, and Donovan realized that if he stopped here now, that would be it. They would lose sight of their quarry, and with it, they would lose Gabriel. He couldn't allow that to happen. There was only one option.

Donovan yanked the steering wheel hard to the left and the car banked. "What are you doi—," Ginny wailed, but her question became a warbling scream as the car bounced violently up onto the sidewalk at speed, its undercarriage scraping against the curb. Pedestrians scattered in every conceivable direction as Donovan fought to maintain control of the vehicle, swinging first left, then right as he tried to avoid a hotdog stand and then the awning of a women's clothes store. He could hear people cursing and shouting behind them as he left a wave of minor injuries and terrified civilians in their wake.

A little farther along the sidewalk a congregation was spilling out of a church, and Donovan barely had time to throw the car back onto the road before mowing them all down. Coal spilled from the hopper at the back of the vehicle as it rocked dramatically from side to side.

Keeping the raptor and its burden fixed squarely in his eye-line, Donovan managed to pull the car back on course.

They were nearing the docks. In the distance, Donovan could see the bright lights of the fairground, the Ferris wheel slowly revolving against the nighttime sky.

"Quickly, Donovan!" Ginny screeched, and Donovan looked up in horror to see the raptor swing around and dip beneath the roofline of the nearby buildings, disappearing from view. He pressed on, maintaining his course, hopeful it would reappear again a moment later.

"Where did it go?" he called to Ginny as he tugged the car around another bend, heading straight toward the spot where they had last seen the creature.

"I don't know!" she gasped in frustration, and Donovan felt a sinking feeling in the pit of his stomach. "Head toward the fairground. It seemed to be heading in that direction. Maybe we can pick up the trail there. Hurry!"

He did as she suggested, fighting down the sense of panic and the bucking steering wheel, but he already knew it was no good. They'd been too slow. They'd lost it. They were in the right neighborhood. That much was sure. They'd tracked it as far as the fairground, and there, somewhere, the raptors must have established their lair. But Donovan hadn't been quick enough to see where it was.

His hands were shaking as he pulled the car around the corner and brought it slowly to a stop on the fringes of the fairground. The crowds here were huge, a heady mix of people of all ages, from all walks of life. They wandered aimlessly between the brightly colored stalls and rides, with children carrying bags of cotton candy, soft toys dangling from their little fingers. Uniformed policemen guided the traffic and kept a watchful eye on the citizens, on the lookout for pickpockets and other petty criminals. But none of them were looking up at the sky. None of these people could have seen the raptor flitting by, the limp form of Gabriel Cross clutched in its talons, so intent were they on the boisterous activities surrounding them.

There was nowhere left to drive. The street ahead was closed, and beyond that, the dark waters of the Hudson River. He had no idea where to even start. They could be anywhere in the Battery: miles away, or within a few feet.

"Shit!" Donovan cursed, slamming the heels of his hands down hard against the steering wheel. "Shit!"

Ginny turned to him, her eyes wide with panic. "What are we going to do? Gabriel . . . ?" She was still clutching the two pistols in her fists.

Donovan didn't know what to tell her. "We get out and look. They have to be around here somewhere. We leave the car here and comb this place until we find them. You start with the fairground. I'll see if I can't get those uniformed men to help." He leaned over and put his hand gently on her shoulder. He hoped she couldn't see in his eyes that he was as panicked as she was. "We'll find him, Ginny. Mark my words. We won't let him down."

He reached over and popped the car door open. His heart was slamming against his rib cage in panic. He only hoped when they did find Gabriel, it wouldn't already be too late.

—•—

The pain in his shoulder was almost too much to bear.

The raptor had skewered him with its razor-sharp claws, burying the tips of its talons in his upper arm. Gabriel could feel warm blood flowing from the puncture wounds, trickling down his arm, soaking his shirt.

He swooned and everything went black, but the pain brought him round again a moment later and he fought to hold on to consciousness. He focused on the stinging rush of cold air as they swept across the rooftops, on the two immense eyes he could see, watching over him in the distance. He focused on the thought of Donovan and Ginny in a car somewhere far below, powering through the streets in pursuit. He focused on the thought of what he would do to the raptor when they finally arrived back at its nest.

Gabriel scanned the rooftops beneath him. He was used to identifying the city from above; he knew it best from up here. They were close to the docks. Down below, he could see the bright, gaudy lights of the fairground, close to the water. The Ferris wheel turned languorously, creating a stuttering vortex of flashing lights.

The raptor swept low, dipping beneath the roofline of the nearby buildings. For a moment, Gabriel thought it was heading toward the fairground itself, but then it veered sharply to the right, keeping to the shadows to avoid being spotted by the press of people below.

Gabriel fought a wave of disorientation, shaking his head, trying to maintain his bearings. His safety might depend on it later. He wouldn't allow himself to lapse into unconsciousness now. He couldn't.

Close by, the dark water of the river lapped at the shore of the island, and the lights of the crossing ferries twinkled in the middle distance. Wherever was the raptor taking him? He had a sudden, shocking thought that they might not actually be based on the island at all, but somewhere offshore. He felt a wave of panic rising in his chest. If the raptor took him off Manhattan Island he was as good as dead—there'd be no hope then of Donovan and Ginny ever being able to trace his whereabouts. He'd be on his own, with only a handful of the Ghost's weapons to protect him. He began to wonder if Donovan hadn't been right all along, if this wasn't just some foolish venture he'd talked himself into as a way of proving himself—or worse, that he'd been wrong, and he really did have a death wish. The pain in his shoulder prevented him from dwelling on the thought for too long, however. Now was not the time for philosophizing. Now was the time to make sure he survived.

Presently, it became clear that it was not the raptor's intention to leave the island, and Gabriel allowed himself a short sigh of relief. They were heading toward two enormous hangars that sat squat and fat among the other warehouses and storage facilities down by the docks. They were a recent development, erected with a skin of corrugated iron plates over a shell of girders. The raptor made for the one on the left, its engines stuttering to a stop, its wings unfurling to their fullest extent, so that the two of them could glide slowly toward an opening that became apparent in the roof.

Elegantly, the raptor twisted and angled its brass frame toward the hatchway, pulled Gabriel in close, and dropped fluidly into the dimly lit warehouse below.

Gabriel barely had a chance to get an impression of the large space before he was dropped heavily to the ground. He landed awkwardly, tumbling over and bashing his head on the concrete. He cried out in pain and tried to stifle it immediately. He had the sense of being surrounded by others, and he could smell the tang of spilled blood.

Gabriel rolled onto his back, peeling open his eyes. His shoulder felt like it was on fire, and now that the raptor had released its grip on him he could feel more blood streaming from the wounds. High above, among the rafters and exposed girders, four or five of the raptors chattered and hissed, leaping from one beam to another, screeching in their shrill, inhuman fashion, like carrion birds awaiting the opportunity to swoop in. Their red eyes watched him threateningly from above, as if warning him that if he took his eyes off them for even a moment they might set upon him, tearing him apart with their vicious claws.

Gabriel pushed himself up into a sitting position, taking in his new surroundings. The far end of the hangar had been fitted out like a workshop, a larger version of the workroom he kept at his apartment on Fifth Avenue. This one was filled with a similar array of assorted components and tools, valves and weapons. Only this workshop appeared to be as much that of a butcher as an engineer.

A flayed human corpse dangled by its wrists from a rope tied to a roof support, rocking gently back and forth like a grotesque pendulum. Human bones, too, lay scattered on the ground around the corpse's feet, the components of at least four or five other people. These would be used, Gabriel presumed, in the construction of the raptors and the unholy binding rituals that animated them. He screwed up his face in disgust.

He became aware of the sound of someone laughing. He turned to get a better look at the man who stood just a few feet behind him, watching him, eyes flashing with amusement.

He was a short man, with dark hair and a protruding, equine nose. His eyes were piercing and emboldened with a mad gleam, and the amused sneer on his lips suggested to Gabriel that he was quite insane. The flesh around his mouth and eyes was swollen and marred by unsightly lesions, and his forehead protruded, giving him a heavy frown. Gabriel recognized almost immediately the blight of the leper.

Perhaps more disturbing than this evidence of the man's illness, however, were the signs of what he had done to his own body. His limbs had been replaced by bizarre mechanical contraptions, like those of the raptors that scuttled about in the eaves overhead. His legs were piston-driven constructions that hissed and sighed as he moved and had entirely replaced their biological counterparts. His arms were mechanical, too: one of them was still almost skeletal, a fusion of brass and bone, rubbery tendons working through tiny brass eyelets to control the talons of his new hand. The other was sheathed in interlocking brass plates, dulled and marred by use.

The man was some sort of bizarre hybrid of man and machine. Gabriel wondered how much of the original man was still left beneath all of the machinery. He was, Gabriel presumed, the progenitor of the raptors, and the man responsible for the abductions and the heap of grisly body parts at the other end of the warehouse.

He was watching Gabriel intently. Gabriel was about to speak, to challenge this horrifying vision of a man, when he heard a woman whimper from somewhere behind him. He turned to look.

The woman and two others—a young man and a boy of no more than twelve—were chained to the wall, bound around the wrists by iron cuffs. The woman was clearly distraught, and when Gabriel followed her gaze, he realized, with horror, the reason for her sudden outburst.

A large pit had been sunk into the ground, designed, he presumed, to allow mechanics easy access to the underside of the airships that would have been constructed or maintained here, had the warehouse been put to its intended use. This particular pit, however, had been given over to a much more sinister purpose.

Even from where he was squatting on the ground, Gabriel could see three ropy, translucent tendrils probing hungrily over the sides of the pit. Each one terminated in a pair of dripping, snapping jaws. He felt momentarily paralyzed with cold, oppressive fear.

No . . . it couldn't be. It couldn't be this. Not here.

The man with the mechanical legs walked over to him, the pistons in his thighs hissing with a pneumatic wheeze. "Get up," he said, but Gabriel remained transfixed on the probing proboscis of the beast in the pit.

"Get up!" the man screamed, grasping hold of Gabriel's bloodied shoulder, pinching the wounds and sending lancing pains down Gabriel's arm. "And don't even think about trying anything. My pets will be on you in seconds."

Gabriel resisted the urge to thrash out at the man, to grab him by the throat and throttle the life out of him. Of course, he was right. Gabriel had barely been able to fend off *one* of the mechanical creatures without help, even armed with the Ghost's full array of weapons. He stood no chance against a whole flock of them. Not alone.

No, this was when he had to maintain his cool, to pretend to be nothing but an innocent civilian until the time was right. Donovan and Ginny would be here soon, and with them all the back-up Donovan could muster. But then, there was the creature in the pit to consider. . . .

He got to his feet.

"There. Much better," said the man, his tone utterly patronizing. "Now, over there with the others."

Cautiously, Gabriel did as he was told, edging his way around the pit toward the other abductees. He could barely believe what he was seeing. The alien creature languished in the bottom of the hole amid heaps of rotting human remains. It was fully manifested, unlike the example he'd fought with Celeste beneath the mansion of the Roman.

Also unlike its kindred, however, this one was in a sorry state, half-dead, five of its limbs lying paralyzed and necrotic among the human waste. Its flesh, too, was puckered and covered in open sores, and he could see its black organs pulsating weakly inside its strange, translucent bulk. It had clearly been poisoned, but kept alive in this weakened state, for what purpose Gabriel could only begin to imagine. It was probably being fed on the discarded captives, such as the three poor civilians chained to the wall now. He'd wondered how the raptors were disposing of the abductees once they were finished with them—now he thought he had the answer, as horrifying and unwelcome as it was.

Surely, though, there was more to the abductions than the need for a simple food supply for the creature? Why did the leper have it here at all? It wasn't like it would make a good pet. . . .

It was clear the man was using the abductees to conduct experiments of some kind—the equipment and the cadavers in the workshop proved as much. Components from the corpses were being used to fashion the raptors, too, at least in part—the occasional rib bone, and the flesh, stretched out and cured to make wings. Was that it, though? It seemed unlikely. But, Gabriel reminded himself, the whims of madmen were near impossible to fathom.

None of that even began to explain the presence of the alien beast, however, and Gabriel didn't even know where to begin trying to understand where it had come from, or what terrible purpose it was being put to. How on earth had a man with such limited resources, a leper locked away in a warehouse by the docks, managed to manifest and control one of these creatures, something even the Roman, a semi-immortal warlord, had failed to do? It seemed utterly unthinkable. He simply couldn't be working alone.

The man with the mechanical legs beckoned to one of the raptors, which fluttered down from among its kin. It landed neatly beside him on its hind legs, its metal claws clacking against the concrete. It leaned forward and hissed at Gabriel, its wings twitching nervously. He met its lifeless, demonic gaze.

"Tie him up with the others," said the man, and the raptor stepped forward, reaching out its talon and shoving Gabriel backward toward the other captives. He stumbled but managed to retain his footing. He could hear the young boy was weeping quietly in terror. He vowed to free the child—and the others—just as soon as he was able.

For now, though, his choices were limited. The most he could do was kill the man and incapacitate the raptors by shredding their wings with his fléchette gun. He only had limited ammunition, though, and even grounded, the things were deadly. That wouldn't buy him enough time to free the others, and it still left him to deal with the thing in the pit. This time, there was no Celeste to come to his aid, and even Donovan and Ginny wouldn't be able to do much about the alien beast, regardless of how many reinforcements they brought with them. The only tiny spark of hope was the fact that the creature was already weakened. Whatever had been used to poison it might have left it open and susceptible to injury, judging by the puckered scars on its flesh. But that was a hell of a maybe. Without Celeste and her remarkable blood . . . well . . .

Gabriel felt a sudden, acute pang of loss. He buried the emotion. It would do him no good here, not now.

With little else he could do, Gabriel submitted to the raptor, allowing himself to be forced back against the wall beside the woman. The mechanical beast proved quite dexterous as it clamped the rough iron cuffs around his wrists, pinning his arms behind his back. For a moment the raptor leaned in close, pushing its face close to his so that it was only inches away, cocking its head and studying him. Did it recognize him? Had he fought this one on the rooftops of the city? Gabriel couldn't tell.

The raptor opened its mouth, baring its brass fangs, and issued a horrific shriek. Then, with a short burst from its rotor blades mounted on its shoulders, it shot back up to the roof, landing on one of the iron supports, from where it could keep a watchful eye on the proceedings below.

Gabriel turned to the woman. She was pale and thin, and she, too, was weeping. He could see she was trying stoically to hold the tears at bay, to prevent herself from becoming hysterical, and he admired that stoicism. He was not sure that—if he hadn't gotten himself into this mess, if he hadn't at least had some experience of the terrible things he was witnessing here—he would be able to do the same.

"I'll get us out of here," he whispered to her as softly as he could so as not to be overheard. "I'll get us out of here alive."

The woman turned to look at him, and he could see from the expression on her face that she thought he was just as insane for believing that as the part-mechanical man who had been holding her captive. He guessed she'd seen firsthand what the end of her life was likely to look like, and all hope of survival had already been lost.

As if to underline this point, their captor came forward, eyeing his four prisoners with an appraising look. "I think . . . yes, you'll do." He stood over the male prisoner, who shook his head and began to babble in protest.

"No . . . no . . . no!"

The man drew his hand back and slapped the prisoner across the face, his metal claw raking long furrows in the soft flesh of the prisoner's cheek. Blood bubbled to the surface, and the prisoner cried out but then bit back on it, repressing it to a whimper.

"Better," said the part-mechanical man. "Remember, if you run you'll only make it much worse for yourself. The raptors are waiting." He reached around and unlatched the prisoner's shackles and then grasped him by the elbow and dragged him to his feet. The woman beside Gabriel turned to stare at him, fixing her eyes on his, resolutely refusing to watch what was about to happen to the other prisoner. She'd seen this before, Gabriel realized.

The man led the male prisoner to the edge of the pit. "Stand there," he said, "and don't move." He held the other man back, just out of reach of the writhing tentacles that still probed hungrily around its perimeter. He took the prisoner's left arm and held it out over the pit, rolling back the sleeve of the man's crumpled suit to reveal the milky white flesh of his forearm. Then, grasping the prisoner by the wrist, he used one of his sharp, talonlike fingertips to draw a long, bloody line across the man's palm. Blood blossomed almost immediately from the wound and the man yelped in pain and shock.

The mechanical man waited, still clutching the prisoner by the wrist, watching the blood in the man's palm gather until it became a little tributary, until it began to drip into the pit below. He stood, studying the beast's reaction with interest.

Gabriel couldn't see, but he could hear enough to tell the blood was driving the beast into a wild frenzy. Its surviving tentacles thrashed at the sides of the pit, and he could hear it bucking and rearing up, trying to get at this new source of food. The prisoner's blood was like a drug to it, and the creature craved it beyond all else.

The mechanical man sighed, and without further ado, grabbed his prisoner and shoved him over the edge of the pit. The man screamed, howling in fear and agony as he fell into the monster's embrace and its snapping, snarling limbs latched onto him, burrowing into his flesh, draining his body of its lifeblood in a matter of moments.

All of this happened out of sight of the other captives, of course, but the sounds of it were enough to turn Gabriel's stomach: the crunch of bones being snapped, the wet rasp of rending flesh. He'd seen before what these creatures could do to a man, and he had no desire to see it again.

Gabriel fought ineffectually against his bonds. He wouldn't allow another of the prisoners to die. He would rip out the mechanical man's throat before he let that happen, whatever the consequences to himself. But for now, there was nothing he could do. The shackles held firm, and with his arms tied behind his back, he couldn't even activate the fléchette launcher strapped to his forearm.

He tried instead to focus on understanding what was going on. What was his captor doing? Why had he cut the man's hand before pushing him into the pit to feed the beast? Was he simply teasing it? Or was he testing it?

Yes! That was it, Gabriel realized with a start. That was exactly what the man had been doing. He was testing the prisoner's blood to see what effect it had on the creature. To see if he was like Celeste.

Was that what this was all about? All of these abductions? Was he attempting to find someone whose blood would poison the creature? Clearly at some point he had obtained some of the correct blood type, judging by the state of the beast, but did he now need more?

The mechanical man was eyeing the remaining prisoners. For a moment, from the way he seemed to hover over the child, Gabriel thought he was about to select the young boy to be his next victim, but instead he turned, looking up to the rafters where his pets were bobbing nervously on the iron beams. "Never mind," he called up to them, shrugging dismissively. "Never mind. Your brothers will return shortly with more test subjects, and then, my children, I'll allow you to play."

The raptors squawked and chattered anxiously at this, and Gabriel wondered exactly what game it was they were hoping to indulge in. He probably didn't want to know.

He looked to the door and hoped Donovan and Ginny would be along soon.

—•—

Rutherford had been following Senator Banks for over thirty minutes, and so far, he thought he had managed to evade being discovered.

The senator had been driven directly from his hotel to a plush-looking apartment building on 64th Street, where he had alighted from his vehicle and gone inside. At first, nervous that he might miss something important, or that the senator might switch transport, Rutherford had considered doing the same, parking and following Banks on foot. If Banks realized he was being followed he might use an alternative exit from the building to shake Rutherford off the scent. But then Rutherford had noticed the driver, waiting by the curbside, the car engine still idling. Banks wasn't intending to stay for very long, and in his arrogance, probably hadn't even considered he was being followed.

So Rutherford had waited, keeping a watchful eye on both the door to the apartment building, and the driver. His patience had paid off, and within ten minutes Banks had returned in the company of another man, a tall, lean, gray-haired man dressed in a blue woolen overcoat with a red scarf wrapped around his lower face. He had a military bearing, and Rutherford had assumed he must be a retired soldier, or at least that he had spent a great deal of time in the armed forces.

The newcomer had shared a number of words with the senator on the sidewalk before heading to his own, parked vehicle a little way farther along the street. Banks had returned to his driver, and presently both cars had moved off, convoy fashion, Banks's car in the lead, heading downtown.

Rutherford had eased his own vehicle out behind them, careful to establish enough of a distance between them so as not to appear suspicious.

Now, a short while later, they were nearing the docks, approaching two large, modern hangars that were nestled among a smattering of similar industrial buildings. Nearby, Rutherford could hear the bustle and frivolity of the fairground, but such things remained far from his thoughts. He was entirely focused on the task in hand: putting a stop to the schemes of Senator Isambard Banks.

He pulled over, sliding his stolen car into the shadows of a warehouse wall as the two cars ahead of him came to a stop. He watched the thin man climb out of his vehicle and approach a bus that was parked on the concourse awaiting them. The driver of the bus jumped down to greet him, and Rutherford realized for the first time since arriving that the bus was full of men. At a signal from their driver, they began to disembark, spilling out of the bus like worker ants. There must have been fifteen or twenty of them, all wearing matching gray boiler suits. They were workmen of some kind, and Rutherford wondered whether they were connected somehow to the weapon, or were perhaps there to man and maintain the airship that would transport it to London.

Rutherford regarded the two hangars. It was likely the airship itself was housed in one of them, he thought. The airship that he had to prevent from ever making it across the ocean.

He reached over and wound the passenger window down, hoping

this would be enough to allow him to hear snatches of the conversations taking place outside. The workmen caroused and jostled each other, but Rutherford was intent on watching the thin man, who had now crossed to where the senator was waiting for him beside his car.

"Tell your men to prepare the vessel," said Banks, and the other man gave a sharp nod of acknowledgment at the order. "I want you airborne as quickly as possible. No delays, Joseph." He glanced at the buildings looming over his shoulder. "I'll take care of Abraham."

Banks held out his hand, and the thin man took it, shaking it firmly. "Good luck," said Banks, "it is a fine thing you're doing, for the honor of your country. It will not be forgotten."

"Thank you, sir," replied the thin man, before turning to his men. He barked a couple of sharp commands and then led them off to the hangar on the right.

Banks watched them go, a wide grin spreading across his face. Then, sighing, he turned and made for the other hangar, his shoulders slumping slightly, as if he were reluctant about to brave the lion's den.

Rutherford waited until he was out of sight and then cracked the car door open and climbed out. He was momentarily torn. He had two options—to go after the thin man, Joseph, to see if he could put a spanner in the works of the airship, or to follow Banks and attempt to ascertain the entirety of the man's plan. Both were equally as important. Both were equally as risky.

Rutherford had known all along that Banks was the key to all of this, however, and he needed to see it through. He would follow Banks first of all, try to find out exactly what he was dealing with, what this superweapon was actually capable of. In the meantime, he hoped that would give him a chance to consider what the hell he was going to do to stop that airship from ever getting off the ground.

CHAPTER SIXTEEN

Gabriel looked up at the sound of a car engine purring to a stop just outside the hangar. He felt a sudden rush of fear. Was it Donovan? If so, he hoped he'd been able to acquire some assistance, otherwise the raptors would make short work of him, or else Donovan and Ginny would find themselves chained up alongside Gabriel and the others, ready to be fed to the monster.

A few minutes passed, and Gabriel began to think that perhaps the vehicle had moved on again, or that the occupant had left the car and moved on to a different destination.

The mechanical man seemed not to have noticed the arrival, or if he did, he paid it no heed. He was busy now in his workshop, tinkering with some device or other, a component he had earlier removed from his upper arm. He looked up, however, at the sound of footsteps coming through the doorway behind him.

The newcomer wasn't Donovan, as Gabriel had hoped, but rather a tall, portly man in a thick woolen overcoat and porkpie hat. Gabriel recognized him almost immediately from the photographs he had seen at the apartment of the British spy. This was Senator Isambard Banks.

"Hello, Abraham," said Banks, sauntering over to where Abraham remained hunched over his workbench. The senator seemed not to notice the dangling human corpse, just a few feet away from where he was standing. If he did, he appeared not at all disturbed by its presence. "Enjoying your little games?"

So, that was the name of his mechanical captor: Abraham. Gabriel watched Abraham's reaction to the other man, noting with interest the sudden change that seemed to come over him. Where earlier he had been energetic and arrogant, almost hyperactive, even, now he appeared meek and afraid in the shadow of the other man. He was utterly in Banks's thrall.

"Senator Banks," Abraham replied quietly, so that Gabriel had to strain to hear. "I wasn't expecting you until tomorrow."

Banks grinned. "Ah, well, we like to keep you on your . . . toes, Abraham," he said, glancing down at the man's mechanical feet. "After all, you do hold all of our futures in your hands. And besides, need I remind you that you're being very well compensated for your haste?" He smiled again, but it was sinister, almost threatening.

Abraham laughed nervously. The raptors twittered overhead, scuttling around on the iron beams. Something about the presence of the senator set them on edge, too, it seemed.

Banks reached up, retrieved his hat from his head, and placed it pointedly on the workbench over the component that Abraham was working on. Abraham frowned, and looked as if he was about to say something, and then clearly thought better of it, instead rising to his feet to face the senator.

"Is it ready?" asked Banks.

Abraham frowned again. He gave the slightest of nods. "The device is ready. I've fitted it into the loading bay of *Goliath* as agreed. But there's still no solution. The search for an appropriate donor is proving . . . taxing."

Banks shrugged. "Very well," he said.

"The raptors are still out. I'm expecting them to return with more subjects shortly. I'll keep testing them through the night."

Banks shook his head. "No. The time for that is over, Abraham. *Goliath* leaves tonight."

"Tonight! No! You said tomorrow!" Abraham sounded desperate, panicked by this new development. He stood wringing his strange, mechanical hands before the senator. "Senator Banks, you must listen to me." His voice had now taken on a pleading tone. "We *need* that solution."

Banks laughed. "Things are moving, Abraham. We've run out of time. There's a British spy running around Manhattan. He knows much of our plans. We can't risk him warning anyone in London."

"But without the solution we can't control those things. You've no idea!" Abraham was nearly hysterical now. "They're monsters, Senator. Deadly monsters. If you give birth to an entire army of them without a means to control them, you're damning us all."

Banks reached out as if to put a reassuring hand on Abraham's shoulder, but then thought twice, grimacing at the sight of the man's bloated, necrotic flesh. When he spoke his tone was conciliatory, condescending. "I'm sure that's entirely the point of the weapon, Abraham. We *want* to unleash those monsters on the British, don't we? If these things were easy to contain, they would be of no use to us."

Abraham was literally pulling at his hair in frustration. "But you're missing the point!"

Gabriel took a deep breath and then let it out again, trying to remain calm. So, that was their plan. They intended to unleash an army of those things—those alien monsters—on the British. That, too, was the reason for the abductions. Abraham was searching for the right blood type to be able to control the beasts. Clearly he had intended to somehow synthesize it, or otherwise use the blood to develop a solution that could be used to immobilize the monsters once they had done their work. Without it, they wouldn't be able to stop them once they'd set them free. They would devastate the British and then, when they had exhausted the food supply of those tiny islands, they would turn their attention to the rest of the world.

Abraham was right: Banks really didn't know what he was dealing with.

Gabriel wished Donovan were there, hearing this. Clearly this was the business the commissioner was mixed up in, too. That's what had gotten them so worked up about the man known as Jerry Robertson, the British spy. In posing as a political activist he'd been able to get close to Banks and had probably been privy to things Banks would now rather he hadn't heard. They were trying to stop him getting word to London or otherwise interfering with their plans. In trying to locate the spy, Donovan wasn't working for the good of the nation, as Montague and Banks had so succinctly put it. Rather, he was unknowingly aiding and abetting them in the execution of their scheme. Gabriel knew that if Donovan were fully aware of the facts, he'd be the one handing the spy the holotube receiver.

A preemptive attack on London would be all that was needed to incite a full-blown conflict with the British Empire. With weapons such as the alien beasts at their disposal, the senator and his friends had every reason to believe they'd be victorious. It would bring an end to the cold war, certainly, but it would also bring an end to the British. It would leave America dominant, the ultimate power on the world stage.

Banks was playing a dangerous game. Gabriel knew firsthand how dangerous just one of those creatures could be. Unleashing an army of thousands of them on the world would amount to Armageddon, whether

Abraham had a few vials of solution or not. Even if they *could* work out how to control them, the loss of human life would be monumental. The British Isles would be reduced to a wasteland. The empire would crumble, and millions of people would be left dead. It wasn't so much a military strike as an attempted genocide, all for the glorification of one man and his power-hungry friends. Banks and his cronies had to be stopped. Gabriel had seen enough death for ten lifetimes. He couldn't allow these men to continue with their plans.

Abraham was growing more and more agitated, and Banks was beginning to lose patience with the mechanical man. "Just one more day, Senator. One more day!" Abraham pleaded. "I understand that you're anxious for *Goliath* to be under way, but I really think it's for the best."

"Oh, do be quiet, Abraham," Banks snapped, clearly close to the end of his tether. "I'm growing tired of your prattling. The decision has been made. *Goliath* is already being prepared for launch."

Abraham took a step back toward his workbench, fearful of the senator's tone. "I'll . . . Call it off or I'll set the raptors on you!"

Banks's shrewd smile turned at once to a taut mask of fury. "Are you threatening me now, Abraham? Well that's a very stupid thing to do. I'm most disappointed. I had thought there would be a role for you in the new world order. But perhaps not. Perhaps your usefulness has already come to an end."

Abraham stared at the senator, wide-eyed, as if he couldn't quite believe what he was hearing. He looked up, beckoning to the five raptors still clinging to the rafters above. "Kill him!" he screamed in desperation, pointing at the senator. "Kill him!"

But the raptors did not respond, other than to flutter their wings nervously and hop from foot to foot, mewling like frustrated kittens.

The senator laughed. "Don't you remember, Abraham? The raptors were keyed to obey me, too. That was one of my stipulations when I built you this place."

Abraham stared at the senator with barely concealed panic as Banks waved both of his arms above his head and shooed the raptors away. They started like a flock of birds at the sight of a predator, buzzing into the air with the groan of rotors and the flapping of wings. Within seconds they had chattered off through the hole in the roof, every single one of them disappearing into the night.

Banks was still laughing, evidently pleased with himself.

"Senator," Abraham warned, his tone now resigned, serious, "you're going to destroy us all."

"Don't be so damned melodramatic, Abraham. I'll do no such thing. Those creatures will be no match for the might of the American military machine. Unlike the British we'll be prepared for them, we'll know what we're facing. The British will be caught by surprise, and once the creatures have consumed their capital our armed forces will move in. The creatures will be dealt with swiftly and efficiently, and we shall lay claim to the territory of our former masters." Banks sounded as if he were giving a speech to the Senate. He clearly believed in this madness, in the inherent superiority of his people.

"The creatures are impervious to anything the armed forces could throw at them!" Abraham stressed. "They simply cannot be harmed, not without the poison, without the solution. It weakens them, Senator, makes them susceptible to our weapons."

Banks was having none of it, however, and Gabriel could see from the look in Abraham's eyes that he knew what was coming next.

The senator reached forward and grasped the squirming Abraham by the throat. All of Abraham's posturing, all of his confidence had gone along with the raptors, and now he gasped and begged for his life. The senator, however, showed him no mercy. Lifting Abraham from the floor, ignoring the ferocious scrabbling of his artificial limbs, Banks carried him toward the pit by his throat.

The diminutive scientist was struggling for breath, trying to call out, to appeal to the senator to set him down, to show him mercy, but Banks had made up his mind, and a moment later he pitched the part-mechanical man over the side of the pit toward the waiting monster below.

Abraham managed to catch hold of the lip of the pit with one arm, scrabbling frantically at the concrete, but within seconds the creature had buried a proboscis in his back and he was dragged down, screaming, toward the hungry mouths.

Gabriel heard the creature shriek in pleasure at the unexpected treat and tried to block out the sounds of its multiple, dripping jaws as they found purchase in Abraham's remaining flesh, rending it from the brass and bones that now comprised his skeleton, lapping at the warm blood beneath.

Abraham emitted one final, shrill cry before whatever served as his heart gave out and he sputtered and choked on his own spilled bodily fluids. The mechanical parts of his body continued to pop and jerk at the bottom of the pit as the monster drained the remains of his torso of blood.

Banks stood back, dusting his hands, a grim expression on his face. He did not even look over at the three remaining captives chained to the wall, but promptly turned, strolled back toward Abraham's workbench, retrieved his hat, and left.

——•——

Gabriel didn't even wait for the sound of the senator's car engine firing up before he began trying to extricate himself from the iron cuffs. They were roughly hewn, and the rusting edges bit painfully into his flesh as he tugged and wrenched, bashing them against the wall to attempt to shatter the latch.

With Abraham and the raptors gone, the only thing he had to worry about—for the time being, at least—was the creature in the pit, and he'd hoped its two recent meals had been enough to sate it for a short while. But no matter how hard he fought against his bonds, he couldn't figure out how to break himself free.

He tried getting the woman to reach over and snap the catch free, straining against the chain to get himself as close to her as possible, but Abraham had not been an unintelligent man and had evidently considered that possibility, spacing the chains just far enough apart so that the prisoners couldn't help each other to escape.

Just as he was about to resign himself to the fact that he wasn't going anywhere, he heard the scuff of a booted foot by the doorway and looked up, panting with exertion. His first thought was that the senator had returned, his second that Donovan had finally arrived. But neither of these two eventualities was true.

The man who stood in the doorway was perhaps the last person Gabriel had expected to see. He was lean and wiry, evident even beneath the wintry overcoat he was wearing. His hair was blond and well groomed, and he was handsome, around forty years of age. He was standing beneath the harsh electric light and staring in horror at the grisly scene before him, at the swinging corpse on the rope and the heaps of discarded bones: a rib cage, a femur, a handful of skulls.

"My God . . . " he said, and his British accent confirmed what Gabriel had already suspected. He looked a little older than he had in the photographs Donovan had shown him, but he was, without doubt, the missing British spy.

"You're Jerry Robertson," Gabriel called out to him, and the man looked up, his eyes narrowing with suspicion. When he saw the three of them straining against the iron cuffs—Gabriel, the woman and the boy—he started over toward them. He stopped short when he caught sight of the tendrils creeping slyly around the lip of the inspection pit.

"That's their weapon," Gabriel said. "The weapon they're planning to unleash on London."

The spy stepped closer, staring down into the hole in the ground. His eyes widened at the sight of the writhing beast, and it lashed out at him, three of its proboscises snapping out, their slavering jaws gnashing at the air.

"What is it?" the spy asked, incredulous. Gabriel could see he was an intelligent man, but he was struggling to come to terms with what he was seeing. "Some sort of sea creature? The result of a eugenics program?"

Gabriel shook his head. "No. It's one of a race of creatures that live in a dimensional space that exists alongside our own. There are thousands of them, all around us, all of the time, but we cannot see them, or interact with them, because they are spatially out of phase with us." He sighed, trying to figure out how to explain it to this man in a way that didn't make him sound utterly crazy. "Look, I know it's hard to swallow, but the evidence is there, right before your eyes. The people who did this are planning to set thousands of these things free over London. It'll be a massacre. They're almost impossible to stop."

Robertson was still staring at the thing in the pit. "Who are you?" he said.

"I'm . . . my name is Gabriel Cross," Gabriel responded, determinedly. "You might know me better as the Ghost."

Robertson turned to look at him. "From the newspapers? The vigilante?"

Gabriel shrugged. "Yes. If you let me out of here I'll help you to stop them."

Robertson looked uneasy. "How do I know I can trust you?"

"You don't," Gabriel said drily. "But I'd imagine the fact I've been chained up by the bad guys gives you an idea of where my allegiances lie."

Hesitantly, Robertson edged around the pit to stand before him. "With the British?"

Gabriel shook his head. "No. I wouldn't go that far. But certainly not with Senator Banks. I don't believe in this war he's trying to start, and I won't allow him to unleash those things on the world. Not while I still have a breath in my body."

Robertson smiled. "All right. I'll let you out. But no funny business."

Gabriel laughed at the man's accent, his plum-in-the-mouth Britishness. "Free the others first," he said, and Robertson nodded, setting about unlatching the woman's cuffs.

"My name's not Robertson," the spy said as he worked. "It's Rutherford. Peter Rutherford." He turned to console the woman, who was now weeping openly with relief. She was barely responsive. "She's in shock. She's going to need help."

"She can find help," Gabriel said, firmly. "Her and the boy. We have to stop that weapon leaving for London."

Robertson—or rather Rutherford, Gabriel corrected himself—gave a brisk nod of agreement and started work on the boy's cuffs. A moment later he had popped the child free, and he put a hand on the boy's shoulder. "Take this woman and find a police officer," he said. "Get away from here as quickly as possible. You'll be able to find help at the fairground. Tell them everything."

The boy looked terrified and didn't say a word, but he reached out and took the woman's hand in his own. She allowed herself to be led quickly toward the door.

Gabriel watched them go while Rutherford set about freeing his cuffs. "I promised I'd save her," he said. "I promised to get her out of here alive."

"And you did," Rutherford replied, dropping the cuffs to the floor with a clang.

Gabriel rubbed at his sore wrists. "No, I didn't. You did." He met the other man's gaze. "That was a timely arrival."

Rutherford smiled. "I followed Banks here. I've been trying to work out where they'd housed the airship. I've been piecing together their plans for weeks."

Gabriel nodded. "I know, I saw the wall at your apartment before it was burned to the ground."

"Montague," Rutherford replied, and he almost spat the name of the commissioner in distaste. "I'm sure he's responsible for that."

"It seems he has a lot to answer for," said Gabriel. He liked the British man, and he could tell from the haunted look in Rutherford's eyes—the same look he saw in the mirror when he cared to bother with it—that the man knew pain and suffering. Gabriel guessed he'd been a soldier too, during the war, like so many men of their generation, and like Gabriel he would stop at nothing to prevent it from happening all over again.

Gabriel turned to the creature in the pit. "What about this? We can't just leave it here? Somewhere round here there's got to be a vial of the poison that'll destroy it."

"We'll have to come back for it," Rutherford said urgently, already making a start toward the door. "Can't you hear that? We might already be too late."

Gabriel could hear it now: the sound of chugging propellers and the grating of metal plates. The roof of the other hangar was sliding open, and the airship was already lifting toward the skies. He ran after the British spy.

Outside, the cold air hit him like a slap to the face. It was dark, with only the shimmering orb of the moon and the lights of the nearby fairground by which to see. But the scene before them was all too clear. The airship, *Goliath*, was rising steadily into the Manhattan night, a great, fat lozenge, a shining silver cylinder, pristine and new in the moonlight. The silhouette of its immense form blotted out much of the sky, stark against the frozen mantle of yellow-gray fog that hung above the city.

Gabriel watched as the behemoth finally cleared the hangar and ascended fully into the night. The passenger gondola was brightly lit with stark electric light, and innumerable propellers whipped and chopped the air as it turned slowly about, circling above the warehouses and hangars far below.

Gabriel felt his heart sink. *Goliath* had taken flight, and with it, the weapon that would ignite the war and destroy millions.

They were already too late.

—•—

In the hangar, unbeknownst to the two men, the creature in the pit began to stir.

Its surviving tendrils curled like serpents over the side of its prison, grasping for the discarded cuffs and chains and using them to heave itself up, sliding its bulk over the ruins of its victims, the heaps of rotting carcasses, bones and mechanical limbs. Within moments it had levered itself over the side of the pit, and with surprising agility, it began to drag its bizarre, bloated form across the concrete floor of the hangar, trailing dead tendrils in its wake. It could smell humans, the stench of humanity; hear the fresh blood pounding through their veins. Nearby there were thousands of them, pressed together in close proximity like a vast herd of cattle, an enormous swarm of rats. It felt drawn to them, unable to prevent itself, every fiber of its damaged body singing out for the taste of fresh blood. It was hungry, and close by, the tide of humanity was waiting.

CHAPTER SEVENTEEN

Ginny didn't know where to look or what to do.

She'd been wandering the docks for an hour now, searching frantically, and there was still no sign of what might have become of Gabriel, where the raptor might have taken him. Without mounting a search of every building, warehouse, hangar or moored vessel in the area, they'd have no way of being sure. They could be anywhere by now, lost somewhere in the steaming metropolis.

She bit her lip in frustration. God, she needed a drink.

Ginny pushed her way through a crowd of people who were meandering about the fairground wearing cheery, carefree expressions. She envied them that naïveté—that unburdened state so at odds to her own. She was wrestling with feelings of guilt and responsibility. She wished she hadn't agreed to this ridiculous enterprise now. What had she allowed to happen? She'd enabled Gabriel with her enthusiasm, even argued to go along with him, to be abducted from the rooftop just as he was. Part of her wished she had been, too—at least that way she'd know what had happened to him. But part of her knew she'd been selfish to encourage him. She'd longed for adventure, for excitement, for meaning. She'd longed to be a part of something dangerous and important. She hadn't ever considered that it might go wrong, that it might end up like *this*.

Was Gabriel suffering somewhere, tortured by the raptors and wondering where she and Donovan were, why they hadn't come to his aid as they had promised? Was he already dead?

She tried not to consider that. She had to focus on finding him. She had no idea what she'd do if she did, of course. Confronted by a nest of raptors, without Donovan and any backup—would she even be any use to Gabriel at all? Perhaps she'd be more of a burden.

Ginny crossed behind a stall selling cotton candy. The people in line were gabbling noisily and pointing at the Ferris wheel, revolving slowly against the evening sky. "You can see all of Manhattan from up there," she heard someone say. And then: "I hear it's not very safe. People have been getting stuck up there for hours in the freezing cold."

For a moment Ginny wondered about trying to get a place in one of the cars. Would that elevated perspective offer her a better chance of finding Gabriel, perhaps the opportunity to glance another raptor returning to the nest? But then she saw that the line of people for the wheel was even longer than the line for the cotton candy, and she couldn't bring herself to simply stand around waiting. She had to *do* something.

Donovan was off somewhere else, at the other side of the fairground, doing much the same. He'd said he was going to attempt to enlist the help of some of the uniformed men who were policing the fairground, tell them he'd seen the raptor abduct a man and get them combing the area too. A few extra pairs of eyes had to be of help, she supposed, but they needed to be smarter than this. Simply wandering around hoping they'd catch sight of something telling, or hoping they'd happen upon a likely site for the nest, wasn't going to get them anywhere. They needed a plan. They needed Gabriel.

Ginny looked up at the sound of chugging rotors overhead, thinking for a split second that it was the sound of another raptor, but her heart sank when she realized it was just a large dirigible taking off, rising out of its hangar toward the frigid skies. The lights from its passenger gondola cast lengthy shadows across the fairground as it slid fluidly overhead, turning around in a wide circle.

It seemed unusual for an airship of this immense size—a passenger liner—to be operating from here at the docks. Typically they'd be tethered at the birthing fields in New Jersey, from where they'd make their jaunts across the Atlantic to Europe and beyond. She supposed it could have been a cargo vessel, but even that seemed an unlikely proposition. It had no clear markings or liveries, and wasn't even a displaying a flag to indicate its nationality. Whatever the case, she didn't have time to concern herself with the irregularity of it now.

Ginny watched the airship for a moment longer as it drifted lazily overhead, and then returned to her search for Gabriel. She would do all that she could. She had no other choice. She would scan the skies for more raptors, anything that might give a clue as to the location of their nest. She would also continue to look for anything unusual in the vicinity of the fairground, anything that could suggest where the raptor bearing Gabriel had gone when it dipped below the cover of the buildings.

She had to hope that would be enough, that somewhere close by Gabriel was still alive, and that Donovan was having more success than she was.

—•—

Gabriel watched the airship rise above the nearby rooftops with a dawning sense of dismay. Could this really be it? Had Banks really managed to pull it off? If *Goliath* made it to England then everything would be lost. Millions would die, the world would once again be engulfed in war, and worse, thousands of the alien creatures would be set loose to slowly consume the planet. There'd be no stopping them. They would wash across the world like an inexorable tide, devouring every living thing in their wake.

Of course, there'd be people who would work out how to stop them, eventually, but they'd be as dust motes on the wind, tiny specks of hope adrift on a sea of destruction and despair. No one would survive. He was sure of it. Banks had unwittingly engineered a catastrophe on a biblical scale.

Gabriel cursed himself for being unprepared. If only he'd had his rocket canisters with him he could have gone after the vessel, tried to fight his way on board, *do* something. As he was, as Gabriel, he felt weak and ineffectual, unable to act. Gabriel was nothing compared to the Ghost, a rich playboy with too much money and no real friends, a pilot invalided out of the force in his prime.

It was then that it struck him. He was a pilot. There *was* something he could do.

"Can you fly?" he said to Rutherford, who had the panicked look about him of a man trying desperately to work out what to do next, and failing.

"What?" said Rutherford, clearly distracted by the progress of *Goliath*.

"Have you ever piloted an aircraft?" Gabriel asked, his tone firm and deliberate.

Rutherford shook his head. "No, I was a foot soldier during the war."

Gabriel grinned. "Then I'll have to drive. Come on, there has to be a launch ramp around here somewhere."

Rutherford looked confused. "You mean we're going to go up there?"

Gabriel had already set off at a run, searching the rooftops of the nearby buildings for any sign of a biplane emplacement. "We need to get up there, Rutherford, to stop that thing. We need to try to get on board. We can't do anything from down here."

In truth, Gabriel wasn't entirely sure they'd be able to do anything up there, either, but it was the only chance they had. Any aircraft they managed to find down there at the docks would be designed for carrying cargo. They'd have to rely on their wits, and on the weapons they had about their persons.

"There!" Rutherford bellowed, and Gabriel spun about to see the British spy pointing up toward the roof of a redbrick building about two hundred yards away. He could just make out the silhouettes of three biplanes propped on their launch ramps, high above the ground. He ran over to join the other man.

"How do we get up there?" Gabriel said, trying to work out the quickest route to the roof. He glanced back at *Goliath*, watching the vessel scud lazily beneath the clouds, edging its way out over the docks. They'd have to break in to the warehouse and find the stairs to the roof.

"There's a fire escape. It looks a bit rickety, but it might hold." Rutherford had already started toward the building, and Gabriel followed behind. Rutherford was right—a tall iron ladder resolved in the gloom, affixed to the brickwork with iron bolts. It terminated a few feet from the ground, so that Rutherford had to leap up to catch hold of the bottom rung. The ladder shook dramatically, swinging loose from the wall, and he called out in shock but managed to maintain his grip.

The ladder clanged back against the side of the warehouse, scattering rusted bolts and plumes of brick dust. But it held.

"I think we'd better take it one at a time," Rutherford called down as he began to heave himself up, his feet scrabbling for purchase on the brickwork as he pulled himself up, one hand over another, until he managed to get one foot on the bottom rung. "I'm not sure it'll take the weight of both of us at once."

"Hurry, then!" Gabriel called after him, glancing back at *Goliath*. Soon the airship would begin gathering momentum, and once it was out over the water and picking up speed, they'd be hard pushed to catch it.

The ladder swung out again as Rutherford almost lost his footing. Gabriel nearly jumped up to grab hold of the bottom rung in an attempt to steady it, but he was concerned he'd pull the whole thing away from the wall if he did.

Rutherford seemed unfazed by the danger, however, and continued his climb, quickening his pace when he realized he was nearing the top of the building. A moment later he disappeared, hoisting himself over the lip of the building. A scattering of tiny stones rained down on Gabriel from where Rutherford's movements had disturbed them, shaking them loose from the rooftop. He brushed them away from his face.

"Come on up!" Rutherford bellowed down to him, and Gabriel did as the British spy suggested, leaping up to catch hold of the ladder and pulling himself up. The going was precarious, and more than once he thought the whole thing was going to come down, sending him crashing to the concrete far below. Still he persevered, and within a few moments he was pulling himself up onto the roof to join Rutherford, who was waiting for him and leaned over, grabbing him by the shoulders and helping to pull him up.

Gabriel scrambled to his feet, dusting himself off.

Up here they had a much better view of the airship and could see almost directly into the brightly lit interior of the passenger gondola. Dark shapes moved around inside—members of the crew, no doubt, buzzing about preparing *Goliath* for her long journey across the ocean.

Below, the lights of the fairground were almost hypnotizing, so gaudy, lurid and bright. Gabriel could see swarms of people mingling like worker bees in a hive. He turned his attention to the three aircraft, all sitting ready on their perches like large, mechanical birds.

"This one looks like it's in the best shape," Rutherford said, indicating the one on the far right. Gabriel walked over to it, running his hands along its flank. It was in poor condition and didn't look like it had been airborne for weeks, if not longer. The wheel blocks were caked in a thick rime of dirt, and there was no windshield, leaving the pilot and passenger both open to the elements. Nevertheless, compared to the other two, which were in more of a sorry state, it was the best option they had.

"I'll try to get it started," Gabriel said, clambering into the pilot's pit at the rear of the vessel. He didn't bother wrapping the webbing around himself, figuring that he might need to quickly fling himself free if things didn't go to plan. Not that he had a parachute to hand if the occasion did present itself.

He wiped the controls with the sleeve of his jacket and grabbed hold of the ignition lever. "Stand clear!" he shouted to Rutherford, and waited until he could see the Englishman had given the rocket engine a wide berth. He gave the lever a sharp tug and felt the aircraft buck slightly in its moorings, but the rocket failed to ignite.

In the distance, over the nose of the biplane, he could see Goliath slowly sliding away into the night. He pulled the lever again, and this time the rocket shaft burst into life, a bright plume of roaring flame gushing out of the launch tube.

"Get in!" he called to Rutherford, who ran up the steps to the side of the plane, placed his hands on the edge of the passenger pit and vaulted in. Gabriel gave him a moment to right himself and then pulled the second lever on the control panel, slipping the wheel blocks and sending the plane darting forward, up and over the nose of the ramp, riding away into the sky on a plume of searing rocket flame.

Gabriel grasped the rudder controls and fired up the propeller. The polished wooden blades gave a single, pathetic revolution, and then stuttered to a stop. He tried the controls again, but got only the same response: a fitful start, and then nothing. He cursed as the rocket flames—only ever intended to launch the aircraft over the side of the building to dispense with the need for a runway—guttered and died, and the biplane went into a steep nosedive toward the ground.

He heard Rutherford cry out in surprise as he fought with the controls, trying desperately to both pull up the nose and force the propeller to start working. He yanked furiously at the start lever, listening for the telltale whine of the engine firing, and, just as he thought they were about to crash headlong into the concrete below, the propeller caught. He heaved back on the controls with all his strength, and the nose of the aircraft came up, slowly. They swept along the ground, only twenty feet above the concourse, narrowly missing losing two of their wings against the corner of a hangar. Then they were arcing up into the sky once more, twisting around so that the vast bulk of *Goliath* hove into view.

"Did you always cut it that fine?" Rutherford called back to him. His voice was nearly lost on the wind as they sped toward the leviathan that hung low in the sky above the fairground, and Gabriel noticed with a smile that the Englishman's knuckles had gone white where he was clutching the edges of the passenger pit.

"No," Gabriel called back. "Sometimes I actually *hit* the ground, too."

He heard Rutherford laughing as they banked sharply, the engine groaning in protest.

As they drew closer to *Goliath*, Gabriel couldn't help but feel dwarfed by the sheer size of the thing. The biplane was like a tiny mote against the vastness of the great liner, a flea buzzing in the ear of an immense beast. He felt the tug of an almost prehistoric fear in his belly—the feeling of being in the presence of something huge and dangerous, something that caused him to feel utterly insignificant. His instinct was to turn the biplane around and flee, but he fought it, holding the controls firm, remaining focused on his goal.

He had to find a means of getting them aboard the airship, or else somehow grounding it. He didn't know where to even start. Without any weapons he couldn't take out the propellers, and his fléchette gun would barely scratch the surface of the things. Likewise the rudder. The vessel was pretty much impervious to anything he could throw at it.

Gabriel wrestled with the controls and the biplane lurched, climbing up around the girth of *Goliath*. He swept up and over the top of the liner, studying its smooth, silvery skin for any signs of weakness, any Achilles' heel that he and Rutherford could attempt to exploit.

He looped the biplane around, circling the airship like a pilot fish dancing around a shark. He drew parallel to the control car, suspended beneath the belly of the great beast, and through its lighted windows he could see the figure of a tall, thin man at the controls, slowly turning the great wheel that operated the rudders at the rear of the ship.

Up here, high above the docks, the air was icy cold, and Gabriel's fingers were growing numb. The cold air was so sharp that he felt as if the flesh were being flensed from his face as they tried to keep pace with *Goliath*.

He heard Rutherford call out to him, but the words were lost on the wind. When Gabriel didn't respond, however, the Englishman twisted about in his seat and gestured frantically toward the passenger gondola beside them. Gabriel turned to see, following Rutherford's gaze.

Two men in matching gray uniforms stood at the windows, pointing at Gabriel and calling out animatedly to someone else who was out of view. He couldn't hear what they were saying, but he got the general gist—they'd been seen, and things were about to get very hairy indeed.

As if on cue, Gabriel heard the sputter and bark of a machine gun and threw the biplane into a steep dive to avoid the flashing spray of bullets that threatened to chew their aircraft, and the two of them, to pieces.

The *rat-a-tat-tat* continued, and Gabriel brought the biplane round in a tight loop, swinging beneath the airship in an attempt to get out of the line of fire. He hadn't expected to encounter gunfire—forgetting, of course, that *Goliath* was a warship, and had been suitably armed for any such eventualities. Banks had obviously been concerned that Rutherford, or someone else, might have gotten a warning to the British, and had armed *Goliath* to the teeth in anticipation of the crew having to fight off any welcoming committee when the vessel arrived in the skies over London.

Beneath the passenger gondola hung a massive, bristling cannon emplacement that now roared to life, spitting huge gobbets of hot metal at Gabriel's plane.

"Hold on!" he screamed to Rutherford as he sent the aircraft into a long spiral, twisting away like a corkscrew to avoid the powerful discharge of the cannons.

The tumbling cannonballs slammed into the Hudson with a series of almighty whooshes, sending towering waves cascading over the docks and rocking the moored steamships in the harbor back and forth like children's toys. One of them struck the ground near the water's edge, sending plumes of concrete and dust into the air. People scattered in its wake.

More machine gun fire rattled and barked as Gabriel fought to maintain control of the biplane as he danced and weaved around the giant airship. He could see the muzzle flash of weapon emplacements all over the fat lozenge of the vessel, puncturing its silvery skin.

Rutherford had twisted around again in the passenger pit and was staring at him, wild-eyed. Gabriel knew the question that the Englishman was desperate to ask—how the hell were they going to get close enough to the ship to do anything without getting themselves killed?

Gabriel had no idea.

CHAPTER EIGHTEEN

The first thing Ginny knew about the monster was the sound of people screaming.

One minute they were filled with all the cheer of the fair, bustling and cajoling one another, laughing and kissing and eating and smiling; the next they were screaming shrilly and scrambling over one another to get away.

At first, Ginny had no idea what had happened. She'd been standing close to a carousel, watching the brightly painted wooden horses gallop their way sadly around their perpetual circuit, when she'd turned to find a middle-aged man barreling into her, almost knocking her over in his haste to get away. Cursing, she'd looked up to see others swarming in her direction, and she'd been forced to take shelter behind the ride, watching in confusion as the crowds of people suddenly turned on one another, clawing at each other's clothes, shoving each other out of the way.

Whatever had spooked them was clearly terrifying, and it occurred to Ginny with a sudden rush of hope that it might have been one of the raptors. So, shoving her way out into the press of people, fighting against the tide, she had forced her way through, past the screaming, stampeding hordes, to where the monster had attacked a line of people at an ice cream stall.

Now, standing there watching it, transfixed to the spot, she wished that she had stayed where she was.

The thing was enormous—a great, tentacled behemoth, dragging itself across the asphalt as if it were a fish out of water, unused to the cold, oxygen-rich environment of Lower Manhattan. Its flesh was thin and translucent, and Ginny could see its pulsating organs deep inside its immense bulk. It was like something akin to a squid, and her first thought upon seeing it was to wonder if it had crawled out of the Hudson. Yet it seemed somehow *alien*, like nothing that could have been born via the normal evolutionary process. She had no idea where it could have come from, but the sheer sight of it terrified her more than she had ever been terrified before.

The monster was pulling four or five dead, leaden limbs behind it, but the others, at least six of them, were still febrile and strong, surmounted by snapping jaws that darted about as it moved, searching for prey. It looked deadly, and Ginny wondered how anyone would be able to stop it.

Nevertheless, it was clear from the appearance of the dead limbs and puckered scars and welts that covered its body that something had happened to it. Ginny wondered if they were battle scars, or perhaps the symptoms of some ravaging illness.

Whatever the case, it was the most ugly, terrifying thing that she had ever seen, and every inch of her body was telling her to turn and flee, to hot-foot it away from that place, to find somewhere safe where she could lock herself away, pretend this was all just a figment of her overactive imagination.

But it wasn't. It was terrifyingly real.

Ginny jammed both hands into her pockets. Her fingers closed on the butts of the Ghost's twin pistols, which he'd handed to her earlier that night, before all of this madness, before he went and got himself abducted by the raptors. She wished he were there with her now, and hoped beyond hope that he was still alive.

Ginny watched as the myriad darting mouths of the beast thrashed out at the throng of people, who were now reduced to blind panic, trampling over one another as they attempted to flee the fairground. She wanted to scream at them to slow down as she watched them crushing each other to the ground, exacerbating the problem, blocking all of the possible escape routes so that they were penned in like so many cattle, ready for the slaughter.

All the while, behind the beast, the Ferris wheel continued its luxurious revolutions, lighting up the skyline with its dancing, flashing lights.

Ginny raised her pistols and stalked forward toward the beast. The ice cream stall had been overturned by its thrashing, and now pools of creamy, yellowish fluid were pooling on the flagstones all around it. It held two people in its grasp, each one speared on the end of a flickering tendril, a man through the stomach, a woman through the throat. Ginny could see the thing was draining their blood, gulping it down hungrily as if trying to quench some unslakable thirst. The dark fluid coursed through its translucent limbs, pooling in its torso inside what Ginny could only assume was its stomach.

She had to try to do something. The police would be along soon, probably the army, too. But in the meantime she had to try to stop it killing any more people. She was shaking as she held the two pistols out before her, one in each fist, and squeezed the triggers.

At first, nothing happened. She couldn't even tell if she'd managed to hit the creature or whether her aim had gone wide as she'd shook with fear. She thought it unlikely, though—the thing was so big it was impossible to miss. Whatever the case, it simply continued to drag itself relentlessly forward, farther into the crush of people, its tendrils whipping out to snap at anyone who wasn't quick enough to get out of its way.

Ginny took aim again, firing shot after shot until she'd emptied the chambers of both weapons. She realized with frustration, however, that she hadn't even managed to attract the monster's attention.

She lowered her weapons and backed away. What *was* that thing? She'd emptied two handguns into it and it hadn't even flinched. And now it was coming toward her, following the stampede of the crowd.

From overhead, the roar of engines mingled with the sounds of the chaos below. Ginny became aware of the thumping of cannon fire and the chatter of machine guns, and she glanced up, assuming the airship—which she'd originally thought to be a passenger liner or cargo vessel—had opened fire on the creature, too. She was dismayed to see that was not the case, however: the fat, cylindrical airship drifted lazily in the sky, harried by a tiny biplane that buzzed around it, dancing away from the flashing guns. Explosions flared briefly, casting sudden, intense flashes of flight on the scene below.

The monster had now finished with the two corpses it had been draining of blood, and it cast aside their pale, exsanguinated remains, its tentacles probing the air for fresh fodder. Around it, people had fled into the night, some even diving into the river to avoid its terrible reach. But those trapped in the still turning Ferris wheel had no chance of escape.

Ginny heard a woman shriek as one of the beast's tendrils snaked inside the car in which she'd been cowering with her date. The monster plucked them out like ripe fruit from a vine, gorging itself on their spilled blood. The woman's scream fell silent as the creature's gnashing mouth chewed a hole through her chest.

Then, as if drawn to the easy pickings of the other dangling cars, each one of them filled with whimpering people, the creature wrapped its other tentacles around the spokes of the Ferris wheel and began hauling itself up, slowly probing the cars in turn, searching out the warm bodies inside.

From one of the cars above the creature, a man jumped, crying out as he hurtled toward the paving slabs below, dashing himself across the ground rather than face being eaten alive by the monster. Ginny averted her eyes.

She had no idea what to do.

—•—

Donovan had been trying to find Ginny when the panic ensued. He'd come to the conclusion that they needed to call off their search for Gabriel, to reconvene and try to come up with a more cohesive plan. What they needed was a systematic door-to-door search of the area, and that would take time to organize. If he could get to the precinct and find Mullins, perhaps they could make a start that night. It would need the commissioner's approval, though, and Donovan knew how difficult that was going to prove—especially if the commissioner didn't want him to find the raptors at all.

He'd spotted Ginny standing by a carousel looking forlorn, and he'd realized she must have come to a similar conclusion as he had: that there was no hope of the two of them alone being able to trace Gabriel and the raptor that had taken him. Even with the help of the scant few uniformed men he'd been able to round up from around the fairground, there was little hope. There were literally hundreds of buildings that could have housed the creature's nest, and Gabriel could be in any one of them.

It was then, as he'd made his way over toward her, that the situation had changed, and the crowd of people had suddenly gone wild, screaming and stampeding as they fled something over by the ice cream stall.

When Donovan had finally caught sight of it, his heart had nearly stopped in panic. He'd had to fight for breath, leaning against a lamppost to fight the sudden wave of dizziness that came over him. He could barely believe his eyes.

The beast was exactly like the creature he had fought with Gabriel and Celeste in the basement beneath the Roman's mansion. Had it somehow survived? He didn't think so. He'd watched its death throes at the hands of Celeste, after she'd sacrificed herself to poison it with her blood. Gabriel had incinerated the corpse and destroyed the gateway through which it had been summoned. No, it couldn't be the same beast, although it was clearly a specimen of the same race, which begged the question of how it had suddenly appeared here, at the docks.

Whatever the case, there was little time for those sorts of questions now. The beast was already chewing its way through the crowds of civilians, draining their corpses of blood and tossing them away like used candy wrappers.

Donovan tried to focus, tried to muster the last reserves of his strength. What would Gabriel do? He'd get people to safety. That had to be his first priority.

He'd lost track of Ginny in the ensuing panic, but he knew she'd make her way toward the scene of the attack. He barely knew the girl, but he knew that much about her. She had gumption. She wouldn't stand by and watch people die if she thought there might be something she could do about it, whether Gabriel was at her side or not.

In the event, it was the muzzle flare of her handguns and the ringing of her shots that drew his attention, and he'd struck out, pushing his way through the crowds toward her. As much as anything, he needed to warn her about the creature. He knew what it was they were dealing with here, and he knew that whatever good she thought she could do, she'd only result in putting herself in grave danger. He needed to get her away from there and then help to evacuate the fairground. Gabriel would have to wait, wherever he was. He'd understand. He'd do exactly the same, Donovan was sure.

As for what they were going to do about the creature, Donovan had no idea. He didn't know how they could contain it, let alone kill it. They'd have to bring in the armed forces, see if any of their weapons might be able to cause it any harm. He was doubtful. From what he'd seen in the basement beneath the Roman's house, there was very little that could even cause a blemish on the creature's flesh, let alone put a stop to it altogether.

Donovan cursed. He'd hardly had time to consider what the hell was going on overhead. A battle appeared to be raging in the sky, a massive airship going head-to-head with a biplane. The crack of gunfire and the flare of explosive rounds was lighting up the sky. He couldn't help wondering if Gabriel had anything to do with it, as unlikely as that seemed. Unless he'd managed to get away from the raptor.

He caught sight of Ginny, crouching behind a garbage bin, and ran to her side, panting for breath. "Ginny! Are you okay?"

She looked up at him, terror in her eyes. "What is that thing?"

Donovan dropped to his haunches beside her. "A monster," he replied, "like nothing of this Earth. I've fought them before, Ginny, with Gabriel. There's nothing we can do to stop it, not now, not here. We have to get these people to safety, and then we'll go for help."

Ginny looked back at the Ferris wheel, at the horrifying, tentacled monstrosity that was steadily devouring the civilians in the cars. "But what about them? What about the people on the ride?"

Donovan shook his head. "They're already dead," he said sadly, unable to offer her any hope. "That thing is virtually unstoppable. We have to leave them." He rose to his feet, taking her by the arm and pulling her up beside him. He could see she was still shaking with the shock. He didn't feel much better himself, but he repressed it, hoping he could hide it from her. He needed to be strong, now. "I need you to help me to marshal these people. Can you manage it?"

Ginny nodded, weakly at first, and then more definitely. "Yes. Yes, I can manage it."

"Good." He tried to sound decisive. "Now, keep out of its reach. Whatever you do, give it a wide berth. Everyone on that side of the Ferris wheel, try to persuade them to head that way, out through the park. They can get back into the city that way. I'll move the rest of them round the other way. Let's try to bring some order to this chaos."

He put a reassuring hand on Ginny's shoulder, but she shrugged him off, not unkindly. "Let's get to it, Felix. We have work to do."

He nodded in agreement. Yes, didn't they just.

—•—

"Christ!"

Gabriel couldn't believe what he was seeing down below. Left untended, the creature from the pit had somehow managed to find its way out of the hangar and was now embarking on a full-bloodied massacre on the streets below. He'd seen it topple an ice cream stall as he'd passed beneath *Goliath*, weaving upside down to avoid the flash of its machine guns, and now, coming back over the top of the airship again and glancing down over the side, he could see the creature had mounted the Ferris wheel and was happily plucking the civilians out of the cars.

Rutherford, too, had seen what was occurring below, and seemed as torn as Gabriel about what to do. On one hand, Gabriel's instincts told him to abandon their pursuit of the airship, to break free and head for the fairground to see what they could do to help. But on the other hand he knew that this was just a minor taste of what was to come if *Goliath* was ever able to deploy its weapon.

The *Goliath*'s weapons were taking increasingly bold potshots at the little biplane, but the cannons were firing wide, the missiles streaking harmlessly away through the air. The falling cannonballs had managed to destroy a number of warehouses and other industrial buildings below, but had so far, mercifully, remained clear of the fairground and the civilians below.

The two aircraft were stuck in a deadlock, Gabriel knew, and it was not a deadlock he could win. Sooner or later one of the weapons would strike home, or else the biplane would run out of fuel and go spiraling toward the earth, out of control. It was a light craft, built only for ferrying cargo around the tristate area, no match for the airship, which was built to have stamina—a warship designed to carry its precious payload right across the Atlantic.

Gabriel felt the zip of a stray shot strike the fuselage by his legs, and he glanced round to see a man leaning out of a window in the flank of the passenger gondola, brandishing a snub-nosed rifle. He sneered at Gabriel and brought the sight up to his eye to ready another shot. Gabriel took the controls in his left hand, holding the plane steady for a moment, and flicked his right arm up and around, allowing the barrel of his fléchette gun to flip up onto his forearm beneath the sleeve of his shirt. The trigger bulb landed neatly in his palm and he squeezed it, setting loose a shower of tiny metallic blades.

The fléchettes struck home, splintering the glass window and embedding themselves in the man's chest and face. He jerked suddenly, dropping the rifle and crumpling to the floor.

The biplane veered, and then Gabriel grasped the controls with both hands once again and eased the aircraft away from the belly of the great *Goliath*. He couldn't hold out this stalemate much longer.

Gabriel pulled back on the controls and the biplane climbed. He needed a moment to think, to work out what he needed to do. That was when he saw them, bright and shimmering on the horizon. The eyes.

He stared into them, and they seemed to imbue him with warmth, with calm. He could hear Rutherford shouting something, unsure why they were climbing away from the airship, climbing higher and higher, but Gabriel ignored him.

He thought he realized for the first time what those eyes represented. They were nothing but a mirror, reflecting everything back at him. They belonged to Gabriel Cross. The *real* Gabriel Cross, the man he had buried so very long ago. They were a reflection of the man trying to get out, the man who now sat behind the controls of the biplane. Perhaps that was it. Perhaps that was why he was now seeing them properly for the first time. His buried conscience, the hidden things that defined who and what he really was—they were surfacing now because he had dropped his mask, because he'd allowed himself to become Gabriel Cross the man, rather than *Gabriel Cross* the pretender or his alter ego, the Ghost. All those myriad facets of his life had merged into one. He felt whole again for the first time in years.

Suddenly, Gabriel knew what he had to do.

"Are you prepared to die for your country?" he called to Rutherford, who glared back at him, incredulous.

"Yes," the Englishman nodded. "Of course."

"Then brace yourself," Gabriel shouted above the whine of the engines. "I'm going to get us onboard that thing, or I'm going to kill us both in the process."

He didn't wait for a response. Taking a deep breath, Gabriel jammed the controls forward as far as they would go, sending the biplane into a sharp dive, a direct collision course with *Goliath*.

Gabriel doubted the impact of one biplane would be enough to bring *Goliath* down: it was simply too big and too sturdy to buckle beneath that, even with a full tank of fuel to generate an explosion. If he could aim it right, though—if he could puncture the pliable, silvery skein of the airship and drive the biplane in between two of the aluminum ribs—there was a chance, a very small chance, that they might survive at least long enough to clear the wreckage before the plane went up in flames.

Rutherford was bellowing now as the bulk of *Goliath* hove into view. Gabriel twisted the controls, fighting furiously to align the nose of the biplane with the flat expanse of the airship's flank that he judged to be their best chance. If there proved to be a gasbag behind it, everything would be over.

The nose of the biplane impacted with the airship with a loud crunch, and Gabriel released the controls, flinging his hands up to cover his face as the aircraft chewed its way into the side of the liner, drilling its way down like a corkscrew as if aiming for the very heart of the beastlike vessel.

Everything was sound, confusion and pain. Gabriel couldn't see. Something struck him hard in the head, and he lolled backward in the pilot's pit. His legs felt numb.

There was a moment of serene silence, of nothingness. To Gabriel it felt as if he were floating in water, drifting quietly in empty space.

And then the world crashed back into being, and he was fighting for breath, choking on the blood that was pooling in his mouth. He opened his eyes, and all he could see was twisted metal. The biplane had caught in the steel spokes beneath the surface of the silvery skein, forcing itself partially inside the airship so that it hung there, partway inside *Goliath*, partway out, like a fly caught in a spider's web.

Gabriel could see that Rutherford was still alive. He was sporting a large gash in his forehead, and he was shaking his head, dazed by the impact that had caused it. Otherwise, he seemed to have survived the crash in one piece.

Gabriel spat blood and noticed at least one of his teeth went with it. "Can you move?" he barked to the Englishman, and his voice sounded tinny and harsh in the huge space. He looked down over the side of the wrecked biplane to realize they were suspended above the main storage bay. He could hardly believe the irony: down below stood the large, oval form of the gateway, the weapon itself, Abraham's portal through which the creatures would be birthed. Around it, two banks of Tesla coils stood ready to be fired up, providing the massive electrical charge that would be needed to open the dimensional rent and allow the monsters through. Gabriel knew that it worked—the creature attacking the fairground below was evidence enough of that. Now he had to find a way to destroy it.

"Yes," Rutherford called weakly in response. "Yes, I think I'm all right." He shook his head again and then wiped away the dripping blood with his sleeve.

"They'll be here soon," Gabriel said, trying to ease himself out of the ruined pilot's pit. "We need to move." He glanced up at Rutherford, who was watching him, a vacant expression on his face. "Now, Rutherford! Move!" Gabriel bellowed, and this seemed to bring the spy round, snapping him out of his reverie. He started, realized that Gabriel was levering himself out of the wreckage, and did the same, pulling himself free of the ruins of the biplane.

The sudden movement seemed to unbalance whatever tenuous equilibrium the biplane had found, and it shifted beneath their feet, the nose breaking free of one of the airship's support struts and dipping dramatically. Gabriel managed to grasp hold of one of the steel rods as his footing went from beneath him, and a quick glance told him that Rutherford had done the same, leaping up to grab hold of an aluminum rib. The biplane bucked and then seemed to settle once again.

"She could blow at any moment," Rutherford called over. We need to get down there." He nodded to indicate the floor of the hangar bay. Gabriel nodded. Together, the two men began their descent, using the steel supporting rods to find purchase as they scrambled as quickly as possible toward the hangar floor.

Gabriel could hardly believe they were still alive. It had been a reckless move, born out of desperation, and he hadn't really expected to make it out alive. Now they were here, actually on board *Goliath*, and the only plan he had was to somehow find a way to ground the leviathan vessel.

He heard shouting from below and looked down to see three men, dressed in the same gray uniforms as the others he'd seen earlier, burst into the hangar bay wielding shotguns. One of them dropped to one knee, raised the twin barrels and squeezed off a shot, which reverberated loudly in the open space. Gabriel was surprised they'd risk shooting inside the vessel in case they damaged it, but he supposed the large rent he'd opened with the biplane had emboldened them to risk it.

The shot pinged off the fuselage of the biplane close to where Rutherford had been climbing, and he swung out on the support strut, trying to reach into his pocket and free his handgun to reply.

Gabriel was quicker to the draw, however, and bracing himself against the nearest rib, he squeezed off a volley of fléchettes. The tiny blades sparkled in the electric light as they whizzed through the air, showering the three men and felling two of them instantaneously, blood oozing from multiple wounds in their faces and throats. Their shotguns clattered harmlessly to the floor. The third man managed to squeeze off another shot before Rutherford dropped him with a bullet to the chest, but it went wide, sparking off the metal skeleton of the airship and tearing a small gash in the silver skin.

Gabriel and Rutherford wordlessly continued their descent.

It wasn't until Gabriel reached the ground that he allowed himself to breathe. His body ached all over from the exertion and the battering he'd taken in the crash. His shoulder was still bloody and sore from the abduction earlier that evening, and more than anything else, he needed a cigarette. But he had to go on. He had to plumb every reserve of strength he had left. They were so close.

Rutherford was looking up at the gateway with something approaching awe. It was similar in shape and size to the ancient marble artifact the Roman had used for the very same purpose: a large, oval gateway impressed with a plethora of unusual occult runes. Only this time, rather than being carved into a block of ancient marble, the portal had been cut and shaped out of strips of polished steel, the runes etched carefully into its surface to form a gleaming archway that looked more like it should have formed a doorway in a contemporary skyscraper than a device for summoning interdimensional beasts. Power cables trailed from the base of the device, snaking away toward the banks of Tesla coils from which the power would be fed.

"So . . . this is it. This is the weapon," said Rutherford, still clutching his handgun and looking as if he was trying to work out where to shoot.

"Yes," said Gabriel. "This is it. This is what they're planning to deploy over London."

"Then we have to destroy it." There was no compromise in Rutherford's tone. They'd come this far. This should have been the easy bit.

"The best way to do that, Rutherford, is to bring *Goliath* down. Even if we jettison the weapon, the airship can still go on, can still turn its cannons on London. Banks will still be able to start a war, even without his superweapon. A preemptive strike will be enough to encourage a swift retaliation. Things will escalate from there. Banks will still get what he wants." Gabriel clapped a hand on Rutherford's shoulder. "We have to finish the job."

The Englishman nodded. "You're right. Let's find the control car and work out how to ditch this thing in the river."

Gabriel smiled. "Oh, I have a much better idea than that."

Rutherford shrugged. Despite everything, he seemed to be enjoying himself. "In that case, lead on."

Gabriel circled around the weapon, looking for the doorway through which the three men had come in. There would be more along momentarily, he was sure. He held his right arm out before him, ready to cut them off with a spray of deadly fléchettes if they came for him.

Rutherford, following behind, sidestepped over the bodies of the dead crewmen, stooping to claim one of the shotguns and pocketing his hand weapon for the time being. Gabriel nodded his approval.

The gangway led down from the hangar bay to a long keel that appeared to run the gamut of the entire vessel. It was remarkable, Gabriel thought, how little of the space inside the airship was actually occupied. It had the air of a cathedral about it: hollow, desolate and empty. Only a single passageway ran along the spine of the ship, surrounded by the enormous aluminum rings and webwork of steel supports that gave the whole thing structure.

Silently, keeping their own counsel for fear of giving themselves away, they crept through the belly of the great ship, passing through empty crew quarters and cargo rooms.

Gabriel had been right, however, and it wasn't more than a few minutes before another gang of men came barreling down the gangway, obviously dispatched to the site of the crash to ascertain what had happened to their fellow men. They, too, were armed with shotguns, and there were three of them, rough-looking types who Gabriel presumed had been hired more for their muscle than their experience.

Gabriel and Rutherford ducked behind a stack of crates, pressing themselves against the wall as the men, intent on getting to the hangar bay as swiftly as possible, jogged past, their boots ringing out on the metal concourse.

Rutherford waited until they had almost disappeared from sight before leveling the shotgun at their backs, clearly intending to take them out, but Gabriel reached over and stayed his hand. He didn't want to bring the whole crew down on top of them in a corridor where they could find themselves hemmed in with nowhere to run.

They waited a moment until the sound of the men's boots had faded out of earshot and then pressed on, winding their way farther toward the nose of the ship.

The passenger gondola, when they found it, wasn't, of course, fitted out as such, but instead had been converted into a map room, a viewing gallery and a kitchen area. Gabriel and Rutherford hung back by the doorway, peering inside.

At least five crewmen were flitting about inside, studying maps, peering out of the windows or hurrying about with plates of food. To Gabriel's astonishment, the man he had shot through the window still lay in a crumpled heap on the floor, and the other men were working around him, none of them having bothered to shift his body or show him even the slightest sliver of respect. Above his prone form, the wind was gusting in through the shattered window, noisy and chill.

Rutherford tapped Gabriel on the shoulder and made a gesture for him to look forward to where a wooden door presumably led to the control car. Flanking the door, to Gabriel's utter dismay, were two of Abraham's raptors. They hovered a few feet from the ground, their engines droning, their wings sheathed by their sides.

Banks had clearly been telling the truth, back at the hangar. The senator must have had Abraham make any number of them for his own, nefarious use.

Gabriel and Rutherford locked eyes. Both men knew what had to come next. The likelihood was that one of them was going to get killed, torn apart by the mechanical beasts or shot dead by one of the crewmen, but they had to get through that door.

The men first, Gabriel decided. He usually balked at killing others like this, always waiting for them to shoot first, to prove to him they deserved to die, before he let loose with his armory. These men had already shown their hand, however, throwing their lot in with the senator, manning the cannons that had taken potshots at their biplane, and worst of all, preparing to commit genocide on the British people. Gabriel would not mourn their passing, and he would not punish himself for it, either.

He hoisted the barrel of his fléchette gun, nodded his head to Rutherford to indicate he was going left, and then launched himself through the open doorway, bellowing insanely at the top of his lungs and squeezing the trigger bulb to release a hail of tiny razors into the air. One man dropped, clutching his throat as gouts of blood sprayed between his fingers, decorating the galley wall and spattering the pots and pans ranked up beside the sink.

Beside Gabriel, Rutherford went right, taking out two of the men with consecutive blasts from his shotgun before ditching the weapon and drawing his handgun, rolling to avoid a burst of retaliatory fire from a crewman who produced a pistol from his belt, and another who was standing beside the window and quickly bent to retrieve the dead man's snub-nosed rifle.

This latter was too slow, however, and was caught across the chest by Gabriel's second wave of fléchettes, felling him where he stood, the rifle still clutched tightly in his hands.

Gabriel dropped left, falling to one knee to avoid a swipe from one of the raptors, which had come for him almost immediately, unfurling its wings and gliding across the gondola above the pounding gunfire. It shrieked and lashed out with its talons, catching him in his upper arm and raking suit fabric and flesh alike.

Gabriel swore and rolled, trying to get away from the raptor's grasping claws. He caught a momentary, stuttering glimpse of the last remaining crewman collapsing across the floor, and then Rutherford was being wrenched into the air by the other raptor, slamming him hard against the galley wall.

Gabriel had to think quickly. He had limited weapons, and he knew his fléchettes could do little but puncture the creature's wings. At least, he supposed, that would be a start.

From his position on the floor, Gabriel sprang up and over the corpse of one of the dead crewmen, landing heavily on his side. He came up with his weapon arm aimed directly at the raptor and the still-warm corpse covering his body as a makeshift shield. He let fly with the fléchettes, spraying the creature's wings until the taut panels of human skin were shredded in their frames.

The raptor howled and dropped awkwardly to the ground, losing its balance and stumbling over onto its side. Gabriel took the opportunity to jump to his feet.

Rutherford was just about managing to keep the other raptor at bay. They were locked in a stalemate, with the spy still pinned against the galley wall but successfully grasping the raptor's wrists, preventing it from raking at his flesh.

Gabriel looked to the door. The other raptor was blocking the way, scrambling to its feet in the gangway.

If he could only get to the bird . . . Gabriel's experience in Greenwich Village had shown him the bird was the key to the raptor's animation. If he could find a way to kill it he could stop the mechanical beast in its tracks. But he'd never be able to get close enough to prize open the little door in its torso before the raptor took his head off.

He glanced around desperately for anything that might serve

as a weapon. And then he spotted it, right there in the galley beside Rutherford: a pan of boiling water, still bubbling on the stove.

He had only seconds to get to it before the raptor was on him again. He leapt across the gangway, taking great strides toward the galley. He heard the raptor closing in behind him, its rotors still spinning with a frantic whine as it tried to lift itself off the ground.

Gabriel's fingers closed on the pan handle just as he felt the creature's claw bite into his already-damaged shoulder, and he called out in pain, barely managing to hold on to the pan. Then, grimacing, he twisted around, allowing the creature to drive its talons even deeper into his flesh and muscle, and hurled the boiling water into its chest.

The sizzling water splashed across the brass skeleton, drenching the tiny doorway that housed the bird. The pan clattered noisily to the floor.

For a moment, nothing happened, and Gabriel thought he'd made a terrible mistake, that the raptor was about to reach forward and rip out his throat, but then its claw went into spasm on his shoulder and it staggered back, its hands going to its chest, clawing at its rib cage as if trying to get at the pain inside.

It issued one final shriek of dismay, and then the light in its eyes blinked out and it crumpled to the floor, nothing but a pile of brass and bone.

Gabriel didn't stop to celebrate. He turned to Rutherford, still grappling with the final raptor. "Keep it busy," he said, and then made for the door.

The captain—the thin, gray-haired man that Gabriel had seen earlier—didn't survive long enough to issue more than a start of surprise as Gabriel burst through the door boot-first and cut him down with a short burst from his fléchette gun. The man slumped over the wheel, dripping blood, and Gabriel stepped forward and heaved the body to the floor. There would be time to consider his actions later—right now he was running out of time to make a difference.

The tall, panoramic windows that flanked the control car provided Gabriel with a spectacular view of the city below. The scene at the fairground, however, was one of utter pandemonium. The creature from the pit was still engaged in plucking civilians from the cars attached to the Ferris wheel, and the crowds that swarmed around the thing were in utter chaos, with people attempting to flee in all directions at once but managing none.

Gabriel grasped the main steering wheel and spun it hard to the left, feeling *Goliath* groan in protest as the propellers fought to keep up with his demands. The gondola bucked violently as the liner slewed around. He ran across to the other wheels, spinning them wildly, forcing the rudders to bend to his will, dipping the nose of the airship so that the vessel pitched forward, slowly diving out of the sky . . . directly toward the Ferris wheel and the alien beast.

Gabriel hoped it would be enough. The monster was half-dead anyway, poisoned and weakened by Abraham's ministrations. When *Goliath* hit, there would be an explosion unlike anything he had ever seen, a massive, roiling ball of gas. If anything could destroy the monster, it had to be that.

Gaining momentum as it began to slowly fall out of the sky, *Goliath* plummeted toward the earth.

Gabriel looked to the door. He hoped Rutherford hadn't finished off that raptor.

—•—

Ginny saw it coming. She saw the airship bank in the air, apparently out of control, and begin its inexorable dive toward the earth. She saw that it was headed directly toward the Ferris wheel, and she saw hundreds of people who were going to die in the ensuing explosion.

Not knowing what else she could do to warn the people around her of the terrible danger they were in—they had failed to listen to her pleas, her shouts and her screaming—she withdrew one of Gabriel's pistols from her pocket, along with a handful of loose bullets, and began loading the gun with shaky fingers.

A moment later, when she'd managed to slide six bullets into the chamber, she climbed up onto an overturned garbage can, hoisted her arm above her head and squeezed the trigger, firing off all six shots in rapid succession. The sound was incredible, even against the backdrop of screaming and stampeding feet.

A handful of people turned to look, hopeful, she supposed, that someone had finally arrived to tackle the beast, someone with military training. But instead they saw a small woman in a pink cloche, standing on a dustbin firing bullets into the sky and pointing toward a falling airship that was growing larger with every passing second as it loomed over them, gaining momentum.

It was enough to clear the area, finally, as people fanned out, spreading away from the crush to put enough distance between themselves and the site of the oncoming collision.

Ginny saw Donovan hurtling toward her, and she leapt down from the garbage can, allowing him to take her hand as they rushed off toward the river. Donovan didn't even speak—he didn't need to.

Ginny could hardly breathe. She was waiting for the moment the airship was going to strike, waiting for the sound of the explosion, waiting for . . .

And then it happened, and it was at once the most devastating and most beautiful thing that Ginny had ever seen. She heard it first, her back still turned as she fled the scene, trailing after Donovan, who pulled her along behind him as he ran.

She released his hand and spun about, and everything she saw from that moment on seemed to occur in a sleepy haze of slow motion. It was as if none of it was real, as if she had somehow entered some dreamlike state as she stood there beside the river and watched the massive liner *crumple* into the Ferris wheel.

At first, everything was silent. The nose of the airship came down at an acute angle, striking the beast and then collapsing as the rear of the vessel folded in on itself, forcing the Ferris wheel over. Then the gasbags exploded with a detonation the like of which she could never have even imagined. She covered her eyes involuntarily as the flash seared her retinas, and all she could hear for seconds afterwards was the ringing of the explosion in her ears.

When she finally peeled the crook of her arm from her face, the Ferris wheel, toppled to a jaunty angle, was alight and spinning like a giant pinwheel, and the beast—that strange, alien creature—was writhing beneath the ruins of the liner, squirming in pain as its flesh burned with a sickly-sweet stench. It issued a terrifying screech, an inhuman wail, and then lay still, its body roasting in the intense heat of the flames.

The wreckage of the airship was like the massive, shattered carcass of a whale, its aluminum ribs jutting toward the sky from which it had fallen so dramatically. The silvery skin had been all but incinerated in the explosion, and now, Ginny found, it was hard to imagine the wreckage had ever been an airship at all.

Around the fallen vessel a number of trees had caught alight as the gasbags had gone up, and they burned with gusto, their wintry branches cracking and popping in the ferocious heat.

Ginny stepped forward, taking it all in, feeling the warmth of the fire upon her face. Beside her, Donovan was surveying the scene with a blank expression. He clearly didn't know what to make of it all.

She heard someone call out, and she looked up to see an object hurtling out of the sky. It glinted in the firelight, and at first she couldn't make out what it was. But then she felt as if her heart had stopped in her chest, and she was running, sprinting across the grass verge to where the projectile was about to strike the earth.

"Ginny!" Donovan called after her, and she sensed him break into a run behind her. But she wasn't about to be stopped.

Seconds later the object slammed into the ground with the crunch of buckling metal, rebounded twice from the flagstones and then finally came to rest after a long, grating slide across the dock.

The object then broke into three distinct components, each one rolling away over the ground. Near to her, the remains of a raptor, still sparking and twitching, the rotors of its engines spinning fitfully, came to a dramatic stop.

A little farther away, two men, both bruised and covered in spattered blood, lay panting—and laughing—on the ground.

"Gabriel!" gasped Ginny, as she ran to his side. He looked up at her through barely open eyelids. His face was streaked with black soot, and his shirt was torn open, exposing a chest that had been shredded by the claws of numerous raptors.

He grinned. "Hello, Ginny," he said. "Found me at last, then."

She grinned, crouching down and placing her cupped hand to his face. "Something like that," she said, before kissing him brightly on the forehead. Then, bracing herself, she took his hands in hers and hefted him to his feet. He stumbled slightly, and she took his weight for a moment while he righted himself. "How did you steer that thing?" she said, glancing at the remnants of the raptor.

"We didn't," replied Gabriel, laughing. He looked over at Donovan, who was helping the other man to his feet. "So you've met Jerry Robertson, Felix?" said Gabriel, still smiling. "Or rather Peter Rutherford, our missing British spy." The other man, looking just as haggard as Gabriel, was brushing himself down, which Ginny found faintly ridiculous given the torn and bloodied state of his suit. He smiled at her expectantly.

Donovan's eyes widened in surprise, and Ginny laughed, suddenly caught by how incredible the whole thing seemed. Gabriel had just come tumbling out of the sky on the back of a raptor, and now he was standing there introducing them to the British spy they'd spent so long searching for the last few days.

"I take it the two of you had something to do with that?" Donovan asked, nodding toward the burning wreck of *Goliath*.

"Well . . ." Rutherford started, but Gabriel cut him off with a wave of his hand.

"We'll explain in the car, Donovan. We'll tell you everything. You need to know the truth." He paused for a moment. "You do have your car, don't you?"

Donovan laughed. "Somewhere around here. If it hasn't been flattened by falling aircraft, that is."

Rutherford approached Gabriel, clapping a hand on his shoulder and causing Gabriel to wince in pain. "It's over, Gabriel. Thank you."

Gabriel shook his head. "No. It's not over yet. We still need to stop Banks." The look on Gabriel's face was telling. Ginny knew what that expression meant.

Rutherford nodded. "Yes. You're right. We need to finish this." He turned to Donovan. "You say you have a car? I know where we can find Banks, and most likely the others, too, if you'll help us?"

Donovan didn't hesitate. "Of course," he replied.

Gabriel stepped forward. "Then let's go," he said, taking Ginny by the arm. Behind him, the burning wreckage of the Ferris wheel was still turning lazily against the skyline, dripping flames as it was slowly consumed. The husk of the monster had all but disappeared, leaving nothing but a dark stain on the concrete where it had once been. "First, though," Gabriel continued, "there are some things I need to collect on the way."

Donovan nodded in understanding, and together, the four of them made for the inspector's car, leaving *Goliath* to smolder on behind them.

CHAPTER NINETEEN

Donovan's car slewed to a stop before the main entrance of the Plaza Hotel, and the four of them—Donovan, Ginny, Rutherford and Gabriel, the Ghost—climbed out onto the sidewalk. It was late, the dead of night, and a hush seemed to have settled over the city. Whether it was news of what had happened at the docks spreading, or whether it was simply the city itself, holding its breath in anticipation of what was to come, the Ghost didn't know.

They hadn't stopped for long at his apartment on Fifth Avenue, long enough only to collect the Ghost's things, for Gabriel to assume his mantle, and for Rutherford to dress his wounds and change into a borrowed suit. Gabriel had outlined everything to Donovan and Ginny as they had driven through the city streets, with the Englishman filling in the occasional gap, helping to establish the full picture.

Everything they'd imagined had been true. Banks, Montague and seven other men had formed a cabal. They had plotted for months, if not years, to bring their plans to fruition. They were intent on instigating the downfall of the British Empire and the rise of the American Republic in its stead. They would assume control of its colonies when it could no longer govern them, they would establish the British Isles as a new state of America, and they would look to Senator Banks to lead them through the political and social upheaval that would follow.

It seemed incredible to the Ghost that nine men and a single airship could pose a threat to an entire nation. But Banks had planned to play on the political fears that already existed between the two superpowers, to take advantage of the rivalries that had given birth to the cold war in which they were now locked.

Donovan had accepted all of this with a resigned weariness. The Ghost didn't know what it meant for the police inspector, to be going after his own commissioner, but he doubted it would end well. Nevertheless, even when offered the opportunity to walk away, Donovan had thrown his lot in with them. He would do what he knew to be right, and damn the consequences. The Ghost admired Donovan for that, more than he might ever say.

The four of them, each holding their weapons ready, lined up before the revolving doors of the hotel. Inside, from what he could see through the windows, the lobby appeared to be abandoned. The Ghost wondered if perhaps they were expected, that Banks was lying in wait like a spider at the center of his vast and intricate web. Had he cleared the hotel in anticipation of their arrival?

Of course he'd be expecting them, Gabriel considered, or expecting someone at least—whoever it was who had foiled his plans down by the docks, who had caused *Goliath* to end her maiden voyage in the midst of a raging inferno.

Tired, but filled with the heady rush of adrenaline and the desire to bring the matter to a close, the Ghost burst through the revolving doors, sweeping the barrel of his fléchette weapon back and forth across the hotel lobby. The Plaza was as opulent as he'd anticipated, all marble and glittering chandeliers, prints of old masters and classical statutory. There was no one at the reception desk, no porters, no guests. No one at all. Everything was silent and still.

Until, that was, he heard a familiar shrieking sound and glanced up. Two raptors came diving out of the sky, their wings extended like blades, slicing through the air as they swept down toward him.

Gunfire erupted from all around him as Rutherford and Ginny snapped out shot after shot with their handguns, puncturing the wings of the creature on the right and causing it to tumble heavily to the marble floor. The Ghost didn't have time to watch it clamber to its feet, however, before the other raptor was upon him.

He waited until it was no more than a few feet above him and then reached into his trench coat and pulled the cord that ignited his rocket canisters. He couldn't suppress a smile as he shot up and forward, his arms extended, catching the raptor around the midriff and forcing it up and backward toward the balcony above. Its legs kicked and wheeled uselessly as they slammed into the decorative railing with an enormous crash, sending debris pitching to the lobby below. The two of them—the Ghost and the mechanical beast—slid across the carpeted walkway above, driven on by the force of the Ghost's rockets.

The raptor was strong, however, and it thrashed out, striking him hard in the face and causing him to reel, losing his grip. The raptor twisted out from underneath him, fluttering away over the balcony, and the Ghost, still hurtling along the carpeted walkway, was forced to break into a dangerous roll in an attempt to stop himself colliding headfirst with the oncoming wall.

Shielding his face with his arms, he crashed through the railings once again, spinning through the air, out of control. He struck one of the chandeliers, sending a glittering rain of cut glass tinkling to the marble floor below.

Donovan, he saw, was still standing by the marble doors, but a snatched glance told the Ghost that the inspector had finished assembling the weapon he had brought with him in the trunk of his car: the portable rocket launcher he had taken from Rutherford's apartment.

He swung the stocky barrel around on its tripod, tracking the progress of the downed raptor as it stalked across the lobby toward Ginny and Rutherford, who were standing shoulder to shoulder, their weapons still barking, their bullets pinging harmlessly off the raptor's brass skeleton.

The Ghost, still spinning through the air, watched as Donovan pulled the trigger. The weapon belched and juddered as it spat its payload, and a second later the raptor detonated in a shower of golden fragments and body parts.

The Ghost, finally managing to right himself, swung around in a wide circle, searching for the other raptor. Too late, he realized it was above him, and a moment later it was on his back, raking at him, trying to pry open his black suit to get at the soft flesh beneath. He dipped, twisting left and right, trying to shake it off, but it was no use—the thing had him in its vise-like grip.

He heard Donovan call out, loading another round into the rocket launcher, but there was no way he could shake the raptor free.

"Donovan! The elevator doors!" he called, glancing down and grimacing in pain as the raptor tore a chunk out of his lower back. Donovan spun the barrel of the rocket launcher around on its tripod, aiming at the ornately wrought elevator doors on the other side of the lobby. He depressed the trigger, and the Ghost watched the doors implode, buckling inward with the force of the blow and tumbling away into the void beyond.

The Ghost angled his body, forcing his feet together and dipping his head so that both he and the raptor shot forward toward the still-smoldering opening. The raptor screeched in confusion as they shot into the elevator shaft, and the Ghost angled his body, climbing higher and higher and higher, thankful that the elevator car itself wasn't blocking their ascent.

As they hurtled toward the top of the shaft, the Ghost spun, slamming the raptor repeatedly against the walls of the confined space, until its grip on him had loosened and he was able to twist around in its grasp to face it.

There were nearing the top of the building now, and beneath them the elevator shaft fell away into darkness. Facing the raptor, staring into its hateful, glowing eyes and trusting it would not loosen its grip any further, he raised both arms and punched out with all his might, puncturing the fleshy panels of both wings.

The raptor screeched in fury, but the Ghost was relentless, and he knew what he needed to do. He slammed the raptor back hard against the wall of the shaft once more, forcing its head back with his hands. Then, kicking back off the wall to gain momentum, he dragged himself free of its hold.

The creature's talons gouged long furrows in his side and his chest, but a moment later he was free of its reach, and the raptor, its wings flapping uselessly in the confined space of the shaft, was unable to maintain its altitude. It plummeted, shrieking, toward the bottom of the shaft.

Moments later he heard it strike the roof of the elevator car far below. The lights of its eyes, now no more than tiny pinpricks in the darkness, faded to nothing as he hovered at the top of the shaft, watching, waiting.

Gasping for breath but nevertheless feeling triumphant, the Ghost turned and shot back down the elevator shaft to his waiting companions below.

—•—

Rutherford led the way to Banks's suite, taking the stairs now that the elevator had effectively been decommissioned. The suite comprised almost an entire floor of the hotel, a private and exclusive apartment, perfectly suited to the grandiose tastes of the overambitious senator. The Ghost couldn't imagine that the man paid for such sumptuousness himself, but rather that he subsidized his lifestyle on the taxpayer's dime.

The wooden door to the apartment was unmarked. The Ghost didn't bother to knock. Moving the others to one side, he stepped forward and slammed his booted foot into the lock, cracking the frame and sending the door bouncing back on its hinges. Clutching the trigger bulb of his fléchette gun, he strode brazenly into the room beyond.

It was just as Rutherford had described it: garish, overdressed and filled with gaudy baubles and gauche prints. The Ghost's first impression was that Banks wasn't at home. The living space was decidedly unpopulated and eerily quiet. But that didn't chime with the fact there had been two raptors waiting for them in the lobby, nor with the lack of any serving staff.

Behind the Ghost, the others had paused on the threshold, their weapons ready, waiting to see what he would do. He cocked his head at the sound of movement from behind a set of double folding doors and then grinned when he heard the senator's ubiquitous cackle echoing out around the apartment.

Yes, they were clearly expected.

The Ghost crossed to the folding doors and swung them open with both hands. The room beyond was every bit as garishly decorated as the rest of the apartment, but this time, it was full of people.

Nine men sat around a large oval table, most of them still wearing their gray suits and lounging around nonchalantly in their chairs swilling bourbon. Banks was there at the head of the table, and beside him, Commissioner Montague, who looked up at the Ghost as he stood on the threshold, taking in the scene. At the rear of the room, behind Banks, two more of Abraham's raptors hovered threateningly in the far corners, hissing and chattering like insane pets.

The Ghost felt the presence of his three companions as they joined him in the wide doorway.

Banks was still cackling with apparent glee. The Ghost wanted to reach right over the table and throttle the arrogant bastard where he sat, and he hoped he might yet get the chance.

"Ah, what a motley assortment of vagabonds we have here," said Banks, grinning apishly. "A criminal, a police inspector, a foreign spy and . . . a girl." He banged the table with the flat of his hand as if enjoying some private joke, causing the ice cubes in his glass to rattle. But as Gabriel watched, the man's demeanor changed. The lines on his face became harder, the smile disappearing. His palm became a fist, which he banged once more on the table, this time more determinedly, as if declaring his intent. He glowered at each of them in turn, as if sizing them up. "I take it you're responsible for that little show down on the docks this evening?"

The Ghost shook his head. "No, Senator. I understand that pleasure is entirely yours."

Banks's eyes narrowed in consternation, but it was the commissioner who spoke next, addressing Donovan. "I see, Donovan, that you've finally managed to locate our missing spy." The sarcasm practically dripped from his tongue. "I think it best that you leave us now." He glared at Donovan pointedly. "If you walk away now I can make this very easy on you. We wouldn't want Flora hearing about all this nonsense, would we?"

The Ghost sensed Donovan tense beside him. "No," he said sternly, quietly, and the power of the statement was enough to make the commissioner sit back in his chair. Donovan raised his handgun, and his eyes flickered toward Banks. "I'm placing you all under arrest. I'm taking you in. I'm offering you the chance to come quietly, with respect."

Banks guffawed loudly at this, easing back in his chair arrogantly and slowly clapping his hands. "Oh, so I'm under arrest, Commissioner." He glanced at the man beside him, who smiled quietly to himself. "On what charges, may I ask?"

The Ghost took in the others' faces around the table, one at a time. To him they all looked the same—bland, blank-faced businessmen, all here for the money and power alone, having sold their ideals along with their souls a long, long time ago. All of them were grinning as they watched the events unfold around them, all confident that the senator would smooth away any trouble, that they were safe beneath the protective umbrella of his corruption.

When Donovan didn't respond, the senator shrugged and continued. "The airship crash, well—that was a terrible accident, wasn't it? A disaster of a magnitude rarely seen in the city. But no one is to blame, surely? The mechanical malfunction that caused the vessel to drop out of the sky could never have been predicted. It happens all the time, all over the world." He paused, collecting his glass from the table and taking a long draft. "And that creature that people reported seeing at the fair. Well, I understand there's no evidence that it actually ever existed. Surely the reports are exaggerated? Perhaps it was simply a freak occurrence, an alligator that came out of the river? Or perhaps the result of some grotesque eugenic experiment by the madman who'd been abducting people and experimenting on them in his warehouse by the docks? Whatever the case, the only people who died were the ones crushed by the falling aircraft, as tragic as that is."

Banks nodded to himself, satisfied. "I believe I'm right, aren't I, Commissioner?"

"Oh, absolutely, Senator," Montague responded slyly. "That's precisely my understanding of what went on."

The Ghost could see Donovan's finger twitching on the trigger of his gun. He urged the man to do what was necessary, to end it. But even now, even faced with this terrible truth, Donovan was struggling to take the man's life. The Ghost knew that every sinew of the inspector believed in the absolute infallibility of the justice system, believed that these men should be taken back to the precinct and locked away to await judgment by a jury of their peers. But the Ghost saw things differently. He saw what needed to be done if the stink of the senator's corruption was every going to be excised from the city.

For his part, the senator was clearly enjoying baiting Donovan, confident that he wasn't going to crumble, confident that the inspector was too much in awe of both him and the commissioner to be able to act against them. "Oh, get on with it, Donovan. Shoot me if you must. But you do realize that the only thing stopping these raptors from tearing you apart, from tearing apart everyone in this room"—at this he gave an expansive, all-encompassing gesture—"is the fact I'm still alive? They are keyed to my word. They will not act without my approval. But if I die . . ." He trailed off, leaving the implication hanging.

If Donovan shot, he'd be responsible for the deaths of everyone in the room. That was the bastard's failsafe, his final bluff. And the Ghost knew that Donovan would never do it.

The Ghost watched the nose of Donovan's handgun quiver and dip. And then a gun gave a loud report from beside him, and he turned to see Rutherford, his arm outstretched, a determined expression on his face, smoke curling from the end of his pistol.

Senator Banks slumped back in his chair, blood oozing from a hole in his forehead, his mouth hanging open and slack jawed. The whiskey glass slid from his fingers, spilling its contents across the expensive carpet. The wall behind him was spattered with a collage of bright blood and brain matter.

The Ghost moved quickly, shoving Ginny and the others backward, causing her to topple over and collide with a chaise longue. He grabbed for the handles and pulled the folding doors shut behind him, holding them closed for a moment, listening to the excited bellowing coming from the other room.

And then came the sound of the raptors, screeching in delight as they dropped from their perches in the corners of the room, suddenly free to play.

"Time for us to go," said the Ghost calmly as he helped Ginny up from the floor and led her toward the door.

Behind them, the sickening sounds of the raptors' game could be heard echoing around the empty apartment.

CHAPTER TWENTY

NINE DIE IN HOTEL MASSACRE

Police blame malfunctioning automatons for "shocking" deaths

Nine people have died in what police are referring to as a "horrific accident," it was reported at a press conference in the early hours of this morning.

Details remain frustratingly unclear, but it is thought the victims include State Senator Isambard Banks, along with Police Commissioner Harold Montague and a number of other high-profile statesmen, including at least two well-known bankers from Wall Street.

A police spokesperson said the men had been attending a function at the Plaza Hotel suite of Senator Banks when a "malfunction of the senator's automaton housekeepers" is said to have occurred, resulting in the untimely deaths of all nine men.

The police have, as yet, refused to release any further details, but it is thought the automatons may have gone berserk, attacking the men as they sat down to dinner.

The female housekeeper who discovered the bodies has been taken into protective custody for questioning, and the remains of the two automatons have been seized by police for "extensive" forensic analysis.

Commissioner Montague's widow, Patricia Montague, was unavailable for comment at the time of going to press.

It remains unclear what this terrible tragedy will mean for the people of New York. While the city mourns for the loss of its leaders, the search for their replacements is already under way.

—*Manhattan Globe*, Evening Edition, January 13, 1927

CHAPTER TWENTY-ONE

Gabriel surfaced slowly from sleep, languishing for a time in a dreamy, half-conscious state, reveling in the sheer indolence of a lazy morning.

Three days had passed since the wreck of *Goliath* and the subsequent events at the Plaza Hotel. His body was still recovering from the punishment it had taken that night, and as he stirred he felt his shoulder pull painfully where the raptor had buried its claws in his flesh. His body was a covered by a webwork of lacerations and bruises, and he thought he'd broken a couple of ribs when he'd ridden out of the plummeting airship on the back of the raptor.

Nevertheless, for the first time in weeks, Gabriel felt happy to be alive. He and Ginny had spent the last few days enjoying each other's company, back at his house on Long Island. It had been an unexpected relief to find a few moments of stillness and peace in his usually tumultuous life, and he thanked her for that, for proving to him that he still had a life outside of the perpetual party, and the Ghost, and everything that meant.

Now, the events of the crash and everything that had happened after, at the Plaza Hotel, seemed like a distant dream. He had studiously attempted to ignore the lurid newspaper reports regarding the incident at the docks, but Ginny had insisted on pointing them out to him, each and every one, and when he'd chastised her, leaving the newspapers unread on the coffee table, she had changed tack, instead deciding to read them aloud as he drank his coffee in the drawing room.

He knew what she was doing. He'd been trying to push the memories aside, to bury them, just like he had buried so much of his past, so much of himself. He was trying to forget about the death and despair, the monsters that lurked on the threshold, just out of view. He wanted only to focus on the positive things in his life. He'd seen and done so many terrible things, and whatever the cause, however much he had acted for the best of reasons, he refused to dwell on them, to replay them over and over again in his mind's eye. To remember.

Ginny, though, knew that he had to face up to his nightmares—and his actions—just as she was learning to face up to her own. Whatever it was that had happened to her, whatever it was that had driven her to the bottle, it was something she carried with her every day. She knew how those nightmares still plagued him, every waking moment of his life. She knew because she carried them, too.

The loss of Celeste had left him feeling numb and lifeless, lost at sea. Sometimes, in the small hours when only he was awake, lying in bed and staring up at the ceiling, he could still see Celeste, caught in the death throes of the alien beast, smiling serenely as she gave herself up in willing sacrifice to save the people of the city. That was a memory that would never fade, no matter whether he tried to bury it or not. But Ginny had shown him the way toward easing that burden.

Gabriel yawned and peeled open his eyes. The sun was slanting in through the blinds, draping long shadows across the bedclothes. Dust motes picked their way through the air, and outside he could hear the drone of a car engine—Henry, he presumed, running out to the store for supplies. He blinked his gummy eyelids until his eyes became accustomed to the light.

He rolled over, reaching across for Ginny, imagining running his fingers along the subtle sweep of her body. He sat up, however, when his hand encountered nothing but the cold cotton sheets. Her head had left a depression in the pillow where she'd been sleeping. He stared at it for a moment, still trying to blink away the last vestiges of sleep.

"Ginny?" he called, momentarily concerned that she'd fled during the night, like she had all those years before, running away like a scared little girl from something Gabriel had never been able to identify. For a while he'd thought it was him: that she'd been terrified of getting too close to him, or perhaps that she'd seen that darkness within him and it had caused her to run. Then she'd come back, and he'd realized that perhaps it was not.

He heard movement, and sensed her presence in the hallway outside the room.

The door swung open, creaking on its hinges, and she stood there in the opening, framed like a girl in a portrait, the blazing sunlight forming a hazy halo all around her.

She stepped into the room, and he realized she was dressed. She was wearing a red, knee-length dress and matching shoes, and she was carrying her coat folded over her arm. Her lips were painted a bright red, too, and she smiled as she saw him there, still bleary-eyed from sleep. She looked elegant, pretty, and he felt a stirring of longing. Then he saw the case she had placed in the hallway, and he realized she was there to say good-bye.

"You're leaving, aren't you?" he said quietly, watching for her reaction.

"Yes, I . . . Well, the time felt right," she said, as if that explained everything. But it was good enough, Gabriel thought. It was all that she owed him.

He smiled, then. He'd expected to feel saddened when this time came, as he'd known it inevitably would. Instead, however, he felt jubilant, triumphant. He was pleased for her. Pleased that she felt ready to go. Pleased that she had waited to say good-bye, rather than disappearing in the night like before. This time, things were different. This time she really was moving on. But Gabriel knew that somehow, somewhere, he would see her again.

She hadn't come back for him, he realized. She'd come back for herself. But in doing so, she had helped him to heal. The pain he felt when he thought of Celeste—the tightness in his chest, the crashing sense of dismay—had not diminished, but somehow Ginny had shown him that there was more to be had from this life of his than just the endlessly unfulfilling cycle of the party and the violence that plagued his waking hours. That was more than enough for now.

"Do you want a drink before you go? One last bloody mary for the road?" he asked, propping himself up on one elbow. "I can have it ready in a matter of moments."

She smiled brightly, reaching for her case. "You know what? I don't think that I do," she said.

He laughed. "Where will you go?" he said.

She shrugged. "I've always wanted to travel, to see the world. I think I might like to visit Egypt, to see the great pyramids. I've been reading this book, you see. . . ." She trailed off, smiling sadly. She paused for a moment, and when she spoke again her voice was soft and sad. "I think I ought to leave now, Gabriel," she said. "Before I decide I don't want to go."

For a moment he thought about telling her to stay, taking her in his arms and sweeping her up in an embrace, holding her close and not letting her go. In his heart, however, he knew that wouldn't do either of them any good. He nodded.

Ginny crossed to the edge of the bed, leaned over and kissed him, deeply, on the lips. Then, straightening herself out, she turned and walked toward the door.

"Hold on, I'll walk you out," he called after her, but she turned and smiled at him over her shoulder.

"No," she said. "That way it's not a proper good-bye. I'll see you again, Gabriel Cross." And with that she was gone. A moment later he heard the front door close behind her.

Gabriel lay for a while on the bed, turning things over in his mind. Then, laughing, he swung his legs over the side and made for the bathroom. He'd promised to pay a visit to Donovan later that evening, and there was a great deal he needed to do.

CHAPTER TWENTY-TWO

"Still struggling with those stairs, Felix?" the Ghost said, laughing as he dropped onto the roof of the precinct building, his ankle rockets sputtering out in a plume of black smoke.

Donovan stepped out from behind the doorway at the top of the stairwell. "Something like that," he replied, with a heavy frown. He stood for a moment with his hands on his knees, catching his breath.

The Ghost walked over to stand beside him. "Too many cigarettes, perhaps?"

Donovan looked up, grinning, and clapped the Ghost firmly on the shoulder. "It's good to see you, Gabriel," he said, joyfully maneuvering the conversation in a different direction.

The Ghost laughed. "How's Flora?"

"She's getting all hot under the collar about this business with the commissioner," Donovan said, unable to hide his grin. "She's acting like she actually *liked* the guy." He shrugged, turning to look out across the city. The Ghost followed his gaze. The stars were shining brightly in the sky, the first clear night they'd had in weeks. "Truth be told, I think she's more concerned about me, about what might happen."

The Ghost had been considering this. With the commissioner dead, they'd need to find a replacement. "And what *is* going to happen? Are they going to hand you the job?"

Donovan gave a deep, heartfelt chortle. "Not likely! They'll bring in someone new, someone from Brooklyn or further afield. Who knows?"

The Ghost sighed. "And so you have to start again, I suppose?"

Donovan shrugged. "I guess so," he said, but the Ghost could tell his friend wasn't overly concerned by the impending changes. For the first time in weeks, in fact, Donovan seemed to have a spring in his step. There was something different about him. He was hopeful. He turned to the Ghost. "How's Ginny bearing up?"

"Ginny's gone, Felix," he replied.

"Gone? Where?"

"Egypt, of all places!" Gabriel said, laughing. "Said she wanted to see the pyramids, travel the world . . ." He looked Donovan in the eye. "For a moment I thought I might like to go with her, get away from all of this, leave the Ghost behind, spend some time just being Gabriel for a while."

Donovan shook his head. "The city still needs you, Gabriel. Whoever, or whatever you choose to be. The people down there need someone to believe in, someone who's going to look out for them. It sure as hell isn't going to be the police, especially if it ever comes out about the commissioner." Donovan sighed. "Hell, *I* need you. You wouldn't believe what's landed on my desk in the last couple of days. I've got reports of a coven of witches dabbling in blood sacrifice somewhere uptown, a female bank robber on the loose—who seems, apparently, to be able to walk through walls—and word of a dangerous new drug that's been picked up by the mob. I don't even know where to start." Donovan reached into his coat, searching out a cigarette. "So you better not tell me you're going anywhere."

The Ghost smiled. "I'm still here, aren't I?"

"And besides," Donovan went on, apparently on a roll, "some of those raptors are still out there, running wild. Someone needs to round them up."

"Yes, I wondered when that was going to come up. What happened to the two we left in Banks's hotel suite?" said the Ghost. "I saw the newspapers were reporting you'd seized the remains."

Donovan shook his head. "You should have seen that place, Gabriel. My God . . . what they did to those people. There was nothing left. *Nothing.* They'd been completely torn to pieces. And the raptors had gone, straight out the window. They're out there, somewhere." He gestured toward the open vista of the city. "We checked the hangar, of course, but they'd all fled, too. Mullins is still picking over that place. It was just as bad—worse, even—than what we found at the hotel."

"I know," said the Ghost quietly. "I was there. I couldn't stop it."

"You *did* stop it, Gabriel. You and Rutherford. You made a difference. It could have been so much worse."

Both of them were silent for a moment. "What about Rutherford?" asked the Ghost. "Is he safe?"

"Jerry Robertson, the rich socialite from Boston, boarded a steamship for England this morning. He'll be home within a couple of weeks," Donovan said, taking a long draw on his cigarette and allowing the smoke to plume luxuriously out of his nostrils.

"I wonder if they know what he did for them," the Ghost said. "I wonder if they realize what was at stake."

"I don't think any of us realized what was at stake," said Donovan. "I'm not sure we ever do. We just carry on, don't we? Do what we think is right and hope that's good enough?"

"Don't get all maudlin on me, Felix. Not now. Like you said, we made a difference. That has to be enough, for both of us. It was enough for Ginny."

Beside him, Donovan nodded.

The Ghost looked up. High above, two bright, shimmering eyes looked down on him, standing there on the rooftop, his trench coat billowing around him in the breeze. The Ghost knew that Donovan couldn't see the shining orbs, but he took comfort in their presence all the same.

The Ghost turned to Donovan, clapping him on the back. "Come on," he said. "It sounds like you need some help with those reports."

Donovan flicked the butt of his cigarette over the edge of the building and turned toward the stairs. "You can't come in dressed like that," he said, a confused expression on his face.

"I know," said the Ghost, carefully removing his hat. "But Gabriel can."

Donovan grinned. "I'll have one of the men put the coffee on, then," he said before disappearing through the door.

The Ghost—Gabriel—took one last look out across the rooftops of the city and then turned and followed quickly behind.